THE COLLECTOR SERIES

R.C. BLAIDES

Copyright © 2022 by R.C. Blaides

All rights reserved.

Paperback ISBN: 9798365175693

No part of this book may be reproduced in any form or by any electronic or mechanical means, including information storage and retrieval systems, without written permission from the author, except for the use of brief quotations in a book review.

ACKNOWLEDGMENTS

Acknowledgement

Writing a book is not an act of a single person sitting at their desk hammering on their keyboard. Instead, it is a culmination of efforts from many people, which have been fostered over several years, and learned from life experiences and love.

For my part, I want to acknowledge those in my life that made this story possible. First and foremost, I need to thank my loving and beautiful wife, Susan. If it were not for you support, help, and encouragement, this novel would have never been completed. You have been a beacon of love and inspiration for me in so many ways. Trying to explain to the world how would make my words spill from the pages of this book.

To my daughter, Gabriella, I continue to watch you grow in both your beauty and career. Your work in health care has literally touched many hearts.

To my parents, who taught me hard work and self-discipline always pays off in the end. It is this work ethic that has allowed me over the 30 years to continue my barber business, as well as, teaching for the Pennsylvania Department of Corrections.

Finally, I must thank the professional team at Twin Tales Publishing, including authors, Simon King and J.V. Hilliard. Thank you for continuing to provide me with the guidance needed to fulfill my dream. I am fortunate to have two highly regarded and respected authors guiding me on this journey. When I needed mentors, you were there, and I will not forget.

Dedication

The Crime Collector Series is dedicated to my beautiful daughter, Gabriella. I continue to watch your career grow along with your beauty inside and out. You are forever my motivation.

I love you,

Dad

THE COLLECTOR SERIES

CONTENTS

The Crime Collector	1
Blades of Justice	103
Fade Into the Shadows	209
Afterword	313

THE CRIME COLLECTOR

CHAPTER 1

If it hadn't been for me witnessing the accident personally, my life would probably have continued on like before, a mundane existence of work and alcohol. The accident would have more than likely ended up on the third or fourth page of a few local newspapers, while the rest of the world moved on.

It's hard to remember just how things had been before that fateful day, seven long years after my own family had been torn from my life by a drunk driver. Life had a way of numbing a person against events which they had already experienced, and yet, the second I understood what had happened, it felt as raw as if it had been the first time for me.

The thing about the girl was, she had done nothing wrong, a simple victim of the age old "wrong place, wrong time" anecdote. I just happened to be one of a dozen other witnesses, pulled into an event which would leave a thirteen-year-old fighting for life, a battle she was never going to win, regardless of how strong her guardian angel had been.

A small child coming up against an out-of-control SUV was never going to end well and when the driver of said car had like a pound of coke in his system, fate's hand had already won. Little Ivy Tannen stood no chance, mowed down as she walked along Route-422, also known as the Ben Franklin Highway. She was just two blocks from where her friend Linda Pane sat waiting on her front porch, the two of them planning for an afternoon of movies and boy talk.

The road cut through the town of Elderton at an angle, offering a quiet drive for those heading upstate towards Cleveland. It wasn't the busiest of roads, and yet, there had been two other fatalities in recent years, both times the unfortunate souls taken out by wayward vehicles.

The accident occurred just a few dozen yards from a local diner, a place where I would not have normally stopped were it not for my low blood sugar. Diabetes was a bitch I had endured most of my life, handed the diagnosis when I was just four. While I couldn't remember the day of *that* revelation, I had always looked at it as a "detour moment", an event which took me in a different direction entirely. The day a drunk driver stole my family was the second detour day for me. Ivy Tannen's death marked the third.

I was leaning against the hood of my car when the squeal of tires filled the air, followed by the unmistakable scream of terror. When something cut that gut-wrenching sound off as suddenly as an axe to the throat, I knew it meant bad news.

People began coming out from the diner, a few running to where the Jeep sat hoisted over a guard rail. Smoke hung in the air, with steam shooting from the vehicle's front. The market across the street began to spew forth more people and soon, a crowd of onlookers began to congregate.

From where I stood, almost paralyzed by the rush of deja vu flooding my senses, I could see that the crowd's attention wasn't focused on the obscenely angled vehicle, but instead on something a dozen feet further along. It took me a few seconds to get my legs working, but by the time I reached the edge of the growing crowd, I knew there wasn't much anybody could do for the kid.

Several people ran to where she lay still on the edge of the road, one leg twisted back underneath herself at a grotesque angle. A pool of blood grew underneath her and from I could make out, the woman leaning down closest to her was a doctor. She shouted commands to a couple of others and between them, went to work stabilizing the girl. Others turned their attention to the vehicle and to the driver everyone knew would walk unhurt from the wreck.

A slight whisper rose as he fell from his vehicle, the face looking back bloody and familiar to all. It took me a moment to gather my thoughts enough to find the name floating way back in my mind, but when I did, felt a shudder run through me.

Someone bumped me from behind, not bothering to excuse themselves as they pushed towards the front of the crowd. I ignored it, still staring at a man who would shortly face a heavy set of questions from local law enforcement. Judge Gordon Ferris was a man known right across the state, having made a name for himself the previous year when he jailed a congressman for fraud. The case was high profile enough to feature on several news networks, because of the congressman's relationship to Mia Malone, the world renowned Hollywood actress.

Many assumed his links would guarantee leniency, a rumor Judge Ferris turned on its head.

The thing was, I believe I knew the eventual outcome of the accident I had witnessed long before the police eventually dismissed the case as a tragic accident. Little Ivy Tannen had the misfortune of being born into a world where a single unit of currency ruled above all else, guaranteeing unlimited power over those who sought to obtain it. The US dollar.

The cops were paid off, maybe not by Ferris himself, but certainly those serving under him. He knew what it took to make discrepancies disappear and Ivy Tannen lacked the connections and the bank accounts to make herself heard. She died three days later, never regaining consciousness, her single mother left alone to grieve for her only child.

I don't know why, but something made me return to the very spot of her accident almost a month later. It was a Sunday, October 14th. The date was a permanent scar for me, carved savagely across my heart in a way nothing could ever heal. It was the date my own family had been ripped from me by another Judge Ferris, a man not only high on a substance, but also on life.

The day didn't begin with plans for me to make the trip out to the temporary roadside memorial. I didn't plan to travel at all. But it was seeing the little girl's face in an old newspaper which gripped me. I normally use old papers in the bottom of my bird cage, but seeing her face that morning changed everything. Needless to say, I didn't use that page for its intended purpose.

I'm pretty sure that during the trip, my mind was nowhere near the car I was driving, caught up in a place somewhere between the grief for my family and the anger for Judge Ferris. Gripping the steering wheel tight enough for my knuckles to pop, I barely remember the drive at all. Visions filled my mind, the sounds of a horrific scream, repeatedly cut off as the car struck her again and again.

Parking back in the diner's lot shortly before sunset, I walked to where the carnage had taken place. A cold I hadn't felt in a long time hung in the air, the clouds threatening to spill rain the way the Jeep had spilled blood. Just as I knew they would, those weeping for the lost child had built a makeshift memorial from loose bricks. They had assembled them in a circle, filled the middle with white pebbles and arranged a bunch of personal belongings and messages along the outer edge.

A couple of teddy bears sat in the back, one holding a small bunch of flowers under one arm. Several notes had been tacked to a small timber cross, but previous rainfalls had all but erased the pain they had held. That is, all but one.

The single note which had so far survived the weather had been laminated, sealed shut to ensure the photo of the two best friends would never be subjected to rain. The letters BFF had been scrawled along the bottom in thin black marker. Best Friends Forever.

I don't know if it makes any sense, but looking into the eyes of Ivy Tannen at that moment had an effect on me I struggle to put into words. My own daughter, aged just four at the time of her passing, was the one who came to mind. Ivy Tannen represented everything my own child had been robbed of. Long-term friendships, memories, dreams of a life beyond childhood. While Ivy had been robbed of her dreams, my *own* baby had been robbed of the possibility to have them in the first place and that was what cut me the deepest.

Standing in that spot during the twilight hours of a Sunday evening had a way of both clearing my mind, and filling it with possibilities. There was something about the situation which had taken this girl from her mother that bore into me. She deserved justice. Why should a man get away with his reckless actions because of how fat his bank account was? And a judge of all things, a man who had sworn to uphold the law.

My mind was already at work by the time I returned to my car, racing with all manner of possibilities to bring the man to justice. The question was how? It wasn't as if I was a lawyer, or a high-flying politician with a wealth of connections. I was just a simple barber, a broken man with a weakness for the bottle. The irony that I found comfort in the very substance which had played a part in my own grief was never far from my mind.

That night, a dream came to me, one which felt so real, I could almost smell the Colonel Conk oil I used on Ferris. He'd been sent to McSweeney, a maximum-security facility on the outskirts of Somerset. Out of the three facilities in the city, McSweeney was the only one I travelled to, given it's location sitting just inside my forty-mile travel limit.

I had been watching convicted felons groom each other for going on ten years, traveling between twelve facilities across the state. It wasn't where I ever imagined myself ending up when I had first made the decision to attend barber school, but once the offer was put to me, I jumped at it. As strange as it sounds, prisons have their own sense of appeal to the curious mind. For some, the inside of a prison offers as much intrigue as the latest James Patterson novel.

What I found the most appealing thing about my job was the way I could blend in with the surroundings and leave the outside world behind. It didn't make all that much sense in the beginning, but once fate dealt me one of the cruelest blows imaginable, hiding amongst the prisoners gave me a kind of shield. They didn't ask too many questions, which was perfect for a man not wanting to answer any. The thing about my clientele was that most of them weren't overly talkative to outsiders once they got used to their existence.

Cutting hair in prison is vastly different to cutting hair on the outside. For one thing, customers on the outside had their pick of dozens of possible barbers, while inside, they only had each other. There was no need for me to go over the top with meaningless chatter in the hope of building a worthwhile relationship which ensured their return for the next session. Not only wasn't I not the one actually getting down into the trenches, but my role was purely a supervisory one. The inmates essentially cut their own hair.

What many people don't realize is that there is one simple rule when it comes to prisoners. Don't disrespect them. Treat them just as you'd expect to be treated and things will work out fine. They know they screwed up, that's why they're in prison. Being in prison is their punishment. What people sometimes miss is the fact they don't go to prison to *be* punished.

I've come across enough guards, or white shirts, in my time to know who the respected ones are. Those generally stand out as not having a chip on their shoulder, doing their job the way they might run a civilian business. The only difference is, they're aware of the danger.

That danger is something I too, am aware of. There's a scar on my left cheek, about the length of a quarter, which was given to me by a crook who lashed out during one session. He'd managed to grab the cordless clippers from the inmate cutting his hair, stood up from the chair, then threw them into my face. It was one of those lucky moments where a couple of officers just happened to be doing walkthrough. The guards jumped on him before the first drops of my own blood hit the floor.

In the dream I had, it was Ferris who grabbed the clippers from *my* hands. But instead of throwing them at me, he lunged forward, thrusting them into my face as the harmless blades grew in size, each large enough to look more like Freddy Krueger fingers. We struggled for control, with me shouting for the guards to help, but nobody came. The only reprieve came when I shouted hard enough to wake myself just as one of the pointed blades began to sink into my neck.

I woke up screaming, my pillow drenched in sweat as the television continued playing an old Bogart film. The shadows it cast onto the walls danced in silence, much like the movies I liked to fall asleep to. I hated the darkness. It felt almost inhuman to me. Since the death of Tess and little Charlie, I needed light to get to sleep, even if projected by silent black and white movies playing in the background as I explored the bottom of another bottle of JD.

CHAPTER 2

Little Ivy Tannen often visited my thoughts during the following weeks, coming to me whenever my brain wasn't focused on anything in particular. It was as if she hid in the shadows, waiting for every possible opportunity to come forward. I knew what she wanted. It was what we all wanted. Justice.

The thing with Ivy though, was that I think she knew justice for her death wasn't going to come in a hurry. Her mother, Laurie, didn't have the funds to launch any kind of appeal, and when I looked into her life, found a woman living on the very cusp of insanity. Ivy's father had died in tragic circumstances while on a freeway in California, leaving the tightly-knit family torn apart. Nothing was going to save Laurie, and I wasn't surprised to read about her suicide a week after my Sunday evening visit to the roadside memorial. And all the while, Ferris continued on with his life as if nothing had happened.

I was pissed. Not just for Ivy, but the way the system had robbed her family; the way it had effectively swept her under the carpet and pushed a big dresser over the spot to ensure it wouldn't be found. She was what many considered as nothing more than a bump in the road, a person's life so insignificant, it meant nothing more than a short article on Page 3.

While she dropped randomly into my mind during the days watching the inmates, it was during the long nights where I felt she took up permanent residence. As I drank myself to sleep most evenings, her face peered back at me from the dark recesses of my mind, watching the endless reels of bad memories pass by. She hung like a shadow in the background, those innocent eyes watching me like a permanent reminder.

Guilt wasn't an emotion I expected to feel about her death, having played no part in it, and yet that was the exact emotion which continued to ravage me. Like a lost soul seeking vengeance, she continued to plague me for weeks, refusing to leave this world behind. Some nights, I honestly felt as if her spirit was somehow connected to me in a weird haunting kind of way. Stephen King himself couldn't have written a better version of what had happened to me since her death.

The idea of helping her find peace wasn't something which fell into my lap like a boat anchor. It wasn't a light-bulb moment, but rather a slow process of endless daydreams which played in my mind while staring at prisoners' heads. Not all of them engaged with me, and it was during the silence where my mind wandered the most.

I considered just killing Ferris outright. One final hurrah before ending my own dejected existence. What else did I have left to live for? My family was gone and given the torn hole they had left in my heart, couldn't see myself searching for a new one. Yes, there were those who replaced lost family members with new ones. Hell, old

Paul Weir, who lost his entire family in a tragic house fire back in the late 90s, found himself a new bride in the Philippines and now enjoys the company of three new children.

The thing is, I'm not that guy. I can't hide my loss by finding a new place to lay my heart. Tess was, is, and always will be my first love, my high school sweetheart and my soulmate, if such a thing existed. Replacing her with someone else not only felt wrong, but also felt too much like a betrayal. Which left me with very little to live for.

In the years following their deaths, I found myself withdrawing more and more from the world, eventually leading a life which slowly intertwined between work and home. During the day, I would travel to each of the dozen prisons assigned to me, while at night, it was good old Mr. Paul Daniels which kept me company.

Perhaps Ivy Tannen's death had been something of a wake-up call for me.

"Hey, Victor," her voice seemed to call out. *"Why not do something worthwhile with your miserable existence, and avenge me."*

It was almost funny when the thought first crossed my mind, and not for the reason one might assume. The obvious response to such a thought should have been, *"What, actually kill him? I can't do that, it would be morally wrong."* But that wasn't the thought I had. The first question which came to mind, spoken in Ivy Tannen's voice was, *"Do you actually have the balls to do it?"*

I don't know whether I thought I did when the idea first crossed my mind. But rather than dismissing the prospect as some crazy drunk thought, I took the question as a challenge, repeating it several times. *Did* I have the balls? *Could* I actually go through with the idea and kill a man for what he did?

Once I convinced myself of the idea that I think I could, my mind seemed to take over, as if on auto pilot. Further down the rabbit hole I fell, a rabbit hole filled with dark shadows and cries for help, where the evil inside every man's soul hid from the world. This was the place where my purest anger lived, the kind which first showed itself in the days after Tess and Charlie were taken from me.

I think it was because of that dark pit of terror that I found myself drinking the nights away, not stopping until I was safely passed out. The bottle not only had a way of numbing the pain, but also to help me forget about the loss completely. That place; that deep, dark hole where no man's soul can survive, that's the place I feared the most.

Suicide had crossed my mind on many occasions, but I had never considered the idea of taking someone else with me, not since that one and only attempt which had left me scared out of my wits. Judge Ferris seemed like the perfect candidate and I doubt Ivy Tannen would have stood in my way.

"Do you really have the balls to go through with it?" Her voice sounded grotesque as she mocked me from the other side of reality, egging me on for a dare I didn't know I wanted to play a part in.

The idea of suicide continued to plague me, and it was during my morning shave I first considered using the razor. Maintaining a bald head, or a Murder One as the inmates called it, had always given me two distinct advantages. First, it shortened my morning routine considerably.

A bald head was much easier to maintain than a full head of hair. But the real benefit I found was that I didn't need someone else to maintain my mop of hair every four to six weeks. Shaving a head is something most people could do with their eyes closed. Hating uncomfortable silences more than meaningless chatter meant I could avoid sitting in a barber's chair altogether. Bald for me, was perfect. The goatee I sported still allowed me some sense of normality. I don't think I could have gone *completely* hairless.

It felt good to hold a straight razor. Not just good, but wholesomely satisfying in a weird sort of way. This was the sort of weapon most people feared, able to cause massive damage with very little effort. The image of Ferris sitting before me with a neat line running across his throat as the wound gave up his life was one I enjoyed. Visions of him sitting in my chair, of me prepping him for the closest shave of his life, him whispering Ivy's words to me.

"Hey there, Victor. Do you have the balls to go through with it?"

On the morning my life took a definitive turn, I drove to McSweeney, a maximum-security facility located halfway between Indiana and Commodore. For some reason, my alarm clock had malfunctioned and woke me almost two hours before my usual time, leaving me with a choice. I could either try and get some more shut eye, or get my butt out of bed and get ready for work.

Sleep had never been a very strong forte in my life. Tess used to ask whether I was part vampire, unable to sleep through to a sunrise in way too many years. Waking early had been a curse on my life for as long as I could remember and was one of the reasons I snapped up the job when it was first presented to me.

Living in Kittanning meant my home sat smack bang

in the middle of the prisons which were under my watch, the area encompassing the state from the southern tip near Uniontown, up to Erie, and across as far as Pleasant Gap. Twelve prisons, all within a hundred miles from my home. With most of my commute along country roads, it meant I not only enjoyed a relatively stress-free drive from inner city traffic snarls, but I also had enough time to enjoy letting my imagination run free.

The thing about the drive to McSweeney was that it took me directly through Elderton, and right past a certain roadside memorial. I'd left earlier than usual this particular morning, thanks to the rogue alarm. I don't know why, but something made me pull over and return to a place I had sat a few weeks before.

The memorial mostly looked just as I remembered. The cross was still there, holding up several notes and faded photographs. The teddy bears had been moved, but remained inside the memorial's boundary. The laminated photograph also remained, looking just as tough as it had the previous time.

But what had changed was a fresh note someone had left pinned to the cross and judging by its condition, it couldn't have been older than a day or two. A message had been scrawled across it, sounding almost philosophical in nature. My eyes ran across it and at first, I simply passed it off as another mourner's way for dealing with their grief.

Sometimes, an accident is just an accident.

I read it the first time, then looked closer to my feet where a photo had blown from wherever it had been fixed. I was about to lean down and pick it up when the words repeated themselves in my mind. *Sometimes, an accident is just an accident.* My fingers hung frozen in mid air, just a few inches above the photo, as I looked up at the words a second time.

Visions of car accidents began to fill my brain, random events which from the outside, looked like nothing more than the note insinuated. I don't remember rising back up, nor returning to my car. What I do remember is the voice which spoke, a voice wanting me to not only hear it, but accept the guidance it was offering me.

McSweeney had been on my roster for close to eight years and gaining entry into the place had become something of a subconscious routine for me. The staff knew who I was, the process of checking all my gear and entering it into the tool register nothing more than a mundane delay on my way inside. Occasionally, a guard would make small talk with me, but for the most part, they'd be under the pump with a line of staff behind me waiting for their turn.

Thankfully, on the day I realized I mightn't have needed to sacrifice my own life to avenge Ivy's, there was no time for talk. If there had been, I might have raised a few eyebrows with my inability to comprehend their words due to my own distractions. A woman was causing quite the ruckus in the reception area, refusing to follow instructions from the officer trying to help her. When she spat at him in-between a cuss-riddled tirade of abuse, several colleagues came to his aid and crash-tackled her to the ground.

The incident barely registered with me. Yes, I saw it, but for the most part, the thoughts running through my mind were much more dominant. It wasn't until a voice called out to me from beyond the entry gate that I remembered where I was.

"Controne. Warden wants to see you," a young guy named Shelton called out to me. He sounded annoyed and when I looked up at him, saw a number of other guards also staring in my direction. "You awake, man?" I realized he must have called to me more than once.

"Sorry. Late night," I said, not lying.

"Yeah, I can smell your late night," he muttered loud enough for me to hear and I noticed the disdain in the eyes of the rest of his colleagues.

I suddenly had the strangest sensation that I was the only one in the room not in on the joke. It's amazing how much a person notices once they've been made aware of a key piece of information and hearing the tone of that one officer was enough to wake my instincts.

They thought I was an alcoholic. In that brief moment, that microsecond of eye contact, I saw it clear as day, not just in Shelton, but the rest of the guards whom's eyes I connected with. To them, I was a wino, a liability, someone who couldn't be trusted. A panic suddenly awoke within me, a genuine sense of dread that the meeting the warden had called me in for, was one which would effectively end my relationship with the Pennsylvania State Correctional System. How did I not see this coming?

Trying not to show my concerns, I lowered my eyes again, grabbed my gear and headed towards the airlock which led through to the other side. Tom Lockhart's office sat up on the second floor of the main building, right above the entry way I took into the jail.

I had only ever taken the stairs once before, after an incident where I helped a fallen officer. The poor chap had suffered a heart attack in one of the corridors and fallen almost right in front of me. Knowing first aid is a requirement for every person entering the jail in an official capacity and as the first one on sight, I commenced CPR after calling it into Control.

Warden Banks, who retired the following year, had summoned me later that day and shook my hand for what he called "a life saving moment for the officer". I wasn't so sure, but didn't argue the point. If they wanted to believe I was some sort of hero, then who was I to change their mind?

Walking up these stairs now, each clip-clop of boot heels echoing my presence, made the uneasy feeling inside my stomach tighten further. Phantom fingers gripped my insides, twisting and turning with each step, as if prepping me for whatever awaited my arrival at the top. Beads of sweat began to form on my brow, a mix of exertion and panic taking hold.

Fearing I would change my mind and turn back if I paused for thought, I pushed through the door at the top without hesitation. The cold air of the Warden's reception area hung heavy, a suffocating stench of Lysol burning my nostrils the moment I stepped through.

"Mr. Controne, go right in," Lockhart's secretary said from behind her desk. The eyes watching me matched Officer Shelton's tone perfectly, further raising my suspicions that I was the only one not in on the punchline.

"Thank you," I offered, trying my best to sound friendly. Her body language told me it didn't help.

Knocking first, I waited a couple of seconds for my summoner to call me inside. When the office beyond remained silent, I turned the handle and walked through into the blinding light of morning. The wall of windows facing me, amplified the sunshine and I was sure I'd be blinded within seconds of stepping inside.

"Ah, Controne. Take a seat," Lockhart said from somewhere inside the wall of light, the moment feeling a little like God speaking to Moses from the burning bush. I closed the door behind me a little slower than normal, hoping to buy myself a little time for my eyes to adjust to the brightness. I wondered whether sunglasses were optional when attending meetings with the head of the prison.

Taking a seat, I met his gaze for the first time and instantly knew the reason for my summons. A person didn't need a degree in psychology to know when a boss is about to fire them. The worst part about sitting before him was that I knew why, the reason having made itself aware just a few minutes earlier.

"Thank you for coming," Lockhart began, closing a folder and setting it aside. And when he next spoke, the second surprise of the morning slammed into me, waking me up in a way I hadn't experienced in a very long time. "I have a job for you."

CHAPTER 3

By the time I reached the unit two hours later, my brain had taken a significant turn since waking that morning. From where I believed I was headed when first arriving for work, it amazed me at how quickly the direction of not only my morning, but my entire career had taken. I'd gone from betting my house on the fact I was about to be fired, to being handed the keys to my very own training facility.

The idea was simple. It hadn't been the warden's idea persay, but one of the many advisors he met with on a regular basis. He'd just been the one to pull the strings and make the suggestion a reality. I wasn't sure who exactly had put my name in the hat of possible people to lead the project, but wasn't really concerned about such minor details.The fact was, I still had a livelihood, something I had considered gone when I started the day.

The job was a training position to help recent releases learn a skill I had been performing for a long time. In short, they wanted me to teach ex-cons how to cut hair.

"A skilled man is a working man, and a working man is an honest man," Lockhart had said. The man was full of quotes, and I had a distinct feeling he used them to try and sound more intellectual than he actually was. Give me a break already. I had my own quote I wanted to shoot at him, one which I liked to use whenever someone felt the philosophical urge to share.

"Why don't you go and put that on a t-shirt," was what I liked to tell people.

But his offer did sound like something I would enjoy and it definitely intrigued me. The premises I'd be working from had already been located in nearby Indiana. The town sat central to a number of correctional facilities, and combined with some free bus tickets, gave the ex-cons an easy place to reach for their weekly classes. All I needed to do was put in a list of things I needed in order to get the building set up for my needs and I could essentially take the reins of my very own school.

Lockhart took the time to share the building with me in person, and not just on the screen of his laptop. He pulled out all stops to make his case, driving us out to Indiana and actually walking through the building itself. I felt almost like royalty as he drove us to Gompers Avenue, talking excitedly as he maneuvered the whale of a truck along the highway.

The location itself had initially been used as a scout hall, but with the troop's transfer to a newer place, it left the building as a perfect candidate for our little venture. The main hall had plenty of space, enough for half a dozen barber stations to be set up. Lockhart proposed a small room near the back to be my office. He would even have a window fitted to the internal wall so I could keep an eye on things in case I needed to.

Everything he proposed sounded too good to be true. I listened to him talk for almost an hour straight, nodding my head like an over-excited six-year-old. The truth is, I was just as excited as he was, perhaps more so because I would be the one running the show. Yes, I would still answer to him to a certain degree, but for the most part, I would be out here on my own. The idea sounded too good to be true.

We walked around the building with him explaining his vision, while I was busy visualizing the stations and the equipment, mentally building a list of things I'd need in order to make things work. Lockhart told me the contractors were ready to go. All they needed was the right set of instructions and they would bring my own vision into reality.

While the building wasn't exactly Trump Towers, it did offer a workspace I understood. It was open, wide enough to allow traffic through, and with just the right amount of floorspace to give me options. Made of solid brick, it also provided the strength needed to fix anything to anywhere. I wasn't restricted in the slightest by fragile drywall or timber beams.

Lockhart stood watching me as if I was about to take his daughter the the prom. Except in this scenario, he *wanted* me to take her, watching me to see if I proved of what he had offered to me. I could feel his eyes in the back of my head as I took the place in, his gaze burning a hole into me. When I stole a quick glance in his direction, his grin was wide enough to expose teeth.

"So, what do you think?"

I'd seen enough to know I wanted it. Not just a little, but every fiber of my being screaming for this opportunity to be handed to me.

"I like what I see and definitely think we can make this work."

It was what he wanted to hear, giving me a pat on the shoulder as he came to me. I didn't think it possible, but his grin grew wider.

"Good," he said, stretching the word out. "That's what I like to hear."

There was a hint of something in his voice I wasn't quite sure of, the underlying tone hiding something either he didn't want to share, or he didn't realize was there. I pushed it aside as I secretly hoped I wasn't making a bad decision.

The truth is, I think what drove me initially wasn't the opportunity in itself, but instead relief that my previous belief didn't come to fruition. When I had first stepped into his office, I whole-heartedly expected to be fired. Instead, I received what many would consider a promotion, a far contrast from what my earlier expectations had been.

"How long do you think they'll take to get things into place for us?" I had a fair idea of the timeframes involved, but things felt a little uncomfortable as we stood in the middle of the room, the silence hanging a little heavier than before.

"I'm hoping within a month. Think you can get a plan together in time?"

"What sort of plan?"

"Names for your initial crew, to get regular training happening. All you need to do is comply with state education stipulations, submit your evaluations accordingly, and you should be good to go."

"I've never really taught before," I muttered, more to myself, but Lockhart replied anyway.

"That's crap. You practically teach every time you step

into a prison." And then leaning in and lowering his voice, added, "Those men respect you, you know."

"How do you figure that?" Respect wasn't a word I had ever openly associated with how inmates looked at me.

"You haven't had the shit kicked out of you yet, have you?"

He had a point, although I'm not sure I would have gone as far as calling it respect. Personally, I'd have put it down to me watching my step, not treating them with the kind of contempt I've seen guards do. Not all of them, of course, but I've seen enough guard/prisoner interactions to know one side definitely holds a grudge toward the other.

"Fair point," I said. He clapped me on the shoulder again.

"OK, let's get the hell out of here. If you're happy to sign on the dotted line, we can get cracking on getting this place into shape for you."

We shook hands, the ancient tradition more than enough of an answer for him. After a final look around, we headed back to the prison. Once back in Lockhart's office, he took me through the paperwork and I signed where he indicated. The whole thing was finished before lunch and by the time I finally reached the unit for my usual day, I had effectively become an official trainer for the Pennsylvania Correctional Department.

CHAPTER 4

That night should have been reason to celebrate. Given how my morning had taken such a drastic turn from where I initially believed my career within corrections was about to end up, I thought it was a definite step up. But any hint of positive emotion left my body as I drove past Ivy Tannen's memorial on my way home.

I don't know why she held such a presence over me. Part of me got creeped out by the idea she was somehow attached to me simply because I was so close to the scene of her accident. In a way, it felt a bit Stephen King-ish to me, like I had been somehow drawn into one of his books as a plot point, or a character. Was Ivy Tannen somehow haunting me?

The moment I drove past and took just a split-second look in the direction of the memorial, all the positive emotion felt as if it was draining from me, leaking through a puncture wound like a broken barrel. Within minutes, I turned sad, depressed, and by the time I walked through my front door less than an hour later, I was angry.

The first thing I did was go into the den and sit on the

couch. Not just for a minute or two. Whatever had taken my attention during the trip home, continued to keep me preoccupied. Once minute, the final remnants of sunlight shone through the window, the next, I found myself sitting in complete darkness. The wall briefly lit up with shadows as car headlights drove past, pulling my attention back into the present.

I had no clue where I had gone, the only recollection coming to mind being the horrendous sound of tires squealing just before the car hit Ivy. It was as if I had returned to the day of the accident, playing the event over and over again, trying to make sense. Words filled my head, a single sentence, lit up like a neon sign in the background. *Sometimes, an accident is just an accident.*

Something hit me about those words, the insinuation, the hidden meaning, the disregard for what everything else an accident caused. Were the victims just collateral damage to those words? That's what it felt like; as if they were nothing more than an inconvenience for a saying worthy of a place on a t-shirt.

"Sometimes, an accident is just an accident," I whispered into the darkness, the words feeling like crushed glass in my throat. I felt like screaming, the faces of the victims from my past staring back at me. Tess, Charlie, and of course Ivy. Her face loomed the most, her eyes almost burning into mine as I saw them as clearly as the cup I'd left on the coffee table that morning.

Without thinking, I reached for it as I stood, threw it into the shadows and heard the satisfying crunch as it connected with something. The explosion of glass imploding, the ripple of broken china skittering across the floorboards, it all sounded so fulfilling. The anger fed off the sound and I looked around for something else to throw, not caring what it was or where it flew. I needed to hear destruction, the only fuel to feed a rage still lingering deep inside me.

When the sound stopped and silence returned, the scent of coffee filled my nostrils.

"Good one, dumbass," I muttered to myself, the influx of satisfaction disappearing in an instant. This wasn't the way; it never had been. I had spent years controlling the anger inside me, not wanting to lose one of the few emotional links to the deaths of my family. Someone once told that the very essence of my rage needed to be bottled and held deep inside, with me only taking a little sip when it really mattered.

I went over and turned the light on. The damage wasn't quite as bad as it had sounded in the darkness. I'd managed to send the cup through one of the glass doors on the display cabinet. Both had shattered on impact, leaving bits of glass, china, and puddles of day-old coffee strewn across the floor and wall.

This was something Tess would not have approved of. Actually, I could picture her frown as I went to the kitchen and retrieved the implements to clean the mess up, all the while feeling bad for my brief loss of control. I had spent years managing to control the pain and wasn't ready to give it up. Not over something I had virtually no control over.

As I began to sweep up the broken glass, the sounds of the shards filled the den, each tinkle sounding a small part of a musical as I first swept them into a neat pie, then brushed them into a dustpan. Once I was sure I found al of them, I dropped them into the trash and stood looking after it as it lay at the bottom of the bag. Just like that, a cup Tess had held close in her hands on cold winter mornings, was gone, erased from my life in the blink of an eye.

Shaking my head in disgust at such a childish slip, I returned to the den and once again, dropped onto the couch. I still wasn't quite ready to let go of the day. The memory of driving past the roadside memorial kept returning in brief flashbacks, the original accident superimposed over the current scene. As if oxymoroning themselves through my mind, Lockhart joined the trio of faces whirling around in my brain, the sense of triumph from him, intermingling with the depression and rage I felt from the others.

Closing my eyes, I tried to push them aside, feeling guilty as I did, but knowing I needed to. This wasn't the time to lose my sanity, not after feeling as if I conquered a mountain earlier in the day. The emotional train wreck building inside me ended to take a backseat as I contemplated my future. There was more to look forward to, much more. Soon, I would be leading a group of ex-cons through the biggest career change of their lives and hopefully set them on the right path. That was what I need to focus on.

But as I continued pushing the familiar faces aside, a new one came out from the shadows, one I had no choice but to acknowledge. It was my own, sporting the familiar head of hair I had back when I was a family man. Those had been the days after the accident, when the nights were at their darkest and death felt like the perfect way out.

I opened my eyes and looked at the wall behind the television, the one holding the majority of memories in the form of photographs. Frames of all sizes adorned the wall, with Charlie's baby photos flanking our wedding day. There was the vacation to Toledo in one, another from our trip to Hawaii in another. Our honeymoon to Barbados, the weekend in Omaha. All the memories to remind a man of who he once was, and the heartbreaking reality of all he had lost.

But as I stared at the photos, feeling ready to rip my own insides out, the one memory which came through strongest was of one which quite possibly could have been my last. The first couple of years after the accident were the most painful for me, and I spent almost every night beside their graves. The bottle of bourbon I normally took along wasn't anywhere near enough to get me through a night, but I did try my hardest to make it last.

It was maybe nine months after their deaths that I think I really hit rock bottom. Not just hit it, but full-on deep-dived into the very depths head first. One night turned into the next as they became nothing more than an endless blur of grief and pain. I barely remember one day from another, with one thought dominating my consciousness. I wanted to die and join my family. I didn't want to spend another night alone without them, not when they were so close and I could reach them with a single act.

I don't think I ever made the exact decision to kill myself. Yes, there were the pills, but they had been prescribed by my doctor at the time, genuinely wanting me to get a decent night's sleep. I had grown skills in masking my drinking back then, mastering the art of camouflaging alcoholism. Or at least I think I did; I mean, I did manage to convince a doctor of prescribing me a decent supply of sleeping pills in-between bottles of Paul Daniels.

The clearest moment I have from back then, wasn't sitting beside their graves, it wasn't even the grief I was feeling. What I remember so distinctly was the precise moment I popped the cap and stared down into the pill bottle, gazing at the tiny capsules which in essence, were my keys to the door between worlds. They were the train ticket to me joining my family, to once again stand beside them, hold them in my arms.

I swallowed them all, every last one of them, forcing them down as tears and snot intermingled with the rain falling around me. The Paul Daniels made them easy to swallow, the final mouthfuls my last on this earth. To me at the time, there had been no sweeter taste, with destiny waiting for me.

Sleep took me shortly after and I remember smiling so distinctly as my eyes closed for what was supposed to be the final time. It really did feel like a homecoming for me, with the bodies of my wife and child lying just a few feet from me, the only witnesses to an act I hoped would reunite us.

Of course it failed. I woke the next morning with a small lump of pills next to my head, the remnants of a pile of vomit I ejected shortly after my eyes closed. It turned out that the alcohol didn't appreciate the helping hand from the capsules and combined, caused my body to react violently.

It was the one and only time I sank deep enough to willingly end my life in order to rejoin my family. Since that night, I had fought to keep the upper hand over my grief each and every day. I couldn't just throw my life away because of a weakness to live.

The reminder which came forth to tell me that perhaps suicide wasn't a necessary option didn't come from any internal thoughts. Not while I was sitting on the couch staring at the photographs on my walls. It came when I finally switched the television on, channel-hopped across a few programs and found a documentary based in Pittsburgh. It wasn't the program itself which grabbed my attention, but the person currently speaking, looking far different to the day he had robbed a little girl of her life.

Judge Gordon Ferris looked as if he was having the time of his life. I watched the muted Judge talking and instantly felt heat run through me, the man looking more carefree than ever. In this reality, there was no Ivy Tannen in his life, no little girl whose life he'd taken due to his own negligence. I didn't care what the interview was about, no need to hear the words. Seeing the carefree look in his eyes was enough for me to understand that good old Judge Ferris had moved on from his destruction, moved on and continued a life he didn't deserve.

As I sat watching him, seven words continued to roll through my mind, each time louder than the time before. They would be the words which I would come to live by, words which would eventually lead me right to the good judge's door. *Sometimes, an accident is just an accident.*

CHAPTER 5

My plans for Judge Ferris didn't really begin to start growing until a few days later. Back when Ivy's voice had first dared me to act, I had contemplated ending his life, as well as my own, at the same time. Kill him first, and then myself, a classic murder/suicide for the nightly news networks to broadcast to the world.

But those brief words from the memorial, the seven words which had become somewhat of an obsession for me, had been rolling around my brain for days before I understood things didn't need to go the way I had planned. It appeared as if I didn't need to die at all. Sometimes, an accident was just an accident and didn't need anyone else's involvement.

I began toying with the idea of planning some random accident for the good judge. The only problem was, trying to find the right kind in order to fulfill my needs. The bottom line was simple. He had to die. There was no other way around it. Ivy Tannen's soul wouldn't rest until the son of a bitch's ghost stood next to her own and she could confront him herself.

An accident seemed like the best way of getting back at him. Accidents happened every day, many of them found with no real cause or explanation. They were simply... accidents. The ideas rolled through my mind during each shift, watching the inmates going about their jobs as I stood back supervising. The most obvious, of course, was a motor vehicle accident, the same method by which the judge stole Ivy's life. But thinking about a car accident and actually initiating one felt like worlds apart.

How does a person cause a car accident from a distance? I thought about ways of distracting him, of running him off the road myself, or setting up some sort of diversion to get him to a place I had set up ahead of his arrival. But none of them seemed to work. They just *felt* wrong. For each of those ideas to work, it would need the judge to follow certain cues to the letter and that was something I couldn't guarantee.

Next, I thought about a more direct accident. Why did it have to be in a car? If I could just get him to fall to his death, or choke to death, or some other bizarre way unfortunate souls sometimes departed this life, then that would suffice. An image of him laying back in a bath and a hairdryer falling into the water came to mind at one point and it was then I realized things had taken another turn towards the impossible.

For one, I doubted the judge used a hairdryer, much less spent his evenings relaxing in a bubblebath. Gaining entry into his home proved another obstacle standing in my way. It wasn't as if I was a master burglar with skills in breaking and entering. Hell, I could barely gain entry into my own home when I locked myself outside the previous summer. Breaking into his home?

And then there was the surveillance issue, not from me,

but from the environment itself. For an accident to be classed as an accident, he needed to die in circumstances which either couldn't be explained, or appeared to have been caused by fate itself. Any hint of interference and things would turn south in a heartbeat, with an accident quickly taking on the appearance of murder.

Our world had changed significantly in recent years, with surveillance cameras now looming over almost every aspect of our lives. A person couldn't go anywhere without being filmed by at least something. How the hell was I going to get close to the judge without being seen, and then, close enough to do what I needed to do?

I spent so many days trying to think of the right way to create an accident, that I grew tired of thinking about the judge. Even Ivy felt wrong to me, with her constant guilt tripping as she stared at me from the shadows. Things weren't exactly getting easier for me as the weeks progressed, not when one considered the time of year.

There were two times a year when things became almost unbearable for me. It was weird, because birthdays weren't nearly as painful for me as the other two were. Yes, I went to Tess and Charlie's final resting places on each of their birthdays, but strangely, those I could deal with. The anniversary of their deaths was perhaps the most difficult of all, the date which had robbed me of everything I had ever truly loved. And the other was Christmas.

Sitting on Christmas Day amongst the plethora of memories hanging from the walls, there was one image which stood out for me. It wasn't a particularly big one, a small 8x10 fixed next to the door to the hallway. It had been taken just ten months before their deaths, a random moment caught in time, forever reminding me of what true loss really was.

That was the year we had taken Charlie up to New York City for the first time to see the Christmas tree. Not just *any* tree, but *the* tree, the one people came from hundreds of miles away to see. For Charlie, Christmas in Rockefeller Center had taken on a whole new meaning that night. Her face had lit up in a way I had never seen before, captured in a selfie I took on my cellphone.

Tess and I had built the excitement up in the days before, culminating in Charlie covering her eyes until we stood almost directly in front of the tree itself. I held the phone out in front of us and snapped the moment she took her hands away and saw the glitter and sparkles, the lights, the essence of the moment itself. That very image was the one hanging on the wall, a tiny moment in time, holding such a huge amount of emotion.

Since their deaths, Christmas had become another one of those times of the year where I wanted to find the darkest hole and lose myself, to hide from everything to do with the season itself. It was also where I drank the most, the liquor helping me escape the pain better than any counseling session ever could.

By the time Christmas came around, I managed to get myself a week off work, knowing of the struggles I would face. And with the new training role officially coming into effect the first week of the new year, I knew I couldn't take the risk of the drinking hampering my efforts to portray a sober individual. And so, I took a vacation to my own living room, with seven days of absolutely nothing but grief and tears.

The strange thing was, I didn't spend anywhere near as long as I thought I would at the bottom of a Paul Daniels bottle. What I had planned for was a week of giving into my pain. What I ended up with was three days of a blurred mess, followed by the beginnings of an operation which came completely out of nowhere.

It was during the afternoon of Christmas Eve where things took a turn for me, and not in a way I want to openly share. That was the afternoon I took my half-empty bottle to the desk, opened the laptop and googled the interview I had seen the judge give on television a few weeks before.

I must have watched it on repeat at least a dozen times, muted, just as I had experienced it the very first time. It was his eyes I focused on, staring into them as he silently shared his thoughts on some irrelevant topic I didn't care for. His views meant nothing to me, nor did his expertise, or experience, or anything else the interviewer asked of him. It was his eyes which I wanted to see into, to get a glimpse into his very soul as he continued living and breathing, while Ivy Tannen lay rotting in some grave.

Each time the clip repeated, my anger multiplied, the burning in my chest growing with intensity as I failed to find the slightest hint of remorse, or guilt, or some minute sign that he remembered the life he had stolen from a child. My fingers began to shake as the tears flowed almost as fast out of me, as the bourbon flowing in. The knuckles in my hand audibly popped in the silence of the room as my grip on the neck of the bottle increased. The rage boiled over, the scream rising from the deepest part of my soul as I threw the bottle blindly away, tossed aside like the body of a girl now dead.

The initial crash of it hitting the wall went unnoticed as I gripped the sides of the laptop. My hands could barley keep still as they lifted the computer up from the desk, threatening to send it after the bottle, with every fiber of my being struggling to regain control. As I stood with the device precariously balanced on the very edge of a possible launch, the scales of control inside me continued to dip to and fro like a seesaw. It felt like the good side and the bad side, each fighting for control over my conscience.

Squeezing my eyes shut and screaming into the silence, I fought to expel every ounce of anger in a desperate attempt to regain control. This wasn't me, and it certainly wasn't how I had ever envisioned myself to become. The feeling of the negative energy leaving my body genuinely frightened me and I imagined the look of horror Tess would have given me if she had seen me at that moment.

By the time I opened my eyes again, I had managed to scream myself hoarse, the burning in my throat feeling on fire. I looked over to where the bottle had landed and felt the grief multiply as I saw the vacant spot on the wall. In my moment of rage, I had managed to not only knock the photo of us at Rockefeller Center off the wall, but also smashed the frame itself to smithereens as it hit the floor.

Slowly walking over and avoiding as many of the glass shards as I could, my heart sank as I saw a neat cut along one side of the photo, a razor-sharp sliver of the glass having sliced through the heart of the photo. The flap which had been almost completely severed, had taken half of Tess's head with it, a creepy reminder of their accident and the horror I faced when identifying their bodies.

It took me ten heartbreaking minutes to clean the mess and once I was sure I had cleaned up most of the glass shards, I took the photo to the couch and stared at it for what felt like hours. Tears poured from me, feeling like a cheap wine, reminding me of the dumb act which damaged it in the first place.

I knew I couldn't keep sitting in the house constantly killing myself with grief and dread and all the emotions I struggled to contain. If I did, there might have been a chance I wouldn't wake up at all the next day. To try and distract myself, I put on the television and began surfing through a few of the channels, doing my best to find something I knew had the capability of holding my attention. It finally came, about four clicks in, and instantly made me sit up.

Seeing Judge Ferris on the television at that moment felt almost as if fate itself had descended into my living room, willing me to get moving on a mission I knew I could no longer walk away from. He was being interviewed about how he was celebrating the holidays now that he had made such a huge donation to a local homeless shelter. Watching him speak to the reporter with such a fake twinkle of kindness in his eye worked me up again, the feeling of my own failure for not ending him yet rising up into burning rage.

"I'll get him," I whispered into the silence of the room, a part of me believing Ivy Tannen really was in the room with me. I didn't believe in ghosts the way some do, but a part of me hoped a small piece of her essence was still around to know what I was doing.

CHAPTER 6

It took me a little more than a second to know what I needed to do once I saw the judge on television that Christmas afternoon. The answer sat right in front of me, talking to some reporter about how incredibly blessed he felt to have the opportunity to share part of his blessing with those less fortunate. Aside from the financial donation, he planned to help serve Christmas dinner to the less than fortunate later that afternoon, which meant I knew exactly where he was going to be.

What I needed was information. He was a judge working one of the many benches in Pittsburgh, and that more than likely meant he also lived in the city. If he didn't, then he lived either nearby, or somewhere temporarily. Either way, it meant I needed to take a drive from my home I Kittening, down to the city, if I wanted to take the next step.

There was so much I didn't know about the judge, so much I needed to know if I was going to go through with my plan. What I really needed to do was follow him around for a bit, to try and get as much information first hand, before looking further afield for more guarded information. With my new job officially starting on the third of January, it meant I could try and get a few extra days of leave and use the week to my advantage.

Before committing to more time off from work, I decided to take a drive down to Pittsburgh and see if I had what it took to commit to a stakeout. I'd watched enough crime shows to know the basics. Take plenty of food plenty of drink, and something suitable to urinate into. The last think a person on a stakeout wanted to do was leave for a bathroom break and risk missing something vital.

Grabbing a backpack, I began with water, filling two empty soda bottles and placing them inside. I also grabbed a bag of potato chips, a couple of payday candy bars, plus an apple. I wasn't too sure about the latter, not realizing I had any, but found one hiding in the bottom of the fridge. Whether it remained in edible condition would be determined some time during my upcoming operation.

Finally, I grabbed the cable from my cellphone charger, just in case. I wasn't planning on spending my time on the cellphone itself, but with no idea of what I was in for, didn't want to get caught with my pants down. Lastly, I grabbed my baseball cap, sunglasses, and coat. Pittsburgh winters weren't exactly forgiving and again, not knowing how long I would be kept out in my car, figured having it was better than not. As if thinking of the snow itself, I grabbed a folded blanket from the closet, sat it on top of the bag and made my out.

We'd shivered through the worst blizzard of the decade for the previous two days, but as I stepped into the early afternoon, the sunshine reflecting off the snow nearly blinded me. I could feel the heat of it in my eyes, although still shivered as the cold wind blew straight through me.

"The things we do," I mumbled to myself as I climbed into the pick-up.

As I pulled out of my yard and turned for my drive down to the city, I had the undeniable feel of excitement. Something buzzed awake inside me, an air of intense enthusiasm filling the cabin as I set my sights on finally setting the wheels into motion. In just over an hour, I would be within just a few feet from where the judge would be preparing to share his day with the less fortunate.

An hour alone can be a long time, conditions permitting. For me, there was nothing else to think about except the man I was hoping to follow, and the girl who had sent me to find him. This was about nobody else except Judge Ferris, and Ivy Tannen. In my world, one couldn't exist without the other, and that made me the odd one out, the observer, the one standing on the sidelines and watching their worlds collide again and again as he repeatedly sent her flying.

There was one problem with Ferris which I recognized almost immediately after setting off. While I had every intention of following him around to get a better sense of his world, I quickly realized I had done very little when it came to researching the man himself. An hour or two on Google would have told me everything about him I needed to know, and yet that one tiny oversight now haunted me.

I was going in blind, with no real insight into the man I was hunting. What I did know of him amounted to barely enough to be considered an insight. It felt more of just a passing glance. If I had taken the time to really think about it, I would have looked for anything useful, like places he visited, people he hung around with. I did know he was married, but had no clue as to the state of the marriage, whether they had children, or where his extended family came from. I knew exactly nothing.

Shaking my head in disbelief, I continued on, deciding that there would always be more time if I needed it. Google was practically sitting beside me; all I needed was a few minutes of downtime and I could check things out. For the time being, I just wanted to make contact and watch him from a distance.

If there was one thing I knew from the experience of spending forty years on planet earth, it was that people always acted different when they didn't think anybody was watching. Everything from picking their nose, letting a fart fly, to helping themselves to just about anything they found in the streets. A few honest people lived among the crowd, but there were always those who carried an alter ego around for the times they were alone.

There was something else I knew, as well. People in power had a very bad habit of believing themselves better than the masses, with some going far enough to believe they lived behind the scope of the law. I had already seen Ferris display the classic characteristics on at least one occasion, and the unfortunate Ivy Tannen finding out first hand.

By the time I finally reached the city limits of Pittsburgh itself, my brain had begun to run multiple scenarios in quick succession, each offering a possible outcome from me following the judge around. Realizing they were all nothing more than a distraction, I pushed them aside and focused on the road ahead. The snow had begun to fall again and as I parked down the street from the homeless shelter, prepared myself for my first ever stakeout.

CHAPTER 7

The very first thing I discovered in the early stages of my surveillance was just how impatient I was as a person. Not just impatient, but damn near agitated by the prospect of sitting still for a few hours while staring out at the street. My leg began to jitter up and down within minutes as I watched people come and go from the front of the building, the line for a free meal snaking its way around the side and from my sight.

It was freezing, the temperature well below the point where Paulets sufficed for warmth. The people standing in line huddled together to limit the effects of the wind and I couldn't have imagined the misery for those caught up without a home. There were more people coming than goin, which meant more time in line for those waiting for entry. But as far as I could tell, the judge hadn't arrived.

I sank into my seat, considered switching the car off and grabbing the blanket for warmth. But one look at the temperature gauge was enough for me to push the idea well away. The heater was doing a great job of keeping me warm and if I was going to continue, I needed to stay switched on.

Minutes turned to hours and by five o'clock, I began t wonder whether he was already inside. Either that, or the son of a bitch had ditched the idea completely. From where I was sitting, I couldn't see shit, with not only the snow hampering my efforts, but also the building itself. There were no windows on this side, which meant no sneaky look inside. The binoculars I kept in the glove compartment proved useless as I failed to find the man of the moment.

An uncomfortable feeling began to build upon inside me as one distinct realization came to mind. It wasn't something I willfully pulled from the shadows, but something which came to mind the second I understood that I wasn't going to get a look inside from the truck. I needed to go inside and something told me time was of the essence.

The one thing I had always known was that the most important rule of thumb when following someone was to never let them see you. Not just during the actual act of walking or driving behind them, but during other times, like when serving meals to unfortunate souls. I couldn't risk him seeing me and somehow remembering me at a later date. He was a judge after all, and considering he dealt with the correctional department all the time, the possibility of him running into me at work wasn't exactly impossible.

I began to run the idea of getting in line through my mind, knowing it wasn't something I really wanted to do. For one thing, it was freezing and standing amongst a bunch of homeless people, wasn't exactly my idea of a happy Christmas.

"You think they have a choice?" Hearing the voice startled me and it took me a moment to realize it was my own. I shook my head, surprised at the fact a part of me was trying to convince the other part of a job I knew I couldn't avoid. There was no other way around it. If I was going to follow the judge, I needed to pick up his trail and right then, it appeared to begin inside the homeless shelter.

"Damn it," I hissed to myself, pushing the words through clenched teeth as I considered my Paulet. I hadn't planned on walking out in the weather and didn't bring the best option available to me.

Knowing I wasn't going to remain in the car and listen to Ivy tell me I didn't have the balls for this type of job, I pulled the zipper up on my Paulet, twirled the scarf around my neck a couple of times, then pulled on my cap. The icy wind blew straight through the Paulet as I stepped out of the truck, the cold whipping my face with each step.

"Merry Christmas," I whispered, stepped onto the sidewalk and headed towards the building. Whatever reservations I had, fell by the wayside. It was time to move forward.

I did try to cheat a little, an idea growing the closer I got to the shelter. With the front doors wide open because of the line going inside, I figured I could simply walk past, grab a sneaky look inside and find the judge doing his thing. The idea seemed like the perfect alternative to the whole lining up thing, but when I slowly walked past and grabbed a peak, felt my heart sink as the wall immediately inside the door blocked my view.

The line of people snaked through the door, curved around to the left and disappeared through a smaller inside door. The only way to see beyond was to actually walk through the door itself. My ears began to buzz from the cold and when I reached up to touch one, was sure it had frozen solid, my lobe barely feeling the finger.

I briefly stopped and focused on the people already standing inside, and anther thought hit me, but the second I took a step in the direction of that part of the line, a dozen faces turned to look at me, most with a distinct disdain in them. There was no way in hell that I would be able to sneak past them, not unless I tried to lie my way past the crowd. I considered telling them I was another volunteer, but knew my cover would be blown the second I stepped inside and that would raise unwanted attention on me. If nothing else, I needed to remain in the background as much as possible.

Residing myself to the fact there would be no shortcuts to help me, I turned and headed for the back of the line. A few eyes followed me, but for most, the threat had passed. I left their place in the queue intact, and that's what anybody standing there really cared about.

Thankfully, the line didn't extend too far from the door, bent around just a single corner, which meant I still had somewhat of a view to where official arrivals entered the place. It meant that even if the judge turned up now, I would see him and could return to my truck and wait for him to finish his brief stint at charity work.

The guy in front of me tried to initiate some conversation, but I ignored him. For one, I wasn't in the mood for smalltalk, but more importantly, I didn't want a distraction keeping me from watching for the judge to arrive. It took the guy just a single attempt to get the message. Instead, he focused his attention on the woman standing in front of him, leaving me to my own devices.

"Hey, Judge," someone suddenly called ahead of me. I looked up at the same time I pulled the front of my cap lower over my head. A few other heads turned in the direction of the man walking from the building, so me showing interest wasn't anything unusual. The man turned a little sideways, but never slowed, a brief wave with one gloved hand showing the only bit of acknowledgement to the initial caller.

My heart definitely picked up pace as I recognized the face hidden behind a thin scarf, his familiar dark mop of hair dotted with snowflakes as he walked towards his SUV. I hadn't seen it on my approach. It sat around the corner from where I parked, but the second I saw it, chills ran through my body.

There it was, the car which killed little Ivy Tannen. A thick blanket of snow sat on its roof and hood, mostly shielding the color from view, but seeing Ferris climb into it, brought the reality of what it was back to me in a flash. That was the actual vehicle which had taken her life, slammed into her tiny little body and sent it flying into the dirt. The distinct outline of the Wagoneer staring back at me with those ominous LED eyes as he fired it up.

It wasn't until the car began to move that I finally broke free from my paralysis, realizing he was about to disappear again unless I made a move and jumped in my own truck. From what I could tell, he was turning back the way my ride sat and so I didn't hurry, again not wanting to give him a reason to look my way. By the time I reached the truck, he'd barely made it more than a hundred yards up the road, sitting in Christmas traffic.

I caught up easily enough to him once I managed to get turned around. He'd only managed to get a few cars ahead of me and I used them to shield myself somewhat. No point riding his ass. Just as his own ride featured such distinctive lines, mine too had the hallmarks of being memorable. It wasn't that I couldn't afford anything better. I just didn't see the point in getting rid of a truck if the thing still worked perfectly. Who cared if the paint looked a little worn?

We drove for close to ten minutes before the judge took a sudden turn to his right. With the speed he was doing, I had a brief moment of panic, expecting him to speed away from someone he recognized as tailing him. But when I passed by the little parking lot, I felt relief as I watched the reversing lights come on, the Jeep backing into one of the spaces. I continued on for another couple of hundred yards, found a gap, then did a u-turn.

As I parked a little further down on the other side of the street, I felt a little twinge of intrigue. This was the first real insight I had into the man himself and one look at the building he parked outside of told me almost everything I needed to know. It wasn't a building I had ever been to personally, but given that I had spent more than enough time around criminals, knew of its existence long before I saw it in real life.

Waterfalls from the outside, appeared as nothing more than a day spa, a place for weary bodies to go and rejuvenate themselves. Even once inside, there was nothing untoward in the way the place was set up. A reception desk greeted customers, while the rest of the place looked and felt like the real thing. But once a person took the stairs to the second floor, things turned interesting.

With prostitution illegal in the state of Pennsylvania, it left sex workers to find their clients through alternative means and word of mouth played a huge part of that process. The more people who knew, the more clients they received. But word of mouth was just one part, with another side of things needing just as much exposure.

Power. Influence. Control. These were the true ingredients behind successful underground businesses and none held all three more freely than judges. From where I was sitting, it appeared Ferris was taking full advantage of his position. As I watched him walk inside, I knew my immediate future wasn't going anywhere. He'd come for his Christmas dessert, and definitely not the kind he could take home.

I settled in for the long wait, grabbed the blanket and covered my legs. Next, I took out my cellphone, turned the screen's brightness down to bare minimum and began to do the googling I should have taken care before setting off that day. It was time I got to know the man who had not only taken Ivy Tannen's life, but who was also at that very moment, screwing another girl over.

From what I could gather, his marriage didn't appear unusual from the outside. Maria Ferris had stood by her husband for close to forty years, a devoted Catholic, and a member of the local shooter's association. I wondered how she would feel if she knew where her husband was spending his Christmas.

The couple had raised three children, all of whom had moved onto greener pastures around the country. I didn't find anything especially exciting about them and simply put them down as regular people unaware of their father's darker side. It was the darker side I began to research next and it didn't take long to find whispers surrounding the good judge, with mentions of bribes and special favors for those who knew how to win him over.

He wasn't the man I had hoped to find. Up until that moment, a very small fragment remained within me, that perhaps the accident had been a once-off lapse of self-control. People slip up every day, good people, who normally wouldn't stray too far from the right side of life. Unfortunately Ferris wasn't one of them. The more I looked, the more I saw, with the darkness of who he really was growing crystal clear by the time I watched him return to his car.

This was exactly the person I had secretly wished he would be, a vicious piece of shit who so easily moved on with his life after Ivy. There was no remorse, no looking back over his shoulder at the carnage left in his wake. He was the kind of man who would plead for his life once staring death in the face, afraid of everything he would lose.

I tightened my grip on the steering wheel as he came back out a couple of hours later. He was too far from me to be able to see the grin on his face, but I did notice a distinct bounce in his step which definitely wasn't there when he entered the building.

He pulled out onto the road a few seconds later and continued down his original direction. This left me needing to do another u-turn, which I messed up, a tiny hesitation forcing me to hold back. A traffic light further down had changed to green just moments before he took off, leaving me to wait for the brief flood of oncoming cars to deal with. By the time I managed to get to the other side of the road, Ferris was gone.

CHAPTER 8

Ferris disappearing into the Christmas evening didn't matter. With time on my side, it was just a matter of patience, and it didn't take long for me to catch up with him a second time. If nothing else, the man quickly turned into a walking billboard of predictability, returning to the brothel for a second go the very next afternoon.

I did return home for the night myself, preferring the warmth of my bed over the harsh interior of the truck. And it gave me a chance to do a little more research on the man himself, research which I knew I would need. And as if to reward me for my efforts, the laptop offered a few more distinct advantages over the cellphone to an old-timer like myself.

What started off as an innocent question typed into Google, quickly turned into one revelation after another as I began to fall down a rabbit hole of information. *What are the best stakeout techniques* began as nothing more than an off-the-cuff enquiry, but boy, did the answers come thick and fast. A place called Reddit appeared in more than a few answers and when I clicked through, found what can only be described as a noticeboard free-for-all.

Random people offered up all kinds of advice, and a couple included links to some dodgy software a person could download for free. Nothing the richest kid on the block, I liked the sound of free and so followed a couple. The first turned out to be a dud, sending me through to a porn site which instantly opened up several pages in quick succession. I was sure I hit a few viruses along the way, but managed to shut them down just as fast.

The second link took me to a page displaying dozens of links for free software, but there was just one I was after. What I ended up downloading may have included a few additional bits and pieces designed to phish me out of my life savings, but since I didn't keep any worthy information on the laptop, it didn't bother me too much. What I was interested in was the software itself, which I installed onto my desktop with just a few clocks.

Insight was a program which hunted for the kind of information a hunter like me could use to find their person of interest. It scanned millions of pages in the blink of an eye and found personal information. And if I paid an extra $49.99, I could get the Pro version, which included the ability of scanning page held behind firewalls, a truly unique feature I didn't quite understand. Not that it mattered what I knew, because once u paid the extra fifty bucks, I hit the Scan button and sat back to await the results.

Within a matter of seconds, *Insight* managed to find and share everything from the good judge's home address, as well as his office address. There was his driver's license number, previous years' FICA statements, W-2s, his current net worth, and loads more I didn't really need. His addresses were more than enough.

Feeling more than a little intrigued, I ran his home address through Google Maps and stared at the home for almost five minutes as I imagined him spending his evenings inside. It was more than a little modest, two stories worth of brickwork hiding behind an impressive security fence. If I had visions of breaking into his home, they quickly evaporated when I saw what he sat behind. If nothing else, the man was definitely security conscious, with several cameras fixed to the outside walls.

During the brief drive back to Pittsburgh the following day, I began to devise all sorts of plans for keeping tabs on the judge. For one thing, I wanted to make sure I knew exactly where he was every second of the day. To do that meant I needed some sort of tracker. Thankfully, these had become readily available and I had a number of options to choose from.

For one, I could have attached some sort of cellphone to the underside of his car and kept track that way, or used one of those small tracking buttons people attached to their keys. I wasn't sure how viable either one of those would be given the distances involved, the wet weather, plus so many other factors. But just as I had hoped, my savior came again in the form of Google.

It turned out, somebody already faced the same issue as me, and had invented a small magnetized tracking chip. The catch phrase topping the web page read, Don't trust the spouse? Use Magnet Mouse. The picture beneath looked like a small oval-shaped button around half the size of a pack of smokes. For just a hundred bucks per unit, I was guaranteed unlimited range on a state-of-the-art spouse tracker, small enough to be hidden inside any purse. Satisfaction guaranteed or my money back.

I ordered two, opted for the lightning fast, overnight delivery and settled back into my seat waiting for Ferris to reemerge from his playhouse for the second time. He pulled out through his enormous gates around two and made a beeline for the brothel. I followed him at distance and parked in almost the same place as I did the previous evening.

He remained inside for just over an hour and this time when he came out, the grin on his face was wide enough to see from across the street. Whomever had serviced the man, certainly did their job well, his satisfaction visible from a hundred yards away.

Considering it was a Sunday, I wasn't expecting him to go much further than his first stop, but when he pulled back out onto the street, continued in the direction away from his home, opting for downtown. Not wanting to risk getting seen, I hung back a little further until traffic began to build up a little more around us.

As we turned onto Grant Street, I thought he might have been heading into the courthouse, although I wasn't sure why he'd want to go there on a Sunday. But he passed by the building, continued on for a few hundred yards, then pulled into the parking lot underneath the Dillinger Enterprises building. I had no choice but to continue on, again caught blindsided by the sudden turn of events. With no way inside and no nearby options to pull over, I had no choice but to continue on.

An open-air parking lot on the corner of Forbes and Grant turned out to be the best option and I pulled in, but no matter where I parked, my vision of the parking garage's entrance was blocked. The only choice I had, was to get out and start walking. Forty minutes later and with no sign of the judge, I knew I was beat.

I was still too much of an amateur to know what options I could employ to continue my surveillance. Given that it was a Sunday and the building itself offered no reasonable excuses for a man like the judge to show up, I couldn't understand why he'd go there. It wasn't as if an upper-class restaurant or bar lived inside. As far as I could tell, Dillingers was the only business inside, owning the building outright.

Fearing I'd blown my chances for a second straight day, I again headed home. There wasn't much else I could do, not when I couldn't keep monitoring the parking garage's entrance for more than a few minutes. I felt exposed each time I walked past, wondering if a hidden camera was following my movements, in which case my own cover would have been blown.

Home seemed the best option at the time and so I tucked in my tail, returned to the truck and made haste. It wasn't until the following Tuesday that two things happened which would both turn me into a completely new direction, a direction I would have never found if it weren't for a couple of my previous purchases.

CHAPTER 9

Monday turned out to be a complete disaster for me, with zero chance for me to leave the house thanks to a rogue burger I picked on the way home from Pittsburgh. My insides began churning just a few minutes after I popped the last bite into my mouth and by the time I reached the front door to my home, found myself moving at top speed to get to the bathroom.

I couldn't venture more than a few feet from the toilet that entire day, each visit to the porcelain God flanked by me trying to take in as many fluids as I could, then feeling my body evict them again moments later. Monday couldn't end quick enough for me and thankfully sleep came more than a little easy that night. By the time Tuesday morning rolled around, I was almost back to normal.

A man like me likes to keep in touch with his younger self. There were certain things I needed in my life to remind me that the past wasn't such a bad waste of time, the way a lot of the younger generation assumed. Sure, we had Google now, and cellphone technology which gave us all the information we could possibly need in the palm of our hands. But for one thing, the 80s still held the best music ever created, and I don't think I could have given up the tradition of morning coffee and a newspaper. There was just something refined about the experience.

As I sat down to breakfast that Tuesday morning and began to unfold the day's Post-Gazette, or PG, the front page caught me somewhat by surprise, the headline grabbing me in an instant. With the events from the previous Sunday still fresh on my mind, imagine my surprise at seeing the smiling face of Walter Dillinger himself, the CEO of Dillinger Enterprises himself. He stood beaming from ear to ear, shaking hands with Jeff Turner, the city's chief planner; a man not only related directly to the mayor, but also the one in charge of approving most of the city's upcoming projects.

Dillinger Enterprises encompassed a number of businesses, with their construction arm their biggest moneymaker by far. It had been common knowledge that Dillinger's had submitted their own tender for the extremely lucrative UPMC Children's Hospital refurbishment scheduled for the new year, a job promising millions of dollars of turnover to the winning bidder, as well as first option for subsequent refurbishments in other hospitals. In other words, this was like winning the world series.

My coffee remained untouched for almost ten minutes, sitting on the table beside my toast as I read and reread the two associated articles. I couldn't believe that such a huge deal would have been possible given the bad press Dillinger had already received in the weeks leading up to the decision. As the reporter pointed out, something fishy had definitely gone on behind closed doors.

I tried to think back to the day I watched Ferris drive

into the building and wondered whether he had something to do with it. The possibility was there, sure, but I had no other evidence suggesting his involvement. I was preparing to read the article for a third time when a knock on the door broke my paralysis.

The Mouse Tracker turned out to be exactly what I had hoped for and I used my own truck as the initial guinea pig. It attached easily to the underside and when I took to the road for almost an hour, returned to find it still sitting just where I had left it. I did stop by a cellphone store along the way to buy a spare one. This wasn't one of the major stores and when I slipped the salesman an extra fifty, he not only accepted cash for the device but also kept the transaction off the books.

Once back home, I checked the app on the laptop and found the exact route I had taken marked out in red. It even displayed little time stamps whenever I stopped, showing how long I remained stationary for.

Now that I could effectively track Ferris 24/7, I needed to get the mouse attached to his vehicle and I began to consider the best place to get close enough to him for the deed. His home was out of the question. There were far too many cameras for my liking and if I was going to go down the whole accident thing, needed to remain out of sight.

I thought about the courthouse. The judge spent hours inside, his car sitting virtually alone in the building's parking lot. But again the number of cameras watching the building proved too much of a hinderance to me, and I also didn't think a judge would park his car out in the open for anyone to have access to.

It was the brothel which ended up as the best option, a place I knew he would return to again and again. It also gave me more than enough time to work with. On both occasions I had watched him walk into the place, a good hour passed by before he reemerged. That gave me plenty of leeway incase of problems.

I ended up unconsciously passing on breakfast and slid the toast into the trash as I made a fresh pot of coffee almost two hours after the previous one. The thought of finally getting a clearer view into Ferris's life proved to be quite exciting and with fresh coffee in hand, I returned to the laptop.

This time, I turned my attention to the day spa itself, beginning with Google Maps. The small parking lot straddling one side of the building flanked a narrow laneway and thankfully, good old Google had managed to send its vehicle down for a peak, giving me a sneaky stalker's view of the building in question.

The images weren't exactly crystal clear, but I could see enough to know surveillance wasn't at the top of the building's list of needs. I didn't think it would be, given that their highest paying clients needed discretion, and getting filmed walking into an illegal brothel wasn't exactly a smart move.

Scrolling back out to a bird's eye view, I looked for a place where I could park, then walk discreetly to the parking lot, drop down beside the Jeep and slap the mouse underneath. Staring at the screen, I could almost see myself following the plan, stepping down off the curb and following the laneway to where I had seen him park in the spot on two previous occasions.

While I didn't have a precise schedule of what Ferris's day would look like, and I lacked any real history of surveillance, I did know he liked to frequent the brothel and decided to take my chances that evening. It wasn't as if the place was a day's drive from me. I could be parked around the corner from the place in just an hour if I timed everything right.

I made the decision to proceed almost absently, beginning to plan my day to ensure I would be free before I actually confirmed the move. There wasn't much to plan, other than when to leave in order to make it with plenty of time to spare. As long as the tracking mouse was firmly in my pocket, it was all systems go.

The day seemed to drag on and I felt a hint of relief as I left home around four. I knew enough about the judge to know he left the courthouse around five-thirty most afternoons, which gave me plenty of time to get into position. Darkness began to descend by the time I reached the city's outskirts, giving me another boost in confidence. I still needed to actually drop down and make contact with the car itself and still hoped the shadows of the parking lot were enough to shield me from anyone watching.

Thankfully, traffic wasn't too bad, even with Tuesday peak hour in full swing by the time I joined it. My nerves felt more rocky than they had the previous times I'd driven the same streets and reached for my pocket more than a few times, each time expecting the tracker to have disappeared. Of course, it was still there, waiting to fulfill its sole purpose.

I reached the day spa around the same time Ferris would have been walking to his car and began with a quick drive-by. The parking lot didn't have near as many cars as I had hoped, with less than half a dozen. If the judge did think of paying his favorite establishment a visit that evening, it meant he would be parked a lot closer to the building than previous visits.

Following my plan, I again found a parking spot across

the street, pulled in and killed the engine. There couldn't be any sign of life from the truck. I didn't want to risk the judge noticing me at all, and so ignored the cold as it invaded the cabin almost immediately.

Surprisingly, the parking lot began to fill up almost immediately, with cars pulling in every few minutes. From where I was sitting, it appeared as if a party had been planned, with the spots almost all gone within half an hour or so.

The temperature plummeted as I continued sitting in the darkness, my fingers feeling ready to snap off. There was no sign of the judge and by eight o'clock, I figured the night a loss. Imagine my heart skip a beat as the familiar LED's of the Jeep suddenly approached from further up the road and I held my breath as the SUV pulled into the lot, parked between a couple of Rams, and fell into darkness.

It sat silently for a brief minute, and I didn't breathe again until I'd watched Ferris hurry inside, leaving the Wagoneer ready and waiting for me to go and do my thing. Not wanting to jump the gun too early, I stayed put for another fifteen minutes, watching the lot like a hawk for any sign of life. Another two cars pulled up during that time, but from what I could see, nobody remained to watch the cars. As far as I could tell, my moment of action had arrived.

The first thing I did was fire up the truck, drove it down the street some way, then popped a u-turn and parked down a side street. Making sure the mouse was still in its place a final time, I took a deep breath, zipped up my Paulet and jumped out into the night.

There was no traffic on the sidewalk to speak of, but plenty of cars passing by on the street. I pulled down my hat a little more, making sure to keep my face shielded from any potential cameras. While I hadn't noticed any during previous stakeouts, I knew that didn't mean they weren't there.

As reached the corner, I let my eyes scan the parking lot in rapid succession, desperate to notice any movement. I'd need to call my attempt off if anybody appeared. Getting caught wasn't a risk I was prepared to take. Not when I was this close to a win.

The lot appeared empty, with just vehicles waiting for their owners to return. Ferris had parked his Jeep in the middle row, flanked by pick-ups on either side. This not only mostly hid the car from the road, but it also gave me a bit of cover for what I needed to do. If things continued on as they were, I would be finished and out of there in a matter of seconds.

I was about to step off the curb when headlights suddenly lit up the world around me. Panicking, I adjusted my course and continued onward, ignoring the lot as a vehicle started their engine and slowly began to reverse out of their space. Not wanting to risk raising suspicions, I didn't slow, walking onward until I heard the sound of the engine revving as it pulled out into traffic, disappearing into the night as I risked a quick look back.

It was the fear of failure which drove me to finally turn and walk back, this time crossing to the other side of the street well before reaching the parking lot. With time ticking down, I knew each passing second brought me closer to the point where the judge returned to his car. Both of his previous visits had been in excess of an hour, but neither had been on workdays. What of he dropped by just for a quickie?

Finally approaching the corner of the lot, my heart

began beating with newfound strength, pounding away as my eyes darted over the vehicles, my ears fixed on the slightest sound of activity. Each step felt like an eternity, the nearest Ram looking more like paid security. The mouse was already in place, my fingers gripping it tightly for fear of it falling from my hand. I risked a quick look at the building, noting how the second floor had zero windows on this side. There was also no sign of cameras, something I still couldn't completely confirm.

My insides felt tighter than a snare drum as I gripped the tracker tighter, the beating in my chest hard enough to scare me. Just before I reached the corner of the Jeep, I had a brief moment where I thought I was going to pass out, my nerves threatening to get the better of me. As I dropped down to one knee and reached underneath the rear of his car, I instantly felt the magnet on the tracker take hold, popping into place with a short, sharp snap.

Rising back up and continuing on, I held my breath and waited for someone to call out. I was so sure they would, I even slowed in preparation, then silently scolded myself to get moving. And as I neared the far side of the parking lot and back out to safety, I felt the jubilation of reaching my first real milestone. Wherever the judge went from that point on, I would know about it.

CHAPTER 10

The next few days went by faster than I could have imagined and I had one word repeating itself in my mind. Disappointment. In my mind, I had imagined that I would finally get the inside scoop on his life, to be an invisible eye sitting on his shoulder and watching as he went on with his life, completely oblivious to what I was up to. I had even imagined him dead by the end of the week, courtesy of some ingenious plan I drew up from nothing more than GPS information.

Imagine my dismay when the night before I was due to return to work, I was still no closer to finalizing the plan to end him. I knew I wanted an accident to take him, but nothing I worked on came close to feeling right. Everything felt wrong and no matter how much I tried to convince myself otherwise, I ended up in bed that night no closer to his death.

On the Monday morning of my new working week, the depression felt as if it was strangling me, the weight of failure too great to ignore. Ivy's voice rose more than a few times, reminding me of the fact I didn't have the balls to actually go through with things. Maybe she had been right all along. Maybe, I really was nothing more than a washed out alcoholic.

The first day back had me finally walk in to the new barber shop in Indiana, the building completed the previous week. Lockhart had confirmed the official opening with my via a phone call the previous Friday and had arranged to met me there himself.

He was already sitting in the small parking lot when I arrived and after a very brief greeting, handed me the keys.

"This is your baby, Victor. I think you should do the honors." He sounded a little too happy for my liking, but I wasn't about to argue. If this meant I didn't need to go through the rigmarole of gaining entry into a prison, then I'd happily take it.

The smell of fresh paint hit me in the face the second I pushed the door opened. The place sat in almost complete darkness, but a quick snap of the switch and the room filled with enough light to share the workmen's handiwork. Everything looked just as I had requested and I felt a touch emotional as I reminded myself who all this belonged to.

"Think you can work with this?" I looked at Lockhart and smiled.

"It's perfect," I said.

He didn't stay for long, telling me he needed to get back to the prison for an important meeting. I shook hands with him a second time, then watched as he returned to his car. Before he made it back to the road, a new arrival showed up, the first of my new students rolling in to his first lesson. For me, school was finally in session.

The next three hours went by in an almost blur as I had

half a dozen ex-cons turn up for their very first lesson. They seemed like a great bunch of guys and appeared to take the curse serious. It felt so different to the way sessions ran in prison. Somehow, it felt more real.

The morning was dominated by learning, with me focusing on a broad overview of how barber shops operated. Each of my students sat in the barber chairs, keen to take notes as I rattled on about the intricacies of the business. It wasn't until we returned from lunch that the real fun began.

Lockhart had arranged for volunteer clients to drop by throughout the first week. These were guys who received their first haircut free, and then paid just a few bucks on their return. They were assigned a random would-be barber for their cut, giving my guys a real-world experience to see if they truly felt comfortable in the role.

While the morning did keep my mind busy enough to not think about Ferris, the afternoon proved to be the complete opposite. I could barely concentrate as visions of him walking into the brothel returned to me again and again. While I might have been watching the guys cut hair, my mind was elsewhere.

The thing which was still dogging me to death was the fact I couldn't work out how to get him. Not without me getting caught. The weird thing was, when I had first contemplated ending his life, I had been prepared to sacrifice my own as well. Killing myself in the process of taking him down became something of a given, offering me a sense of relief knowing my own suffering was about to come to an end.

But the more time I spent trying to plan his accident, the less I wanted to give up my own life. It was as if hunting him had somehow given me a new lease on life, one I wasn't prepared to sacrifice, which then brought back the whole problem with getting caught.

The accident needed to happen without my direct input. I could plan it, and set the wheels in motion, but the actual point of boom? That had to happen completely on its own. But how? It wasn't as if I had magical powers and could manipulate objects from a distance. And then there would be the evidence. If the cops found a single hair out of place, they would know the accident had been staged, and that would then open the door to an investigation which would ultimately lead to me. I needed something unique, something untraceable.

I watched one of the trainees finish with a client and figured I'd step in and lend a hand. It offered a little distraction to my ongoing problem and I could feel the onset of a headache threatening to ruin my afternoon. Grabbing the broom, I walked over and began to sweep up the hair, listening to a conversation between the two guys in the next station. I wasn't really paying too much attention until I heard two distinct words, words which tore me from my thoughts.

"What do you mean it was nothing more than a hit-and-run," the trainee barber said as he worked the scissors over the top of the man's head.

"That's just how they saw it. A simple hit-and-run."

"But you killed someone." The client gave a bit of a chortle.

"That's why you get yourself a good lawyer," he said and I stole a quick look down.

I didn't recognize him, but their conversation grabbed me anyway. Continuing to sweep up the hair, I slowed down a little to see where their talk led.

"So your lawyer pleads down the fact you were drunk,

blaming it on some traumatic event in your life, pulls the hit-and-run card and the judge bought it?" The seated man laughed.

"Blamed the death of my grandmother for my emotional state. Old bitch flaked it the week before."

"And they bought it?" He sounded way too impressed for my liking.

"I'm out, aren't I? Gave just a couple of years."

"What if her family come looking for you, Paul? Don't they want revenge or some shit?" The seated man nodded as he withdrew one of his hands from under the cape and made a come-here gesture.

"Let 'em bring it," he smirked. "Got my insurance in the car."

I felt sick. Not just sick, but ready to swing the broom at his head. The rest of the world disappeared as my insides tightened, the churning ready to explode in a blast of fury. He was Ferris all over again, a piece of shit who had killed someone with his car; a drunk piece of shit with no regard for anyone else.

It took an enormous effort to pull myself away without lashing out. My office looked to be the safest place fr me, and so I made a beeline for it.

"Vic, you got a sec?" I wanted to continue, to ignore the request and hide in my office. "Vic?"

"Yah?" I turned to see Roger Thomas waving me over. He had just finished his own client and appeared to be trying to clean the clippers he was holding. He held them up for me and I went through the process of dismantling them for a deep clean on autopilot. He said something while I helped, but his words failed to register, my mind still imploding with the revelation of the client.

He was another Ferris, another one living life after

robbing another of theirs. I knew there were others of course, but my attention had been so focused on the judge, that I completely discounted the rest of the vile scum. This wasn't something I had prepared myself for and given the shock, found myself overcome with so many unfamiliar emotions.

I don't even know how I ended up outside. One second, I was holding my hand out for the clippers from Roger, the next I'm standing beside my truck with a hand on the door handle. Why I had walked to my pick-up was a complete mystery, and yet I found myself unlocking the door, pulling it open and reaching inside. It all felt as if I was watching my body from the outside, a witness from the other side.

It was the tracker I wanted, of course. I knew it before my fingers touched the knob on the glove compartment. Reaching for it, I gripped it so tight and thought I heard something inside the small device crack from the force.

"Nah, man. I love it," the man known as Paul called back. He'd finished his cut and was walking back to his car. I had to move fast.

"How did you go," I called out and hurried toward him. His Impala sat a couple of cars down from my own.

"Great, man." He ran a hand over his head. "Best free cut I ever got."

I walked with him, asking whether he had any interest in learning the craft himself. Of course he didn't, and I couldn't care less, using the conversation as a means to getting closer to his car. Once next to it, I leaned against the front fender as he proceeded to tell me about the mechanical workshop he worked at, hoping to one day make it his own.

My fingers continued working the tracker under the lip

of the wheel arch until I felt the familiar snap of it launching itself into place. He never noticed, too engrossed in his bullshit story about running his own show. Once he finished, we shook and watched him drive out of the parking lot.

While the revelation of the man named Paul stirred something awake inside me, it wasn't until I returned back inside that something truly remarkable happened. It was as if I had a sudden awakening, a moment of crystal clarity; as if a light shone down on me and opened my eyes to an idea I wouldn't have come up with in a million years if I wasn't in the very specific frame of mind when I walked back inside.

The moment I was back inside, I grabbed the broom for the second time and began to sweep up the station Ben Brown had used to cut Paul's hair. My brain still felt quite scattered, with separate thoughts twirling around, almost intertwining into each other. On one hand, I couldn't push away my failure for not finding a way to kill Ferris, while on the other, the shock from hearing about Paul's crime still rocked me.

I don't know where the idea came from, but somewhere along the way, I wished I could get one of them to simply kill the other. If Paul whatsisname murdered Judge Ferris, and then turn himself in for the crime, then not only would I be free, but they would both pay for their crimes. And the more I swept, the more the idea began to grow.

It was when I leaned down to sweep the hair into the dustpan that the idea took a turn, one which left me stunned enough to remain frozen as my brain processed the possibility. What if I was to frame one with murdering the other? And that's when it happened, the moment everything changed.

Lying beneath my feet wasn't just the end result of a person's haircut, the discarded remains normally destined for the trashcan. It was DNA, the kind unique to just one person in so many million. This was Paul Whatsisname's calling card, able to be used by anyone needing to point the authority's attention in an entirely different direction.

I don't know why, but something told me to keep Paul's hair separate from the others. It felt right to place some of it in a small bag, then keep it in my pocket for later. What I did know, was that the hair and the ex-con had just joined a plan which had yet to be designed. If my assumptions were correct, this would be the "accident" I'd been looking for.

CHAPTER 11

Driving home that afternoon felt like a new beginning for me. Not only did I have a new tracker to monitor and get to know, but I also held direct evidence in my pocket, the kind of evidence which could make or break a case.

Ignoring everything else completely, I ran for the laptop the second I stepped through my door and immediately began searching for a man I still only knew as Paul. I didn't exactly have a lot to go on, not knowing when the hit-and-run had happened, nor who the victim was. It turned out that there were quite a few of the same crime, spread out over a number of years, but after an hour or so of relentless searching I found him.

His name was Paul Bloome, born 6/9/84, and from the onset I could see he wasn't a person who would be missed by many people. When I ran his name through Google, a number of incidents came back, including the hit-and-run, several assaults, a rape he'd been cleared from, and a number of thefts. Right from the onset, I knew he was my man.

What I needed next were the finer details, the intricate

story behind the death he'd mentioned during his cut. Again, I was surprised with the ease the information fell into my lap, with Google more than living up to its reputation.

His victim had been a fifty-four-year-old woman named Dorothy Lu, the mother of three and grandmother to three more. She had been out walking the family dog after dark when Bloome mounted the sidewalk in a friend's pick-up truck, although said friend denied lending Bloome the vehicle to begin with. He struck the woman doing more than sixty, no easy feat given the narrow street.

Dorothy Lu died on impact, with Bloome eventually caught almost thirty miles away. He hadn't bothered stopping, rambling about some bitch who had damaged his fiend's truck as the cops pulled him from the cabin. He ended up with a twelve-year sentence, reduced to just two on appeal. The more I read, the more my rage grew, feeling just as much passion for this lady as I did for Ivy. Who the hell did these pricks think they were to kill someone and then think they could just wave it away and get on with their own lives.

I needed this to work more than anything. Every piece of my being, every fiber in my body screamed for vengeance for the victims. I picked up the small bag of hair and stared at the contents, rolling the possibilities around my brain. And that's when I remembered one of his other comments, the one about insurance. *Got my insurance in the car*, was what he had said and I felt something click into action inside me. It was a pistol he was talking about, I was sure of it. And if he had a pistol in his vehicle, then that meant it would also have his prints on it, or so I hoped.

The more I thought about it, the more I came to realize

that nothing made more sense than to keep things simple. There was no reason to overcomplicate things with deep planning and intricate details. What I needed was to set the judge up, blow his brains out with Bloome's gun, and then plant the evidence accordingly. It couldn't have been any simpler.

That was the thinking I had as I refocused on the laptop and began looking for the easiest way possible. What I needed first was to get the gun, then lure both men to a location and pull the trigger.

"Why does he need to be there," I suddenly asked, surprising myself with the sound of my voice breaking the silence. The second voice inside my brain reacted almost immediately, confirming what I already understood. He didn't need to be there, not when I would already have more than enough evidence with which to frame him.

I began focusing on where Bloome lived, using the GPS to pinpoint his address, then used Google Maps to get a look at the environment. As I zoomed down to the spot, the car I had leaned against earlier in the day was sitting to one side of the driveway, the Google car capturing it perfectly for me.

The one thing I did know was that I no longer wanted to put things off. I needed to act, to end this once and for all. I could no longer stand idly by as Ferris and this new piece of scum enjoyed breathing fresh Pennsylvania air. It was time to exact revenge.

That night, I ate dinner early, then studied the houses around Bloome's to gauge what sort of security I'd be up against. He didn't exactly live in an upper-class area, his home looking more rundown than his car. I knew he rented the home, but couldn't find whether he lived alone.

From what I could find, I knew he was divorced, no kids to speak of.

The GPS confirmed the vehicle hadn't moved since four that afternoon, and by nine, my feet and had become so itchy to get moving, I knew I could no longer hold them back. It was time to move and I almost ran to the truck in anticipation.

Thankfully, the cold had retreated somewhat, making the drive to Indiana a little more pleasant. It was about the same distance as it was to Pittsburgh and I reached the town limits a little after ten. Traffic was down to just the occasional car, and once I reached the backstreets, it faded out completely.

Bloome lived a little out of town on the northern side, although off a backwater road. This gave me a little extra cover to work with and when I found a narrow track about half a mile from his home, I found the perfect place to park the truck.

His home backed onto bushland and that was how I managed to reach the house without worrying about whether any passing traffic would see me. The going wasn't exactly easy, but with a small sliver of moon to help me, I managed to make it without breaking any ankles. Aside from a distant dog barking its lungs out, there were no other significant sounds.

I stood in the tree line for almost an hour, watching the home for any signs of life. I could see the car from where I stood and gave myself a very good chance of getting inside it. When Bloome had climbed into it back at the barber shop, I noticed he hadn't bothered locking it. Given the state of the vehicle, it didn't surprise me, and I hoped he would do the same here. I couldn't imagine anyone in their right mind going out of their way to steal such a piece of crap, the thirty-year-old car making my truck look like a Rolls Royce.

A single window shone with the distinct shadows of a television, the brightness rising and falling with regular movement. There was no curtain to speak of, and given the occupant, wasn't surprised. Paul Bloome didn't strike me as a curtain sort of guy. And given that the window faced the woods, it wasn't as if it was needed.

I didn't know the man well, but if I knew anything about his type, my guess was he would already be passed out on the couch, the television left on to entertain the rats and the roaches.

My heartbeat kicked up as I pushed myself forward, slowly taking one step at a time as I watched for any movement from the house. The adrenalin coursing through my body felt like nothing I'd ever experienced and a part of me wondered whether it was fear I was experiencing, or excitement. I couldn't tell, every sense in my body turned up to maximum. Listening for clues, watching for movement, smelling the air for the telltale signs of food cooking, feeling each step rise and fall. Even my mouth got in on the act, with the distinct taste of fear filling my mouth.

Something jumped in the brush behind me and I took a step sideways, felt my ankle give way and collapsed as blinding heat ripped up my leg. I tried to catch myself from face planting, and my hand landed on something sharp. As I fought to catch myself again, I felt the faint trickle of blood run across the palm.

"Son of a bitch," I hissed, trying to push the exquisite pain from my hand aside, more concerned about the ankle which felt like it had taken a pounding.

I sat still for a moment, the throbbing heat almost

unbearable as I tried to take inventory. Broken ankle, cut palm, still breathing, house quiet. What mattered was that the only damage had been relatively isolated and I could still make it to the car if I took my time. It didn't look like there were any changes in the home.

Taking my time to get back to my feet, I stood and waited once I was upright again, wanting to make sure I could still move relatively normal. What worried me was if Bloome came out and found what I was doing. If he tried to chase me, I wasn't sure I would have the ability to run very fast.

Realizing I should have put my gloves on before I left the truck, I pulled them out of my pocket; two pairs, with the first thin disposable ones for extra security. I needed his prints to remain on the gun, so reminded myself to take extra care.

With each small step, I tried to put a little more weight on the ankle, and while the pain bit hard initially, I did eventually get used to it. It wasn't as if I had much of a choice. Failure wasn't an option for me and if it meant gritting my teeth for a few minutes to make sure I got the gun, then so be it.

An outside light suddenly came on, the fixture attached to the side of the house. I dropped to the ground, laying as flat as I could. There was zero cover and if someone came out now, I wondered if I stood any chance of not getting discovered.

Strangely, nobody came outside, nor could I see any movement inside the house. The same shadows which were previously dancing across the room's visible wall, continued on unperturbed. My narrowed to get a better view and I thought I could make out the distinctive shape of a small piece of hardware hanging beneath the light globe itself. It was a sensor, meaning anything could have set it off.

I waited a few moments just to be sure, turning one ear towards the back door. An owl began hooting somewhere behind me, paused, then continued. I was no owl expert, but figured if it was comfortable enough to give away its location, then maybe I too was in the clear.

As I got back to my feet, the ankle felt a lot better and as I shuffled past the house and reached the car, I was sure I could run if I needed to. The silence from the night felt almost unnerving as I reached for the door handle, held my breath and took a quick look around. Nothing. Other than the cold biting at my face, I was alone.

The door opened easily enough with a faint click and as I slowly pulled it open, saw a faint hint of why he hadn't locked it. Where the keyhole normally sits was nothing more than a dark shadow, the barrel missing completely. No wonder he didn't bother with it. I leaned inside and reached for the most likely place to keep a gun, the glove compartment. After a few moments of careful rummaging, I came up empty-handed. Aside from a few bits of crumpled-up papers and an empty soda can, there was nothing of interest. I felt that sinking feeling again, wondering if I made a mistake coming out here believing I could just stroll up and find my weapon of choice.

I paused for a moment, looked through the windshield at the door, then reached under the passenger seat. My fingers brushed up against something smooth and cold, but a small tap and I knew it was an empty bottle of sorts and definitely not a gun.

Taking another moment to think, I considered reaching over to the driver's seat and checking beneath it, but hesitated at dropping my head beneath the dash. It would shield me from the door of the house and I didn't want to lose any advantage I had if he came out. I also didn't want to risk walking around and opening a second car door.

Taking a deep breath, I took the first option and reached across, ran my hand under the seat and felt the familiar shape of a revolver's cylinder. A dump of adrenalin sent my heart racing, the pounding almost loud enough to hear as I ran one gloved finger along the barrel until it hit the front sight. With a shaking hand, I took hold and gently pulled it out of the holster that had been fixed to the seat's underside. The ice-cold steel penetrated through two layers of glove and added a touch of atmosphere to the moment.

I was about to climb out again, when a thought struck me, one which had been bothering me ever since deciding to make Paul Bloome a part of my plan against Ferris. The issue of how I could link the two men together. The whole game still felt like amateur hour, with me a complete greenhorn, out of my depth when it came to murder.

What I needed was a plan and as I sat in his car, a faint idea began to bloom, one which would ensure both men played their part in my little game, a game designed to avenge their victims, and make sure neither of them would hurt anyone ever again. By the time I walked through my own front door some five hours later, the countdown to their Armageddon had already begun.

CHAPTER 12

The next few days went by in a virtual haze of excitement and nerves as I began to set the game up in earnest. I had two men to play, each one needed in order to sink the other and without an airtight plan, I knew things could still fail.

The plan was simple really. To coax each man to a specific location, while I took on the role of puppet master. Neither would see the strings being pulled, and neither would be aware of the other throughout the entirety of the game. Only I would know what was going on, and if everything went according to plan, Saturday night would be the big finale.

It began with a single phone call, one I made to Judge Ferris late Thursday afternoon. I waited until I knew he had left work, monitoring his vehicle as it made its way through peak hour. I wanted the call registered on his phone, but kept it neutral on my end via a burner phone I'd purchased for cash the previous week.

"Hello?"

It was the first time I'd heard his voice directly and it

damn near made me hang up. I thought I was stronger than that, and felt the heat rise in my cheeks as I swallowed hard and pushed through.

"Judge Ferris?"

"Yes? Who is this?"

"Someone who knows what you've been up to." The brief pause between me speaking and him processing the words felt like forever.

"What I've been-"

"Save it, you son of a bitch," I hissed, cutting him off. "Dillinger on December 26, the meeting at his office. How much did he pay you?"

"Pay me?"

"Ive got the proof. And let's not forget the repeated trips to Waterfalls. How would dear old Mrs. Ferris feel about her husband getting serviced by a few hookers?"

"Hookers? Waterfalls? I think you have me confused with-"

"A hundred grand, Judge."

"I beg your pardon?"

I knew I was taking a risk, but figured we both knew the truth of the situation. His repeated denials meant nothing to me, not when I knew the reality of his activities.

"One...hundred...thousand...dollars...cash. You and me. Saturday night, 11pm." The silence between us returned and the longer it continued, the more I knew he was falling for the threat. I figured with his career on the line, as well as his marriage and everything else to do with his image, he wasn't about to risk losing everything, not for such a tiny sum.

"How do I know you'll keep quiet?"

"You don't. Be there, or the next Post-Gazette you pick up will feature your downfall." And then, just to be sure, I added, "And if I see anybody else with you, the next call I make will be to Wischnowski himself." Adding the newspaper's Vice President somehow did the trick.

"OK, a hundred thousand. I'll come alone. Where?" I took a breath and sealed his fate.

"Indiana. Fulton Run Road, take a right at the King's Clothing billboard, go to the end and I'll be waiting." I waited for him to process the information.

"OK, Fulton Run Road, right at the billboard."

"A hundred grand. Come alone or else."

I hung up with my heart beating faster than ever, but there was something about the feeling I enjoyed. The adrenalin charging my body, the thrill of what was to come. There were nerves, yes, but not in a bad way.

There was a reason I chose that particular spot for the meeting. For one, there were no cameras anywhere along that stretch of road, not even on the homes themselves. I know, because I painstakingly checked each one. Plus, the location itself sat on the other side of the woods which backed onto Bloome's home. Having him within walking distance was also crucial.

Unbeknownst to the man, I had purchased a small laptop for cash, downloaded the tracking app onto it, and let the system begin recording the judge's movements over several days. I needed history. But the best part came on the Friday night before the main event when I returned to Bloome's house around three that morning, and hid the device under the passenger seat. If he decided to clean his car the following day, the plan would be toast. But to make sure that didn't happen, I left him a gift by his front door.

Having decided to quit alcohol for good, I cleaned out my own supply of alcohol. One bottle of Jack Daniels remained sealed and figuring I'd put it to good use, attached a small bow and message card to it. The note I scribbled on it was simple enough. Let's Celebrate the Win. I figured he wouldn't know any better, and given his taste for alcohol, didn't doubt how he would spend his Saturday afternoon.

As I drove home again, I wondered whether the judge would actually be stupid enough to bring the cash, or whether he would bring backup to take me out. I wasn't sure I could proceed if he brought help, but figured I would feel my way through. It wasn't as if I was any specific timeline.

CHAPTER 13

I must have slept like an absolute baby that night, because when I awoke close to midday on Saturday, I felt as refreshed as I had in a very long time. The faint buzz of adrenalin began the instant I thought about that evening, a distinct weight taking up residence in the pit of my stomach.

Checking the judge's movements, I saw that since my call to him, he had avoided Waterfalls completely, and the first night drove straight home. On Friday, he had driven to the courthouse in the morning, then left around two for a quick drive, parking in the very same spot I had parked my truck the Sunday I followed him to Dillinger's.

As I stared at the screen, I tried to decide whether it was the construction boss he had gone to for help. I checked the time stamp. He remained in the parking lot for just fifteen minutes, more than enough time for him to walk to the building, meet with him and share the details of my call.

But then I zoomed out a bit, not on purpose; more of a

nervous twitch. And when I saw a branch of Chase Bank located on the other side of the parking lot, the dilemma I faced grew. Which building did he go into? The bank, or his pal? I considered phoning him again, but that meant driving out to Indiana. I didn't want to risk creating holes and so pushed the idea away. If this was going to work, it needed to proceed the way I had planned.

As the afternoon wore on, I began to grow increasingly nervous. The pistol sat on the table still wrapped in the towel I'd used when I first got it home. The small bag of hair sat on top, both items needing each other to make this work.

Skipping dinner entirely, I grabbed the gear around eight o'clock and decided it was time to get ready. Hunger was the furthest thing from my mind. I needed to get my butt into position, then monitor my two puppets to make sure each played their part. As I walked out the door, I made a promise to myself that if anyone strayed, I'd call it off and postpone the entire thing.

Ironically, the route to Indiana took me straight past the memorial, and I stopped briefly for a final moment of clarity. Standing by the roadside and looking down at the remnants of what remained of it, I asked myself whether I wanted to continue on. Ivy never spoke in my head the way she normally did, the silence almost uncomfortable as I waited for her to give me her blessing.

At first, it felt a little strange not hearing her at such a critical juncture, but I think that's what finally gave me the courage to commit. Her absence and the reasons behind it, were what had started this whole thing in the first place. It was that very silence which propelled me to act now.

I continued on and refused to consider stopping

myself. I had come too far and the time for revenge had arrived. The main road still carried plenty of traffic, but when I turned onto Fulton Run Road, it faded out almost completely. It wasn't until I turned at the billboard that my stomach began to churn in earnest.

Thankfully, the road was as clear as the day I had first considered the place, with just the single burnt-out wreck still at the end of the pavement. The road itself came to a kind of rounded cul-de-sac, but a narrow track continued into the woods for another couple of hundred yards. That's where I drove my truck, hoping to get far enough away from approaching headlights for anyone to see.

The first thing I did once I stopped was to check the GPS tracker. My stomach dropped a little when it showed the judge's car at the courthouse, but then realized it hadn't updated properly and after a few seconds, the live tracking commenced. He was still at home, a good sign as far as I was concerned. If he meant to bring anyone with him, I would have assumed he'd be meeting with them early enough to devise a plan.

Next, I jumped out of the truck and walked the half a mile to Bloome's house. Again, my heart took a leap when I didn't see the car as I neared the edge of the woods, but then let go of a big sigh as I saw it had simply been moved further around to the front.

Moving in for a closer look, a sense of deja vu washed over me as I saw the same shadows dancing on the inside wall of the only lit window. This time, I needed a definitive answer on whether he was inside and so took my time to get as close as possible.

The window sat above what I assumed was a garden bed in its previous life, with weeds the predominate choice of foliage. I felt my way through until I touched the underside of the window frame and peered inside.

He was home alright, passed out on a recliner chair with the empty bottle of Jack on the floor beside him. From the look of it, the man loved pizza, with multiple boxes stacked up on the coffee table. An episode of the X-Files played on the television, although I didn't stick around long enough to see which episode. For me, time was ticking.

It took me half the time to get back to the truck and when I checked the tracker a second time, found the judge headed in my direction. I closed my eyes, feeling the nerves build with more adrenalin dumping into me. Looking down at the wrapped gun on the seat beside me, I couldn't help but feel the urgency of the situation come to a head.

"Give me strength," I whispered into the darkness of the cabin, hoping for whatever essence Ivy still held in this life to come to my aid.

I took another look at the tracker a few minutes later, watching as the small dot continued toward my location with each update. The intensity felt as if it was strangling my insides, the urge for a bathroom break reminding me of the time I asked Tess to marry me.

"Be strong," I muttered, resolving myself to whatever the future held for me.

The closer Ferris came, the more I was sure I would fail. At one point, I actually reached for the ignition key and prepared to turn it, knowing that if the engine *did* start, I wouldn't have the strength to stay. But I physically reached for my hand with the other and set it back down on my leg, hating myself for the weakness.

To turn my attention elsewhere, I reached for the

gloves and pulled them on. It was time to get ready. And when I looked at the tracker again, I saw Ferris turn onto Fulton Run, with him just a few minutes from meeting his fate.

Not wanting to miss the perfect opportunity, I grabbed my two packages, swallowed hard and jumped out. It was time to move. Walking briskly, I followed the path back towards the end of the paved section, but a hundred yards from the clearing, cut a little to the left. I didn't want him seeing me, not initially, anyway. What I needed was the element of surprise.

The second I saw his headlights pierce the dark, I was sure my ass would let go, releasing all the fear and nerves in one go, along with whatever else was waiting for release. The nerves were unbelievable, nothing like I had imagined. My insides rolled and heaved like a yacht caught in a storm, my stomach carrying a boat anchor. I nearly dropped the towel with the gun inside because of my shaking hands, but I stopped for a brief second to take a couple of quick breaths. And al the while, the headlights came closer.

I remained in the shadows as he reached the very end of the pavement, slowed to almost a crawl, and turned to face back the way he had come. *Smart move*, I thought to myself. If he got spooked enough, he'd simply floor it and get the hell out of there, and if I was standing in front of the car, I had no doubt he'd run me over just as easily.

He stopped and I could make out his shape inside, all the while closing in. What I really wanted to see was whether he looked behind him, or even speak to anybody hiding in the back seat. I didn't notice him stopping anywhere particular along the way and unless he already had someone at home, there was a good chance he was alone.

Once I reached the edge of the clearing, I unravelled the gun, dropped the towel and held the pistol behind me. With my other hand, I began to wave at him, continuing to move closer and closer. When I saw his brake lights suddenly turn off and his door begin to open, I knew I had his attention.

I stopped as he began to climb out, our eyes meeting for the first and last time. He looked a lot older in person and I wondered how much make-up a person needed for a TV interview.

"Got the money?" I called loud enough to be heard over the engine, but he must have been hard of hearing and leaned back into the car and killed the engine. "Got the money," I repeated and he nodded at me.

"How do I know you won't want more," he began, and that's when I revealed the gun. He took a step back from the shock, hitting the edge of the car.

"Because I don't want this lot," I said. He looked at me confused.

"Then why would you-" he began, but time for him had finally run out.

"Ivy Tannen," I called, the name taking a moment to sink in for him. When I saw the recognition in his face, I squeezed the trigger once.

The bullet hit him just below the right eye, the gun not powerful enough to cause the kind of damage seen in movies. His legs held him for a split second, but once the other eye glazed over, they crumpled and the man first fell back, then slid down the side of his car onto the ground. His head hit with a distinctive thud as I stood with the gun held out before me.

It took me a moment to react, caught up in a bitter war of emotions as I struggled to comprehend what had just happened. But once I did manage to move, I didn't waste time. First, I checked his pulse to make sure the deed was in fact done. I held a finger to his throat for a few seconds and felt nothing. Next, I took out the bag of hairs, removed a couple of strands, and pushed them underneath him. Then I grabbed a couple of his own strands and put them in my shirt pocket.

Checking the car, I found the bag and unbelievably, the hundred thousand dollars. It took me a moment to push my own greed aside, promising myself to stick to the plan. I dropped another couple of strands of hair into the car, then slowly backed away.

Picking up the towel on my way back to the truck, I dropped it, as well as Bloome's hair on the seat. Breaking into a run, I returned to Bloome's house, went to his car and dropped the judge's strands of hair on the driver's seat. The gun I slid back into its previous place, the holster waiting for its friend.

The bag of cash I took to what looked like a small doorless shed beside his house. I figured it would be a good enough hiding spot and not one too difficult to find by the cops when they came. Once back in the tree line, I took a moment to pause, turned for a final look and made sure I had completed every task I needed to. Only once I was sure of the plan being followed to the letter, did I turn back towards the truck.

Thankfully, during my initial search for an appropriate location, I found that not only was the small road perfect for my needs, but the small track I now parked on also had a second entrance, turning the tiny path into a thoroughfare.

When I turned back out onto the main road a few minutes later, I began to weep. Once the tears began to flow, there was no stopping them, the eventual sobs coming thick and fast. By the time I walked back into my home, the reality of my deed had finally sunk in.

CHAPTER 14

I didn't think I'd ever get used to the fact that I was now officially a murderer. The initial fallout from the judge's death gripped the city of Pittsburgh and surrounding areas, every newspaper and television network running with the story.

But the real shock came when they announced a suspect within hours of finding the body of Ferris. I still hadn't slept by noon that Sunday morning, my brain refusing to slow down with crazy thoughts of the killing, getting called in for questioning, or even charged with the murder. So when I sat down with my fifth cup of coffee and turned on the television, imagine my surprise when I watched footage of the cops walking Paul Bloome to a police cruiser, his hands cuffed behind his back.

I must have sat stunned watching the report over and over for almost an hour before I took a normal breath again. The thing which hit me hardest was just how much of an amateur I really was. If I had put in just a little more effort, I might have found the link the cops discovered as well.

When they received the call about the dead body from a shocked woman out for an early morning walk with her dog, they went to work immediately. And as soon as they put in the judge's name and cross-referenced it with the area, Paul Bloome's name came up almost immediately. Not because of where he lived, but because of his record.

It turned out that Judge Ferris had been the presiding judge over Bloome's initial hit-and-run case, sentencing the man to twelve years. The cops figured he might have held some kind of grudge and went to pay him a visit. When they did a quick search of the area and found the cash, they called in a warrant which ultimately led to the murder weapon, as well as a laptop linked to a tracker found on the judge's car, a tracker I had been sure to completely reset the night I decided to use Bloome as my scapegoat.

As I sat in my kitchen that afternoon, I looked down at what remained of the hair samples I had taken from Bloome in the barber shop. I don't know why, but something told me that the idea of having access to such a delicate piece of evidence opened the door to something much greater than I could ever imagine.

Ivy Tannen wasn't alone in her tragic death. And neither was Dorothy Lu. They were just the tip of an evil iceberg, one which held the names of countless victims, all screaming for justice against the people who killed them. Hit-and-runs, deadly assaults, drug dealers, burglaries gone wrong, rapists, murderers, all the people who took lives and managed to evade justice. It was them who needed a call from the collector of such evidence, the unique DNA trapped inside each strand of hair holding the power to implicate someone.

I walked down into my cellar holding the bag of hair

and stood before a safe I kept down there. It used to be for a handgun I had bought myself years before, but after selling the weapon, I never looked at it again. Not until now.

Opening the door, I felt something stir inside me, some strange presence filling me with a sense of purpose. I put the bag on the shelf and thought about the possibilities. Was this who I was supposed to become? Some kind of *"Crime Collector"*? If this was what fate had in store for me, then I was willing to play along. With Ferris dead and Bloome on his way back to a very long prison sentence, I had managed to bring justice to two victims at once. I couldn't begin to imagine the possibilities if I decided to take this to the next level.

There was just a single place which I needed to go after learning of who Ivy Tannen had helped me become, and after a quick shower, I took the truck back down to Elderton. I drove in silence, letting the air of accomplishment guide me back to the place where it all began.

The memorial still sat where she had fallen, maintained by a friend she never got to play with on that fateful day. And as I stared down at the photo of the girl who had given me a new lease on life, a single tear rolled down my face.

"I did it, Ivy," I whispered into the wind. "Now you can rest." As if sent by the girl herself, a cardinal suddenly landed on top of the cross, paused and looked at me. It began to sing, its chirping sounding like a sweet song as it rose into the air. And then, instead of flying away in fear, it jumped from the cross, and landed on the front edge of the memorial, just a foot away from me.

"That's the strangest thing I've ever seen," a voice

suddenly said from behind me and I turned to find Linda Pane standing a few yards behind me.

"I was just admiring the memorial," I said as the bird made its escape. "Did you know the girl?" She nodded.

"She was my friend," she said as she walked close enough to lean down beside the memorial. "The best friend I ever had."

BLADES OF JUSTICE

CHAPTER 1

Thirty-seconds. That was the amount of time which could have saved our lives. Just thirty-seconds. If I had just held my daughter for an extra thirty-seconds, took more time to listen to her telling me about her day, she would have still been here, and not lying in some hole in the ground.

It was not their faces staring back at me from the tombstone which was the most difficult when visiting the graves of my wife and child. It was not even that they lay so close to where I would sit; so unbearably, excruciatingly close; almost near enough for me to reach out and touch their mortal remains. What hurt the most was the reason they ended up in that graveyard in the first place. And those thirty-seconds.

As I sat cross-legged on the ground before the graves of my wife and daughter that fresh March morning, it was Caine Dawson on my mind, the man responsible for the storm clouds which descended over my life. He had been the one behind the wheel that October evening, the day everything changed for too many people.

The reason his face was the one floating around in my

mind that morning was not because of where I was. I had spent years thinking about him rotting away in his prison cell way up in Lapeer, Michigan. Lucky piece of shit managed to get himself a transfer from Somerset, on account of what the court referred to as *family reasons*.

Family…just the *word* was enough to churn my insides, the rage reacting to hearing it like a dog at meal time. He had taken mine and for punishment, the courts sent him closer to his sick mom. Even thinking about his location was enough to distract me from just about everything.

The reason Caine Dawson played on my mind for the previous few weeks was because of what I had done to Judge Ferris…the man responsible for the death of little Ivy Tannen, another victim of careless driving. I had shown the judge the error of his ways, shown him permanently, and because of that act, gave a little girl the chance to Rest in Peace, knowing her vengeance had been carried out.

But as the days passed by since that pivotal moment in my life, it was Caine Dawson who continued to plague my mind, with my brain endlessly trying to figure out a way to exact revenge on him the way I did the judge. Surely there was a way. I had spent weeks following Ferris around, working out the best way for him to face judgement without implicating me. Surely there was a way I could do the same to give my innocent family rest.

"I'll never rest, my ladies," I whispered, reaching out and touching the ground before me. It felt cold, with a hint of moisture from the final remnants of dew the sun hadn't yet burned away.

The day after I ended Ferris, this was the place I came to for a bit of reflection. Too many thoughts plagued my mind, each one pointing to a deep-seated fear about getting caught. I couldn't imagine my life behind bars, not now that I had stumbled on a new purpose for my existence. What I needed was to share my story with those who I knew would listen and understand, despite not being able to answer. These were the only two people who I felt a need to share with.

The rumble of a truck driving down Main Street filled the air, briefly pulling my attention from the photos of my wife and child. When I first entered Ford City Cemetery an hour before, the place had been mostly deserted, except for a single car near the back. Now, there were closer to half a dozen, all people out in the sun to catch up with loved ones, including Frank Dunn, whose wife Nancy was buried in the site next to Tess and Charlie.

"Morning, Vic," Frank said as he slowly approached. The man must have been pushing ninety, walking with the aid of a cane I always believed to be on its last legs. The thing looked as thin as a toothpick, hardly strong enough to support the weight of a cat, let alone a near six-foot tall man.

"Morning, Frank," I said, giving him a wave and doing my best to hide any of the emotion which had tormented me earlier. "Hope the leg's better."

The poor guy had had a run-in with a dog the previous month and ended up with half a dozen stitches in his calf. Frank's son, Martin, also happened to be the police chief in nearby Butler, which meant the dog's owner faced some serious questions.

"Oh, it's as good as it's ever going to get."

A number of benches had been erected around the cemetery a few years earlier and one just happened to be situated almost directly in front of Nancy's grave, a definite convenience for a man struggling to kneel. Frank eased himself down onto the seat, sighed and did what he always did when visiting his long-lost wife. He read the newspaper.

The good thing about Frank was that he respected my own privacy during our brief encounters. It wasn't often we caught up at our loved ones' final resting places, but when we did happen to cross paths, we both understood the boundaries of the situation. For a guy who loved to talk, he deserved praise for respecting those unspoken boundaries.

Since I'd already spent a good hour with Tess and Charlie, and covered most of the things I'd come to share with them, I was practically ready to go when Frank showed up. Not wanting him to feel as if he'd pushed me away, I decided to remain for another few minutes.

"What the hell happened to the judicial system," Frank muttered under his breath a few moments after settling in for his read. I hadn't read the paper in days, more content with letting the world pass by without me checking in on it.

"I take it someone got off lite?" I didn't turn, just throwing the question over my shoulder.

"This guy filmed himself murdering his own child and sent it to the mother." That did make me turn around.

"Seriously?" Frank's sullen face sat still, with just his eyes darting across the page as he continued reading.

"And what's the bet he blames a poor upbringing, or some drug dependency."

"Pretty common these days," I said, noting the front page for the first time. It wasn't the headline which caught my attention, but the photo of a man I recognized instantly. Judge Ferris smiled out to me from a time before his unfortunate demise. The headline announced "Life

Without Parole", the sentence for Paul Bloome's new murder charge finally handed down.

A sudden urge to leave washed over me and before I had a chance to fully acknowledge it, was up on my feet.

"You're off then?" Frank asked, peering over the top of the paper.

"I am," I said. "Got work to do."

After a quick wave, I left Frank to do what most men needed privacy for and something none of us wanted to share with the world. By the time I climbed into my car and took another look, Frank had set the newspaper aside, just as I expected him to. This was his moment to grieve, acknowledging a pain time could never heal.

While it was only a five-minute drive back home, I did switch on the radio, more from curiosity than anything else. It was the top of the hour and I knew the news would be shared in bullet-point fashion. It had already begun, the presenter talking about the latest unemployment figures.

The story I was hoping to hear came immediately after, and just as Frank had pointed out, the defense team for Edward P. Ford intended to highlight the accused murderer's own upbringing into question. According to his lawyer, he'd suffered vile abuse during his early years, which ultimately led to a life of violence.

Snapping the radio off again in disgust, I couldn't imagine how much a lawyer's humanity needs to suppress in order to take a case like that one. I found myself gripping the wheel tighter as I swung the car into the driveway.

As I switched the engine off and pulled out the key, I felt the familiar shaking in my fingers and held the keys up in front of my face. They appeared to vibrate in place, the surefire sign of my fingers reacting to low blood sugar.

Not wasting time, I headed inside, went to the fridge and grabbed a Coke, not the healthiest of choices for dealing with Diabetes, but one I could make as an adult. I looked at the photo of Tess hanging near the door to the hallway as I took a swig and imagined her scolding me, just as she was prone to during the early days of our union.

"Sorry, babe," I said as I walked past, kissed my hand and touched her face.

Where I really wanted to go was down into the cellar, back to a place I hadn't gone during the past few weeks. Not since the day I'd watched Paul Bloome get taken into custody on television. That had been the day everything changed for me, and I knew the direction of my life had taken a detour.

As I reached the bottom of the stairs, I paused to stare at the ominous shadow sitting in the corner. The safe looked just as it had that fateful day, almost willing me to come closer and feed it the evidence I was hoping to procure. It would be my partner in crime, my faithful keeper of guilt.

The idea to collect DNA from the inmates I dealt with during my barber sessions wasn't something I easily understood. I knew I needed time to run things through my head, to make sense of the process I needed to follow to ensure my own mortality. Criminals screwed up in a hundred different ways to ensure their failure and I didn't want to be one of them.

It had already been several weeks of thinking, planning, ensuring I understood exactly what I was getting into. I knew what I wanted, where I wanted to take this journey, and also the underlying purpose for everything. This was about vengeance, about righting the wrongs those in power found themselves unable to change. I would become justice, a shadow hiding behind every criminal set free without punishment.

The idea frightened me, churning my insides as I ran the prospect through my mind again and again. But when the name Edward P. Ford returned to the forefront, I knew another child needed my services. I closed my eyes. Reaching out and feeling the cold steel of the safe reminded me of the coldness living inside my own heart, the soulless void left behind through tragedy. Death had become my new partner, a friend to share this journey with. And as I opened my eyes again, felt the surge of a new purpose awaken within me.

CHAPTER 2

For the next week, it felt as if the name Edward P. Ford had become something of an obsession. I couldn't spend more than a minute alone with my mind before his face crept in, willing itself through the shadows towards center stage. It was as if my own subconsciousness knew the direction my life needed to take and he was the latest pitstop.

Vengeance had never been a forte I understood during my previous life. Those whom I considered close had a different view on the world, often talking about moving on after tragedy, not letting the past chip away at a promising future. Now knowing what I did, I couldn't imagine living a life *without* vengeance, where the so-called collector comes calling for payment in blood.

Life returned to almost normal eventually, the fear of getting arrested for the judge eventually fading away completely. This left just one thing on my mind and I found myself ravenously following the case of the child-killer. What intrigued me the most was how keen I was to exact vengeance on the man, which I knew came for just one reason: the premeditated intent of murdering his own baby, a happy three-year-old girl named Mary-Lou, who her mother lovingly called Loui.

Her father, Edward, a twenty-nine-year-old with a history of violence and drug abuse, had been trying to get back with his ex-girlfriend, but after several failed attempts, decided to take things to the next level. He slipped into his-ex's home late one night to confront the woman in bed, but instead, found her already in the company of another man. The pair were asleep and without knowing, Ford slipped into his daughter's bedroom and took the child from her bed.

It wasn't until the following morning that the mother discovered the daughter missing, with just a single handwritten note left on her child's pillow. The message was clear, just a single word scribbled on it in handwriting she immediately recognized. Whore. Fearing the worst, she immediately phoned Ford and proceeded to beg for him to return her baby, but having already ingested enough meth to turn half of Pittsburgh on its head, the father had other ideas.

FaceTime had been invented as a means to opening up the lines of communication in a way which was seen as unprecedented back in the day. I doubt anybody pictured a father using it to execute his child in such a barbaric fashion while connected live to the mother. He made sure to have the handgun in his outstretched hand within the frame as he repeatedly waved it in the crying girl's face.

Like so many before it, the two-minute clip eventually found itself posted online, an "apparent" leak by someone connected to the family. The second I viewed it, I knew I could never unsee the raw fear in the eyes of the child shortly before Ford closed them forever. The horror in those two-minutes of absolute torment is something too many people lay witness to and I for one, knew I needed to act.

The focus on Ford remained right up until the day I had to go in to McSweeney for work. I had spent a week at the shop in Indiana with a large influx of trainee barbers. Seven needed an induction, as well as a few days of introductory training. I could have passed it on to one of my other more senior students, but a new idea had floated during the Monday morning induction and by the time we broke off for lunch, I had a new ambition to pursue.

Collecting DNA from hair clippings wasn't exactly a new idea for me, but as I stood before the group that morning, I noticed how much more I could get through very different means. Throughout the lessons, I couldn't help but notice one guy chewing the end of his pen, another drink from a disposable cup. Once out the side of the building for a quick five-minute break, more samples were created via cigarette butts, the evidence simply tossed aside by those completely oblivious to what they were shedding.

With multiple prisons at my disposal and definite opportunity during my time inside each, the realms of possibility continued to grow the more I thought about it. It wasn't unusual for me to bag trash and take it out with me to a dumpster. Who would notice me slip a few pieces into my toolbox, or pockets?

During the afternoon session that Monday, I not only continued to build my plan for obtaining more evidence, but also about how to store it. I imagined a filing cabinet to sit inside the gun safe, one with enough space to hold dozens and dozens of samples. I would need to catalog each, and then conduct the research needed to understand who each and every inmate actually was. The lists would include as much information as possible, not just an actual database of their crimes.

I mentally played around with multiple ideas and by the time the weekend rolled around, I had a definite plan in mind. The Saturday morning was spent with a notepad and pen, sitting in the backyard as I took in some much-needed sunshine. The fresh air helped me think and I put together a list of things I needed.

The Sunday turned out to be my day of shopping and I hadn't driven but half a mile from my home when I came across a yard sale. Something instinctual made me stop and as I prepared to rummage through another's junk, spotted the very thing I had been thinking about for close to a week.

"How much you want for the cabinet," I asked the man standing behind an old vintage dining room table piled with his trash to sell. He looked up at me as if I had spoken in a language he couldn't quite comprehend, and so I pointed to where the piece of furniture sat between an old fish tank and a vintage refrigerator.

"Oh," he finally said, acknowledging my question with one of his own. I was beginning to think his brain had effectively shut down, perhaps my words part of a secret code written into his subconscious by aliens. "You mean the catalog chest?"

"Yeah, the chest," I said, feeling an urge to walk away. "How much?"

Feeling himself a sale coming on, the guy slowly walked around to my side of the table scratching his balding scalp.

"Wasn't actually going to sell that," he began and again I considered walking away. My mood had been borderline annoyed from a restless sleep when I woke up. This guy was much-needed doing his best to push me all the over the edge towards completely pissed. "My wife doesn't see the value in it."

"Look, I just..." I began, but he didn't appear to hear me.

"Worked in libraries most of my life and this here cabinet used to be part of the catalog system at my first ever job." He let go of a muffled laugh. "Old Mrs. Hanlon had been head librarian back then and Lord knows, she had me standing at this cabinet for more hours than I care to remember."

He slowly pulled one of the draws open, revealing the dusty interior, it was empty except for a thin metal rod used to stabilize the former cards it held.

"Hard to believe this was the only way a person could effectively find a book back in the day," he continued, still caught up in his reminiscing.

"I'll give you fifty bucks," I said, hoping to pull him back from whatever nostalgic vision he was having. Hearing the price seemed to do the trick.

"Fifty?" His tone was enough to announce a failed offer.

"If I *was* to sell it, I'd be asking closer to *one* fifty."

"OK, I'll think I pass." I offered him a smile and went to turn, but contrary to his previous lack of motivation, a hand shot out almost immediately and grabbed my arm.

"Fifty you said?" I turned back, feeling my interest peaked when I felt a new set of eyes on us. One look around and I found the before mentioned lady of the house, standing inside the doorway to the home, arms folded across her sizable chest. One look was enough to tell me she would have been happy to lift it onto the back of my truck herself.

"Make it sixty," I said, feeling just a little sorry for him. I couldn't imagine living with someone who forced me to get rid of something I clearly felt a connection to. The man looked down at his shoes, tried to force a grin and held a hand out.

"OK, sixty it is."

Rather than take it with me, I decided to return home first and drop the cabinet off into the kitchen. It was quite heavy for its size, a sure sign of a quality build. I didn't need a tape measure to tell me it would fit, but when I held one across it, I found the cabinet to be almost purposely made for the safe. It would leave a six-inch gap above, with the sides just half an inch from perfection.

It wasn't until later that afternoon, with the rest of my shopping list taken care of, that I had a chance to truly appreciate the cabinet for what it really was. For one thing, I would have guessed its age to exceed at least seventy years, perhaps more. The timber looked solid, a far cry from the cheap pine used in the majority of mainstream furniture of current times. The craftsmanship also stood out, the dovetailed joins in each draw hand tooled by a person lost to history. This hadn't been machine worked, or put together by some robotic Chinese factory. This was the kind of workmanship people used to pride themselves of.

Four draws across, six draws down, with each embellished by a small metallic card holder to signify its contents. Back in the days of the old library system, this would have been highlighted by a letter, with a bunch of smaller numbers underneath. A person hunting a specific book would have known the author or title and then did a deep dive into the corresponding draw. The cards held inside would have given the hunter a section and shelf destination, directions to follow coordinates like a modern-day GPS.

While those informational cards had long disappeared into the ages of history, the thin metal rods used to keep them in place remained. While a couple displayed distinct bows through some sort of abuse, the majority appeared in just as fine a shape as the day they were fixed into place. Each end sat locked into place through a simple sliding mechanism and it took me all of five minutes to remove them all. I didn't need them. They took up valuable space, space which I needed for my own unique samples.

Once the cabinet sat firmly inside the gun safe, I sat in my chair and just stared at it. I could feel the grin on my face the entire time I sat there, running visions of the intended contents sitting in each draw through my mind. This would be where my future plans would become a reality, with criminals who had managed to beat the system awaiting their turn for justice to come calling.

I already had some samples of course, and those I had bagged and tagged accordingly. At first, I wasn't quite sure on how I was going to catalog them. Of course, by name would have been the most obvious way. Each criminal had one and it would have given me a reasonable starting point. A surname also meant an easy way to keep track of who I held in my catalog of vengeance.

But a different idea came to me later that Sunday night, long after I had closed the safe for the night and returned upstairs for dinner. Funny enough, it had been Denzel Washington himself who gave me an idea and it wasn't anything the man said.

I had been eating my dinner in front of the television

watching a movie version of The Equalizer. It hadn't been one I had any interest watching ahead of time, but when it came on, I found myself too lazy to change channels. Much to my surprise, I couldn't stop watching, not even once I finished my food.

The film spoke to me. In a weird kind of way, I found it speaking to me on a subliminal level, as if fate itself had arranged for the screening and me to meet. I wondered whether it was a way of letting me know that I was on the right path, finally doing what I had always been meant to. Perhaps once I proved my worthiness with the judge, fate itself decided I was up to par and now felt I needed to understand my calling.

It was the crimes themselves which drove me, not the people. If anything, I didn't actually care about the person per se. They were a name, yes, but to me, they would always be known as a crime. Judge Ferris, the drunk driver who killed little Ivy Tannen, a girl doing nothing wrong except going about her life the way any child should. He wouldn't be categorized under Ferris, nor judge. He was a drunk driver, a son of a bitch who deserved what he got.

I jumped to my feet the second the movie ended and almost ran down the stairs into the cellar. I came close to losing my footing halfway down and couldn't imagine what would have happened if I had fallen and broken my neck. I shuddered as I imagined cops walking through my cellar, looking for signs of foul play which took me out, only to find the contents of my safe.

While Judge Ferris had been the first, Edward P. Ford would be my second. But while I didn't have any DNA evidence of his at that time, I did go through some of the samples I already had, hair samples from men responsible for all sorts of crimes. Drugs were the most common, but I also had a forger, two bank robbers, plus a man who did time for assaulting a cop.

None of the ones I had felt like future cases for me, their crimes a far cry from what I was looking. But being an opportunistic shadow, I didn't know whether their DNA would come to some use in the future. Perhaps I would need someone to take a fall, or even just turn attention away from one direction and towards another. If nothing else, it gave me something to put into my new crime catalog and that gave me a feeling of…

After closing the draws again, I looked at my work and tried to recognize how I felt. Fulfilled? No. Accomplished? They were the wrong words. I felt excited, like a person standing in line at Six Flags waiting for the next car on the roller-coaster. There were butterflies in my gut, the kind which knew what was coming and I couldn't wait until the time when the wheels finally began to roll.

CHAPTER 3

Waking that Monday morning, I almost jumped out of bed with an extra spring in my step, even breaking into song as I took my morning shower. It felt good to have a plan and with my own foundations practically in place, all I needed was for the customers to begin rolling in.

My cell phone rang just as I finished giving myself my morning insulin shot and when I answered, I was told by Walter Lightman that I would need to go to McSweeney instead of Pine Grove. It meant almost three times longer in the car to get there, but I refused to see it as a bad thing.

"No probs," I said jovially, thanked him for the call and hung up.

The drive gave me more time to think, broken by the 8 AM news bulletin in which I didn't hear anything of interest. Turning my attention back to the road, I tried to picture the man who I felt would take up the majority of my brain for God knew how long.

"But it'll be worth it in the end," I whispered to myself as I pulled into McSweeney's parking lot almost an hour later.

Not three seconds after stepping into McSweeney's barber unit, I knew that Edward P. Ford wasn't going to be the next person on my newly decided hit list. A new name would fill the spot, perhaps giving the man a bit of a reprieve while I turned my attention in another direction entirely. The worst part was that I already knew about the one who seemed to be on the tip of every man's tongue that morning, and not surprisingly, someone who I hadn't spared a single second of thought throughout the previous couple of months.

Frank Rossi was the kind of man many would cross the street to avoid. He was also likely to follow them over to the other side if he had been paid to do so. The man had been a hired gun in the Pittsburgh area for as long as most could remember, also frequenting the streets of both Philly and Baltimore to a certain extent. I heard he wasn't as keen for the larger population centers as they had enough of their own help already in the phonebook.

Rossi killed for money, and the worst part was, he didn't care who it was, as long as the price was right. Most of the rumors had him at between fifteen and twenty confirmed kills, while some put the number closer to forty. Among his many victims lay a plethora of the kinds of names one might expect to find, mostly those associated with organized crime who always seemed to find their end in some kind of violent affair.

But it wasn't just gang leaders, drug runners, or the kinds of people who deserved hunting by a paid hitman. Sometimes, there were those which turned into news headlines across the country, the kinds of murders which shocked the community. Like Mayor Harry P. Tucker, shot to death in his Lewiston home, right alongside his mother, wife, and twelve-year-old son. I had been working inside

McSweeney itself when news of those killings filtered through, and the whispers began almost immediately.

He was a hitman, a hired gun with no remorse for those he ended. Twelve-year-old Samuel Tucker wasn't the only child claimed to have met his end at the hands of the notorious killer. There were others, four in all, according to those who claimed to know. And as far as I could tell, Frank Rossi hadn't paid the price for a single one.

What the man did for a living wasn't a secret, which meant he was a recognized figure, both out on the street, as well as inside McSweeney. And yet none of his time inside was for the horrendous murders he committed, a seemingly free man to continue his craft without consequences. So, why was he inside?

"To balance the books," was how Johnny Haines once put it. Haines was a drunk, in for his sixteenth time for driving while under the influence. He was what the boys called an old hand, an inmate who'd spent more time inside due to minor offenses. He also knew his stuff when it came to famous prisoners and Rossi was exactly that, a living legend amongst his peers. The man was practically royalty inside, wielding the kind of respect most could only dream of.

The consensus was that Rossi needed to spend some time inside to keep the powers that be happy. Those who could afford the man's services saw it fit to have him serve a few months here or there for minor offenses, like carrying a concealed weapon. His current six-month stint had been for failing to stop for an officer.

What didn't surprise anyone was the network of support the man had behind him. An army of lawyers ready to take on the world stood behind him and it felt as if nobody could ever bring him to the kind of justice he needed to face for his crimes. Not until the day he came into the barber unit for a final cut before his intended release.

After watching the three barbers set up each of their stations, I took up position alongside one of them and proceeded to point out small instructions to a fourth who had come to learn the craft for himself. It was a kind of introduction for the inmate and it gave me an opportunity to get up a little closer to where the action took place. It also meant I practically stood next to Rossi while he was getting his own cut.

The man was an intimidating figure wherever he went. Think DeNiro back in his Taxi Driver years, about three feet taller, and with arms which needed their own zip code. Compared to me, I gave him an extra six inches in height, as well as about a hundred pounds. He was a monster, in both appearance and nature, and I could see him enjoying the notoriety just from looking at him. He never smiled, not even when one of the boys dropped a joke or two, acknowledging the quips with the barest of grins and a slight head nod.

I took it upon myself to take advantage of the situation by sweeping the floor, focusing my effort around the soon to be released inmate. It wasn't a common practice for me, but not completely unheard of. I certainly didn't consider myself above anybody else and wasn't shy of pitching in. I know the guards didn't agree with it, but I wasn't there to impress anyone and sweeping was as much a part of barbering as using the clippers was.

Nobody paid the slightest attention as I swept the discarded hair aside, nor when I bent down to pick up a dropped lid from a wax container. They didn't see me when I reached into the pile for the lid and managed to grab some extra hair for good measure. None spoke up when I fished the lid out of my hand and kept the hair separate, before eventually slipping the precious sample into my jeans pocket.

It took a bathroom break for me to get the sample into one of the small plastic bags I had purchased the previous day and had committed to carrying them with me whenever on the job. Tiny zip-locked coin bags were just the right size for what I needed and half a dozen fit neatly into my pocket without raising too much suspicion. And while I might have been checked coming into the prison, nobody ever gets checked going out.

Rossi left the barber area as quietly as he arrived, again offering nothing more than a slight head nod to those who wished him good luck on the outside. I didn't join in, remaining at my post as I continued watching on from a distance. But inside, I was already imagining myself tracking a man who would kill me in the blink of an eye if he knew the truth, a truth which had already begun with a few strands of hair in my pocket.

CHAPTER 4

I barely made it through the rest of the day, unable to focus on anything else. Each time an inmate called me for help, they needed to repeat themselves, with me standing on the sidelines lost in a world of crazy thoughts running through my head. Four o'clock couldn't come quick enough and by the time I finally managed to climb back into my truck, my insides felt ready to squeeze the very life out of me.

Frank Rossi, the man who had managed to make a name for himself through vile acts of terror had been released out into the community. With each mile closer to home, new thoughts and realizations rose up in my mind, each one an indication of just how huge this operation was going to be.

The thing I couldn't quite comprehend, was just how far his reach stretched, how far those who offered the man protection were willing to go. I knew he had help, of that fact I couldn't have been more certain. Just the fact he hadn't fronted the judicial system for a single murder meant someone was protecting him. Was it the cops? The lawyers? Hell, even certain judges began to flood my mind, each one willing to take a cut of the profits in order to keep the services of a hired gun open for business.

I didn't quite make it back home without a stop. Because of my brain running at an increased rate, I think my blood sugar took quite a hit and I had to make a stop at a BP on the outskirts of Shelocta. It wasn't exactly a desperate situation, but since the truck also needed gas, I figured we could both do with a fuel up. Once I filled the tank, I headed inside to fill my own.

The Coke hit the spot and it wasn't long before the slight shakes also disappeared. They had been one of the best ways of me telling how close I was to a diabetic coma since my younger days. While other sensations could also be used, it was the slight shaking of my fingers which told me when it was time to take action.

It wasn't much further up the road that I decided to make another quick stop, this time to pay my regards to someone who had taken up permanent residence in my heart. Ivy Tannen's roadside memorial, which had initially been nothing more than a homemade job, had been improved rather quickly by a few of the townsfolk. The cross now sitting inside the circle of bricks had been crafted by a local handyman and the photo attached to its front, sat encased in clear acrylic.

The only thing which hadn't changed was the innocence in the eyes of the girl in the photo. Still looking much too young for the horror she faced that terrible day; I did notice the look on her face which had changed from the original photo. If I had to describe that look in a single word, I would say content.

I didn't stay long, just enough to lay a small bunch of flowers on the site. It always worried me that someone might notice my repeated appearances and somehow put two and two together. If they did, and the cops came calling, I knew I would have a hard time explaining things and it was a risk I couldn't afford to take.

Once I arrived back home, I dumped my things on the kitchen table, then made a beeline for the cellar. The sample in my pocket needed to be catalogued and I felt a new sense of urgency as I filled out the cardboard slip which would sit on the drawer's front to classify the contents. I did pause for a moment, holding the marker a few inches above the label as my brain seemed to halt. I couldn't quite decide what to categorize Rossi as. The man was more than just a murderer. He was also a child killer, and that alone put him into an entirely different category. I thought about adding an extra level to the table, like "Grade A Killer". That way, I could give each a distinct level of importance. Child killers would always take top spot, in my book.

But it still didn't feel enough and eventually I went with the most obvious, carefully ranting the name in neat handwriting: Hitman. The word fit better than anything else I could come up with and also encompassed his entire catalog of crimes. As I slid the word into the metallic holder, a new sense of purpose washed over me, the mission effectively under way.

Despite not being hungry, I didn't want a repeat of low blood sugar, so I made my first job organizing dinner once I returned upstairs. There was a ton of work to be done and I wanted to make sure I could get through the evening without unnecessary interruptions.

With a chicken roast, for one, in the oven, I headed to the bathroom for a quick shower. While I did have plenty of things to do, I couldn't pass up the need to wash the remnants of McSweeney off me. There was just something about the smell inside a prison which always remained with me long after walking out of the front gate. It's hard to describe, but for me, it felt as if the very essence of the place stuck to my skin. Not just stuck to it, but somehow embedded into every pore, the stink of the place stuck to the insides of each nostril. Only a shower could wash away the place and it was something I needed religiously after each shift.

The dinner which followed wasn't anything special. It's hard to try and explain, but during the previous few years, food had become nothing more than a necessity. I didn't eat for the taste. Food just didn't hold that kind of appeal for me anymore, not since I began cooking for one. If it wasn't for my Diabetes, I probably would have bypassed food completely, especially during those days of heavy drinking.

For me, food had taken on the role of nothing more than a fuel source. My body needed it to survive and I fed it accordingly. Taste didn't seem to matter and a lot of the time, there were other things to focus on as I shoveled in the meals. It felt a little like filling up the truck with gasoline. Did it complain when I didn't provide it with a certain brand? Of course not, because fuel was fuel, nothing more.

I wanted to conduct my research uninterrupted and so, I finished my meal first. That way, I could sit at the latter without distractions for as long as my body allowed. I knew fatigue would eventually will me to bed, of that I had no power. Plus, I had work the next day. But for the next few hours, I had a big wide world to explore and I intended to take full advantage.

It wasn't long into my first session that I discovered

one fundamental revelation. Hitmen weren't exactly well known while they were still active. Those who had fallen in the line of duty, or had been taken down by law enforcement and now sat inside a prison cell, those had their entire history stretched across hundreds of websites. But those still very much in the game? Not so much.

At first, I was surprised at how little information I could find on the man. Barely any of the murders he'd been rumored to have committed even mentioned him. It felt as if a dark veil of secrecy surrounded him, which stretched far beyond anything most people would consider normal. He had no social media to speak of, or at least none that I could find, no family who included him in their online presence.

His mother had died during childbirth, while his father was unknown. He'd been raised in an orphanage until the age of thirteen, at which time he took his sorry ass to the streets and began to hang out with an outfit called Pen 44, a nod to the street the gang's leader grew up on. As if trying to do her best, the gang leader's mother, a woman named Barbara Chol, gave the gang some direction by pointing them towards various establishments fit for robbing.

Pen 44 kept Rossi within its grips until he reached twenty-one, at which time he came to the attention of a local thug named Roberto Hughes. Hughes had a reputation for being a tough guy who would chase up debts for a fee. He recruited Rossi into his ranks and soon, the young man was hunting down his own piece of the pie.

Driven by a lust for riches, it didn't take Rossi long to gain the kind of experience which would eventually lead him to more serious crimes, before supposedly committing his first paid murder at age twenty-three. Of course, the rumors told otherwise, claiming he'd committed his first murder a lot earlier, while still involved in Pen 44. A security guard had been killed during one particular robbery; the man's skull caved in by a vicious beating from just one of the would-be robbers. While the whispers all pointed to Rossi, it was never proven and the murder still remains unsolved to this day.

I took a break around nine, my head filled with crime scene photos and details of some of the most horrific felonies imaginable. There was a distinct buzz inside me and a serious urge for a drink.

"No drink," I told myself when the idea to whip down to the local bar crossed my mind. "Not ever," I reaffirmed, pushing the urge aside. It wasn't easy, not by a long way. It wasn't called an addiction for nothing and I was more than aware of my alcoholism. Time was the only thing which would help me beat such cravings; that and a few distractions thrown in for good measure.

What struck me as odd, and shouldn't have come to me as a surprise, were the things *not* mentioned in the dozens of articles I went through. There wasn't a doubt in my mind about the people helping the man behind the scenes, and I could only imagine the amount of cash which must have exchanged hands to keep someone like that not only out of the public spotlight, but also out of jail for any significant time.

Organized crime wasn't anything new to a man like me. I practically saw it firsthand every time I stepped inside one of the dozen prisons I worked in. Gangs from all walks of life existed inside, with members making up the majority of the inmate population. When people think of organized crime, they might picture images reminiscent of The Godfather movies, with men in fine suits toting

Tommy guns as they crisscrossed the city in their dark automobiles.

The reality was that organized crime looked nothing like it did in movies. Most people would be surprised by who these people really were. They could be standing next to them in line at the supermarket and they would never know. The boy or girl next door, the person coming to quote for a new set of curtains, or the person sorting their income tax for the year. The truth was, organized crime lived in the very streets of each and every city in America and nobody could ever effectively scrub it out entirely. The influence it had over people was insane, which is why so many in authority ended up a slave to the movement.

I didn't know whether I had achieved what I intended to by the time midnight came around, but I did feel a whole lot better about understanding the job before me. This wasn't going to be easy, of that fact I was more than aware of. As I closed the laptop for the night, I came to one very clear point. Judge Ferris was nothing more than a worm when compared to what I had before me with Rossi. This was like comparing a random ten minutes on a nearby go-kart track to taking pole in a Formula 1 race at Monaco.

Lying in bed that night, I couldn't help but wonder whether I had chosen a target completely out of my league. Hunting down irresponsible drunks with a taste for power was one thing, but trying to turn the tables on a full-on hitman? That was another thing entirely. There was just one thing I knew for sure as I finally closed my eyes and that was the understanding that I would never quit. I wouldn't consider my job complete until Frank Rossi was dead.

CHAPTER 5

Days turned into weeks as my prep for the hit continued. What many might have seen as nothing more than surfing the internet, I called training. Once I really got going, I was surprised by just how much information a person could find when really looking. I even found a quote from Elon Musk stating that a person no longer needed to pay for education, as everything a person needed to know was right there online for Free. Google really did become my new best friend.

By day, I continued working inside the prisons, often stretched out to all four quarters of the state. But each time I found myself looking for possible samples, my brain began to deep dive into a world of possibilities. Why stop at just hair when there was so much more up for grabs. I began accumulating all manner of samples and it surprised me at just how effective I became. It turned into an almost obsession for me, each time trying to get as many samples as possible.

The crime catalog continued to grow and by the time June came around, the cabinet was more than half filled.

This created a problem for me and not one I was complaining about. I had become too efficient in my collection techniques, a virtual conveyer belt of incoming evidence I could use in subsequent crimes.

The realization happened one Friday evening after a particularly good day of evidence scavenging. That was what I had begun to call it, a term I cooked up during one afternoon of high turnover clients. I was in the midst of itemizing my samples, each dropped into the bottom of my toolbox.

My obsession was quickly turning into a full-time job and I already had one of those. And while one served a much higher purpose than I could ever truly comprehend, I still needed the other one in order to survive. Only one paid the bills, the other more of a hobby, unable to fund itself, of sorts. And yet it was that second job which took up the bulk of my free time.

To begin with, each and every sample needed cataloging. OK, so bagging and tagging wasn't exactly overly time consuming, but I needed to understand who the samples came from and that part *did* take up a considerable amount of time. We're talking in-depth research to understand who I had in my hands. Thieves, murders, rapists, they all needed correct files before I could drop them into their appropriate catalog draws. If I didn't, their evidence would be useless.

But the more samples I brought home, the more I came to understand a cold, hard truth. I was bringing home too much. It didn't take me long to realize I was never going to use them all, not in a million years. And that was when I came to the understanding that I needed to be more reserved in my approach. What I needed was to refine my process, to sort through what I had and only retain what I knew I would actually use.

To understand my needs, I went back to the very basics of my existence, the plain, fundamental purpose for what I stood for. I wasn't out to correct wrongly-imposed parking fines, or hunt down rogue graffiti artists. My purpose was to avenge only the most serious of crimes, their victims normally murdered without those responsible facing justice. I was the dark angel of vengeance, the bringer of hell to those thinking they can create such misery and simply move on with their lives.

I wasn't going to need the DNA samples from simple thieves. With a deep sigh, I removed them from their respective draws and threw the small bags of samples into the incinerator. The smell of the burning hair filled the cellar, but it was the sound of the singing fibers which served as a reminder to myself to not lose focus of my intended goal.

The problem was, I had become too confident and the more I thought about it, the more I realized the error of my ways. This wasn't just about becoming good at obtaining evidence. I had foolishly ignored the ramifications of my actions. What if I had been caught? Or worse still, what if I had already been noticed?

I almost panicked as I sat by the light of the flames, thinking back to my previous few shifts and how I had obtained the samples, sometimes bending over in plain sight to grab a handful of the hair I had swept up. Even the act of sweeping itself suddenly felt like an issue. How many had noticed the increase in my kindness to help out with the manual labor?

The reality of the situation hit me like a ton of bricks, all dropped on my head at once. How could I have been so stupid, so arrogantly stupid, in believing myself bulletproof. The chances I had taken equated to one simple thing. I had failed to properly consider the consequences of my own actions before trying to make people pay for theirs.

"Idiot," I muttered to myself as I gripped the handle of my frosted glass tighter than ever, gritting my teeth in frustration.

The answer, however, proved just as simple as the initial mistakes I had made. What I needed was planning, and I didn't mean the things I needed to do each day. What I had to do was consider what I needed, and then come up with a plan which practiced the very traits that would keep me safe. For example, if I needed the DNA evidence from a murderer, then I would find my target and wait until the right moment to obtain their sample. What I would not do, was take whatever samples I could find along the way and within a clear line of sight of guards and inmates.

Cockiness was what had changed in me, thinking myself above the law and untouchable from those who wouldn't hesitate to bring me down. It was time to do things right, otherwise I would end up sitting inside a prison cell myself and I already knew what that would lead to. There was no way I could even contemplate a life behind bars.

CHAPTER 6

June 14th turned out to be the day I would officially begin an operation I had been planning for, for weeks. That was the day I officially picked up Frank Russo's trail for the first time and wow, what a moment it was. For me, it felt like I had pushed my way through a thick blanket of fog and finally made it out the other side. It wasn't easy finding a man who lacked any sort of social media presence.

The twist came in the form of a letter, and not one which anybody had been expecting. As it turned out, a whole lot of tiny screw-ups added up to become a giant one, and one which just happened to benefit me. For one thing, the letter shouldn't have arrived at all, considering the name on the front. But it did and that's all there was to it.

Rossi had been out for a month already by this point, which makes the screw-up even less likely to happen. Someone had sent him a letter, and I don't really know how it's supposed to work, but whoever was in charge of approving the influx of mail must have screwed up, because one turned up for him.

The mistake was simple enough, and something anybody could have made. Inside A-Pod, we not only housed the recently-departed Frank Rossi, but a new arrival also arrived, one Fred Rossa. When the letter landed on the counter of the McSweeney barber unit and I first saw it, someone had crossed the "i" in Rossi and scribbled an "a" over the top. The first name was just the initial, which meant F. Rossi became F. Rossa.

"Ain't me," Rossa said as he looked at the envelope. During most days, a guard would have been with me in the room, but fate again sent me a message by leaving me alone at that very moment. The usual guard was over by the door in deep conversation with one of the few female guards and I could see why. "Easy on the eye" was the elite way of putting it.

"I'll take it," I said and without thinking, slipped it into my back pocket.

The truth was, at the time of taking that envelope, it never occurred to me what the problem was with it. Taking it came as instinctual as someone asking for a Murder One and me handing over a pair of clippers set for the right height. It was something I just did. Rossa finished his cut and the rest of us continued with our day. By the time Taylor the guard returned to his post, the day had effectively moved on.

I didn't come across the letter again until later that day. Actually, it didn't make another appearance until I found myself stepping out of my pants as I prepared to wash that god-awful smell off of me in the shower. As I pulled my pants off, I spotted the top edge of the envelope and remembered where it came from.

The shower took precedence, of course. It always did. Whatever that envelope was, it could wait. It wasn't as if it was going anywhere, and I still didn't think anything of it, except for some junk piece of mail between inmates. Again, it faded into the corners of my mind as I stood under the hot water and let the flow wash away the day. It felt good, almost holistic. It was as close to soul cleansing as I could imagine myself getting, the residue of prison life washing away with the flow of the outside world.

Grabbing the envelope in one hand and the dirty washing in the other, I stopped by the laundry first and dropped the bundle into the clothing basket before continuing onto the living room. Music played in the background, Chris Isaak subdued to just above hearing, enough to take away the silence.

When my eyes first scanned the name on the front, my heart just about stopped as my eyes focused on the scribble over the last letter of the surname. The initial words had been written in black pen, while the scribbler had used red. The change looked more like a drop of blood than a correction, staring back at me like an incredulous eye.

Phantom fingers grabbed me around the middle as I turned the envelope over in my hands and looked at the sender's details. Again, the shock of the moment wasn't lost on me, knowing how hard the man had been to track at all.

Wendy Ranch
521 Pearl Street
Bloomfield, PA, 15224

My fingers felt hypnotized as the rest of me struggled to get them to move. I was beginning to panic, thinking that somehow, I hadn't noticed my blood sugars dropping to dangerous levels, which would explain my lack of control. The shaking of my hands almost confirmed it, but then I finally managed to pull myself back together.

It was plain old nerves which had gripped me, nerves and a good dose of excitement. Finally managing to get my hands moving, I rolled the envelope over and slid a finger into the folded-over lip. With one quick slip, I tore the outer edge open and what I fund inside changed everything.

He was a father. Frank Rossi, the hitman feared by so many, was the father to two little girls. Esther was four, while her older sister Hanna was six. The "letter" was nothing more than a couple of pages of children's drawings, with one of them showing the family unit the artist found herself in.

Aside from the pictures, there was also a note from the before mentioned Wendy Ranch, but right from the get-go, I could tell there were troubles in paradise. It didn't take a genius to figure out that she didn't want anything to do with the father of her children, a woman who sounded close to losing her mind if he so much as showed his face around them.

"Frank. Enough is enough. I have made my position clear to you. We do not want you around here anymore, so please stay away when you get out. The girls and I have moved on and are trying to make the best of a bad situation. We don't want your money; we don't want your so-called protection. It's over between us. The girls are confused and I'm trying my hardest to help them understand this shitty situation. I'm not sure why I included the drawings. Maybe just to let you see that they are

fine without you. We both want what's best for them, so please respect our wishes."

She never signed off on the brief note, the message cut off as suddenly as a slap to the face. I read it no less than three times, my eyes darting across the age as I imagined what her world must have consisted of. I wondered whether she knew what the father of her children was really up to during his "away time" and whether she was the kind of supportive partner every man craved.

Feeling a renewed rush of excitement, I whipped open the laptop and began searching her name on every social media platform I could find. I sat with my mouth hanging open in anticipation of finally getting a breakthrough, but again quickly found myself staring at a blank wall of nothingness.

I didn't think I was ever going to get anywhere with the case and began to wonder whether I had made a huge mistake opting to go after Rossi in the first place. I mean, he was a huge hitter in the underworld and who was I to challenge someone batting way, way, way above my league? There was no denying that I had jumped the gun as such, making my way from the mailroom to the boardroom overnight.

Needing a moment to think, I headed out into the backyard and just stood in the middle of a patch of lawn. Staring up into the night sky with just a half-moon for company, I listened to the city continue on in the distance, the never-ending drone of traffic still rising into the air. The air felt a little cooler than I was expecting, but then again, standing there in nothing but boxer shorts at ten o'clock at night wasn't exactly going to feel like an inferno.

Ferris came to mind again, but not the man himself. Instead, I began to run my side of our relationship through my mind, how I managed to track him down and plan our eventual meeting which culminated in his judgement coming for him. The things I did to make the meeting happen, that was what played on my mind.

And that was when it came to me. I still held the envelope in my hand, the letter itself clasped between two separate fingers. The backyard wasn't exactly bathed in shadows, enough light coming from the street beyond to still show me enough of the envelope for my brain to suddenly open up.

It felt more like an awakening, but once the idea struck me, I felt my whole body begin to buzz with excitement. With the envelope gripped tightly in hand, I practically ran back inside and returned to the laptop, ripped opened the lid and waited for the screen to come to life. Once the usual Google home page greeted me, I headed straight to Facebook and held my breath.

I didn't know whether Wendy Ranch had ever been married to Rossi, or what their relationship had been like during their better days. But what I hoped for was that the woman had family. While her own name didn't exactly ring any bells on any of the platforms, I wondered whether her family did.

For the next hour and a half, I began to scan each and every friendliest belonging to any person with the surname of Ranch. It wasn't exactly the most common name, but there were still enough hits to give me hope. Names like Harold Ranch, Tyson Ranch, Lisa Ranch, all began to form a mini community as I trolled through their friend lists. I began to recognize the same names in several profiles, with the photos confirming their links.

Finally, just before midnight, I struck gold, my heart almost beating in my mouth as I stared at the image of a young woman standing in front of two young girls. She had changed her name to Wendy Rancher, perhaps hoping to give them some kind of shield against online stalkers or would-be threats. Thankfully, my persistence lasted long enough for me to catch a small break and once I had the first part of the puzzle, it didn't take me long to find more.

CHAPTER 7

The address she had on the envelope wasn't her home, but her place of work. Wendy Ranch was a hairdresser and when I ran the business details through Google, found that she was also the owner, which meant Rossi had a way of finding her. It was clear she had been trying to keep a distance from her former partner and I could only imagine the reasons she had.

Instead of struggling to juggle work and my newfound direction in the case, I decided to take a week off work and make the most of trying to get a clearer picture of my target's life. I still hadn't managed to find a way to get eyes on him, which left me with nothing more than a woman trying to do the exact opposite.

What I needed was a plan and I began with the simplest thing of all, walking past the hairdressing salon for a closer look. It wasn't much and didn't give me a whole lot of information, but I wasn't really expecting to crack the case as easily as that. But what those few minutes did give me was the taste. What do I mean? I mean the sense of doing something, which seemed to churn the waters of urgency inside me. It gave me the determination to do more, kind of like setting the wheels into motion and getting me to take the next step.

I noticed that the building across the street was available for rent, the building was a business with an upstairs apartment. Call it what you will, but to me, it looked like a reasonable next step. Instead of hanging around, I went home that first day and hit the real estate agent up for an inspection. A woman named Tara Cox was the agent looking after the property and she was kind enough to meet with me that very afternoon.

"Why waste time," I told her with a bit of excitement and she gave me the fake laugh of confirmation.

The worst part about real estate agents was that they loved to talk, so when I met her later that day, I already had my story all prepped and ready to go. I was a barber (not a lie), looking to open my own shop (kind of a lie). I had a few people working for me (not a lie) and I needed somewhere where I could expand (blatant lie).

I could tell she didn't really care, the woman more interested in getting the kind of information out of me which indicated my capability of taking on a lease for the place. In other words, could I afford it. According to my story, I definitely could, having just received a large payout from the sale of a home in Tucson. I told her my mother passed (not exactly a lie) and that we ended up selling the old family home and split the money between my brother and I.

I didn't think she would check my story out, but I did see her take notes in a small pad. I didn't see the note taking as a bad thing, as it meant her focus wasn't on me and I managed to unclip a sliding window while pretending to check out the view from the top floor while she was still in the next room pulling the other shutters closed.

"Just not sure about the size," I told her once we'd returned downstairs. "I need at least four extra stations."

Fakery wasn't a stranger to me and I could tell she lost interest the second I questioned the building, even more when I asked if she had any others to show me.

"Not a lot bigger, but I do have something similar a few blocks over coming up for lease in about a month, if that interests you."

It did, and I watched her face light up again with a glimmer of hope as I set a second date to view the place. Of course, I was going to cancel it well ahead of time, but I let her hang on to the hope for a few days. After a quick thank you and handshake, we each went our separate ways.

I returned later that night, parked my truck well away from the business and kept to the shadows as I made my way down the alley behind the building. A neighboring shed sat almost behind the window I'd unlocked and I hoped it would give me the boost I needed to reach my entry point.

Something I found out from the very beginning of my life as an avenging angel, was how many dogs suddenly began to appear when a person needed to move in silence. I'd barely laid my hands on the fence separating the two buildings before one began to bark like its life was about to end.

Frozen in place, I sat precariously balanced behind the fence, one foot up on a cross post, my hand gripping the fence picket as I scanned the windows of the houses backing onto that part of the world. It's funny how one notices things otherwise hidden in a sea of information.

The number of curtains I could make out was astonishing. The worse thing about it was that I knew people could see through them and remain hidden, which gave them a distinct advantage. And if any of them saw me, it was almost a guaranteed run-in with authorities.

Carefully dropping down to my knees, I decided to take advantage of the shadows, plus the cover the fence gave me. Time wasn't something I lacked, given the number of hours I still had before morning. 2 AM wasn't exactly the middle of the night, but it was one of those times slots where the majority of the city slept.

Things calmed down again quite quickly, with the dog losing interest after someone shouted for the mutt to "Shut the hell up". I thought I heard someone else open a door a few yards over and whisper something into the night, but I couldn't be sure.

Trying my luck, a second time, it was almost relief when I managed to scramble to the top of the shed and not set off another round of barking. My guess was that the owner had taken the advice of their neighbor and brought the mutt indoors.

The window remained unlocked, and I breathed a sigh of relief as it slid open easily. I wasn't exactly the most in-shape kind of guy, but I did manage to pull myself up enough to slide through the opening. Once inside, I closed the window, slid the curtain back over and paused. Silence. The sounds of the city had been left outside, while inside, not even so much as a fridge hum.

Once sure I was not only alone, but also effectively cut off from prying eyes, I walked through to the front room. Just as it had been the previous afternoon, the curtains remained partially drawn, with just a faint gap on the side. I stopped in the middle of the room and positioned myself in such a way to ensure I could see the object of my needs.

Wendy Ranch's salon sat almost directly opposite, with a street light almost directly in front of her window. From where I stood, I had a perfect view inside, as well as the front door. A slight bend of my torso and I could see everything all the way up the street, which meant I could also spot anyone else sitting in their vehicle.

While there were no chairs to speak of in the upstairs area, there was a small table wedged against a wall in one of the other rooms. Needing somewhere to park my butt, I carried it out to my sniper's nest and positioned it in such a way, that I could see most of what I needed with very little lateral movement.

Once I had the table in place, I took off my backpack and set it aside. I couldn't exactly go on a stakeout without supplies, especially when the reality of a diabetic coma was something which constantly hung over my head. Thankfully, the latest insulin pump sat neatly attached to my back, which meant one less job I had to worry about.

By four o'clock, I was sure I was going to lose the battle to sleep and I ended up dropping down against the back wall. I set the alarm for 7am and closed my eyes, sure I wouldn't sleep anyway. Nerves had a funny way of keeping a person awake and I wasn't expecting any less.

Imagine the surprise when I found myself brought back to the world of the living by the cellphone vibrating in my hand. I felt like crap, my eyes feeling heavier than ever as I got to my feet. The hum of civilization hung in the air as I took my first look out into daylight and wasn't surprised to find the salon still closed. The website stated an opening time of 8.30 and I wasn't expecting anybody to turn up much earlier than that.

As I reached for the backpack to take care of the empty feeling inside me, I reminded myself of the only escape open to me if my one fear came true. Given the place was still available for rent, meant the agent might bring other prospective tenants through. It wasn't something I particularly wanted and so decided on the spur of the moment to try and elevate the issue.

I felt bad sending the message but figured a couple of days wouldn't make much difference to the agent. Pretending to have made up my mind, I sent Tara Cox a text message asking if she was available that Friday morning to sign the paperwork. I figured three days would be more than enough time for me to get what I needed, which at that stage, was still in the air as to what that meant.

She answered back almost immediately, happy to see me at ten that Friday. She asked whether I minded leaving a deposit to hold the place and I said I'd organize one as quick as I could. Of course, I had no intention of that either. The last thing I wanted was to leave evidence of my involvement in anything related to Rossi, including a rental building across the street from a business owned by the mother of his children.

Once I finished with Cox, I took my boiled eggs and the binoculars to the table and leaned against it as I ate. The day looked miserable from my vantage point and almost on cue, it began to rain. I didn't mind. It wasn't as if I had anything better planned.

Wendy Ranch turned up just after eight and I watched from a distance as she prepped her salon for the day ahead. She looked prettier than her Facebook photos, but I also detected a hint of vulnerability in those eyes, a definite sense of awareness I still didn't fully understand. It was a mystery I had every intention of solving before this case was through.

It felt almost surreal sitting behind the safety of my fragile concealment watching a woman who had no idea of my existence. I wasn't even some random thought to her, and yet my entire focus was right there on her as she prepped the cash register.

Was she integral to my plan? Not really. The reasons behind me ending up in a vacant business across the street from her had nothing to do with the woman herself per se, but more to do with her past. As far as I could tell, she was the only real link I had to finding Rossi. With nobody else in my little outfit, I had but a single person I could rely on and I had every intention of keeping it that way. If anyone else became even the slightest aware of what I had been up to, I risked everything, which is why I needed to remain in the shadows.

My intentions, however, were quite clear. I would take each day at a time and go from there. As long as I made progress, I was succeeding, no matter how small. As if to confirm this, I checked off step one, confirming the subject of my investigation actually worked at the place.

"Check," I whispered to myself, drawing a small tick in the air.

Step two was also a simple task. All I wanted to know was how she moved around and if via a car, what one she specifically drove. Once I had the car identified, I could then attach my GPS tracker and find out where she lived. Once that was achieved, I would have a new decision to make. Rossi was the one I needed, after all, and stalking a vulnerable single mother wasn't exactly in my original plan.

CHAPTER 8

Watching Wendy Ranch through a set of binoculars quickly wore thin with me. Boredom was a good word to describe the stakeout, but I did learn one very important thing about her. The young mom had either an endless supply of energy, or an incredible determination for success. By the time four o'clock rolled around, she had worked non-stop for the entire day. Her three assistants each took breaks in turn, but not Wendy.

By the time she walked out of the closed-down salon a little after five, the rest of her team had already gone. I held my breath as I watched her turn left and walk up the sidewalk to where a little Mazda sat parked alone on the side of the street. The dark grey hatchback must have been a far cry from the luxury she would have been used to while in the company of a well-paid hitman. Or so I imagined.

Despite my day effectively ending the second she drove off into the world, I had no intentions of leaving. I knew there might be a possibility I could be stuck in the place for a while and so I packed enough supplies for three days. My insulin cartridge didn't need replacing for another week and I had one in reserve just in case. What I didn't want to risk was leaving and then not being able to come back. And so, I stayed.

Sleep came a lot easier for me later that evening than it had the previous few nights and I put it down to simple exhaustion. I did have my cellphone for company, but there were only so many episodes of Seinfeld a person could watch before the eyes could no longer hold up to the humor. By ten o'clock, I knew I was beat, shut down the phone and closed my eyes. The next thing I heard was the alarm going off.

As I woke to a new day feeling the ramifications of sleeping on a hard linoleum floor, I struggled to understand the reasons for me spending a second night in the empty apartment. I mean, I had the details of her car, right down to the license plate details. What I really needed was to get downstairs and attach the tracker to her car and I wouldn't be able to get that done now, not until at least the following day. Climbing out through the window was no longer an option thanks to the daylight. So, why did I stay?

In a word, instinct. I couldn't deny something inside me telling my subconsciousness to hang around. For what reason, I didn't know, it was just…something. Call it intuition, but there was definitely a reason for me to remain in the building and right from the get-go, I wanted to be prepared.

The first thing I did was take care of my bathroom needs so that they were done with for a good few hours. Next came breakfast, which I ate while sitting cross-legged on the table and peering out into a beautiful day. The rain clouds had vanished overnight, leaving a clear sky with sunshine the likes of which had to be seen to be believed. It was almost a shame to be indoors during such a morning.

The part of the street where we were located had very little through traffic, and parking wasn't exactly in abundance. I could see the previous spot Wendy had parked and as I took a bite of my apple, wasn't surprised to see her roll up in the exact same spot. She drove up in a casual manner and simply turned the wheel slightly until close enough to the gutter, then stopped. From my vantage point, I could see a fair way up the street behind her, far enough to notice the traffic passing back and forth on Liberty Avenue. Which is why I noticed the second vehicle a few hundred yards further up.

The BMW's driver pulled in to the gutter at the same time as Wendy did, mirroring her movements enough for me to notice. My insides tightened with that familiar flutter, telling me I was on the right track. As Wendy climbed out and made her way to the salon's entrance, I kept my binoculars trained in such a way, that I could see the both of them in the same frame. While one might have been more out of focus, I could still see enough to know the second arrival was still sitting in his car when the woman stepped into her salon.

As Wendy repeated her morning chores, I tried my hardest to get a glimpse of the stranger sitting in the car. The binoculars I had weren't exactly on the cheap end of the scale, which is why my frustrations grew exponentially the more I tried to zoom in. The problem was, they weren't powerful enough, giving me nothing but a mere shadow inside the car. I could make out the shape of the person, enough to know it was a man, but the face remained out of view.

The sun visor had been pulled down, not only blocking out most of the light which could have helped my cause, but also came down far enough to cut the man's head in half. Add to that a less-than-powerful set of binoculars and I had failure on a grand scale.

It could have been Rossi. The chances of that, as far as I was concerned, were quite high. But then again, it could have been an Uber driver waiting for his next fare, for all I knew. Either way, I wasn't going to find out by remaining where I sat.

To me, it felt kind of like a stalemate, unable to move and yet the answers to my questions sat just outside my window, within easy reach, so to speak. My cellphone vibrated and I looked down to where I had set it down on the table. An email notification had popped up, but before I could read who it was from, the screen went dark again. As I reached for it, the tip of my finger clipped the front edge, sending it tumbling to the floor.

The crash of it hitting the floor sounded more like a bomb in the silence of the building and I swear the echo alone continued for almost half a minute. I froze, expecting an army of onlookers to suddenly rush up the stairs to see who the intruder was, but then sighed as I reminded myself that the building was empty.

"Dumb ass," I grumbled to myself as I leaned down to pick up the phone and that was when a new idea hit me. The cellphone's camera lenses stared back at me and in that moment, I briefly recalled the advertisements I'd seen about the power of the zoom on these things and a sense of excitement rushed through me as I swiped the screen awake. Wanting to give myself the best chance possible, I got up from the table and took a few steps closer to the window. Unfortunately, by the time I looked for the elusive driver again, the X5 was gone.

"Dumb ass," I repeated, this time with more conviction on the "dumb" part, and while I tried to tell myself that it must have been nothing more than an Uber after all, my instincts told me otherwise. Just how many Ubers drove such a lavish vehicle?

There was just something about the way the car pulled into the spot the same way Wendy did, as if tracing her every move, while trying their hardest to keep their distance. It was that deep emotional twang which refused to let go, telling me that it was the man I was looking for.

The other thing which had also begun to cross my mind, was the fact he was a father. It's amazing how much a man's mind will wander while sitting in the same place for hours on end, with nothing more for company than random thoughts running through his head. And that was one of my biggest obstacles while sitting in that vacant apartment during the stakeout. My stupid, free-running brain going into overdrive like a semi-trailer rolling downhill with no brakes. It was in a practical freewill and it didn't take long for me to start picturing the man with his children. Could I really go through with killing a father, stealing him away from his children?

I tried to tell myself that it didn't matter, that he'd made his own bed when he murdered children himself. There was enough spilt blood already, the scales hanging way too low for him to able to make up the difference. And yet, I also had a conscience I needed to deal with.

Before I had a chance to fully explore my abilities to follow through with my plan, a noise suddenly caught my attention, one which sent a boatload of adrenalin coursing through my system. As the beating in my chest exploded to the adrenal dump, the key in the door lock downstairs clicked hard enough to echo before the familiar creaking of the door opening took over.

"Shit," I muttered, looking at my spread-out gear against the near wall.

"Like I said," Tara Cox's voice began," I may already have someone, but I know how desperate you are." Another voice answered with a faint aha, but I was too busy trying to sweep my things into the backpack to care.

My exit strategy had been simple. The front door was the kind which could be locked from inside, but needed a key from the outside. No deadbolt to speak of. I'd planned to simply walk downstairs and head straight out the front door and back into the world once I knew my job was done. As I silently dropped the final few bits of my things into the backpack, I listened to my escape route close up as the two people now stood just few feet below me.

I knew that most of the person's attention would be aimed downstairs, to where the business would actually exist, but it wouldn't be long before they came up to the apartment. That gave me just minutes, if not seconds, to get my butt into gear. Looking around, I first went to the window which had given me my initial way in. To my horror, a man sat on his back porch just a couple of yards over, a cigarette in one hand, with a cup in the other. Given his body language, I could tell he was there for the long haul. Worse still, he appeared to be deep in thought while staring directly at the window I stood in.

More mumbled chatter floated up to me as I felt my heartbeat begin beating in my temples, the fear of getting caught becoming a real possibility. I almost opened the window to take my chances, but spotted a second person slowly walking along the sidewalk. And then a third woman carrying a washing basket appeared in an adjoining yard.

I was trapped. The worst part was that the real estate agent currently showing the downstairs section to a prospective client knew me. She would be able to identify me and one phone call to the police and I was as good as done for. Panicking, I looked around the room I stood in, hunting for any likely hiding spot.

"And now for the upstairs," Tara suddenly said and I heard the creaking of the first step as they began to climb the single set of stairs.

With no choice, I stealthed my way into one of the two bedrooms and stood with my back against the wall. There was no time to close the door and so I simply did my best to get as flat as humanly possible. Of course, it didn't work, but it wasn't as if I had any choice. A smell suddenly drifted to me, the faint hint of jasmine and I recognized it as the perfume the agent had worn during my own showing.

"Bigger than I expected," the prospective client said and I listened as their footfalls sounded as if they were heading away from me.

Risking capture, I edged my way to the side of the door and took a peek. I wasn't sure who had led who, but I saw Tara's back turned to me as she stood in the doorway of the room I had spent the previous day in. The man was mumbling something about the view and how he would use the huge window as another spot to hang a sign.

It was all or nothing for me by then, and instead of waiting to get caught, I took a deep breath and stepped out from my hiding spot. With my eyes fixed on the agent for any sign of turning back to me, I tip-toed across the floor to the top of the stairs. Just as I reached it, I saw

Tara's back begin to turn as she said something about the bathroom and if she had continued, would have caught me red-handed. Instead, the client asked about the possibility of subletting the upstairs apartment, which drew the real estate agent's attention back to him.

Counting my lucky stars, I continued down the stairs, carefully maneuvering my way through an obstacle course of creaky timber. The trailer came second from the bottom and I heard Tara call out an animated hello, but I didn't stop. With the front door virtually four feet from the foot of the stairs, I opened and closed the door with barely enough time for me to step out into the day. The sidewalk stood empty before me and just as I reached the corner of the building, I heard the open up behind me. Stepping sideways, I rolled around the corner, entered the small alley and broke into a run. I didn't look back until I was safely back in my car.

CHAPTER 9

I must have sat in my truck for close to an hour after my escape while I contemplated my next move. With too many possibilities to consider, and just as many options open for me, I didn't want to risk throwing my advantage away by being stupid.

For one, the agent knew someone was there and if she had half a brain, would probably work out it was me. That was, if she suspected someone of spending a substantial amount of time in the apartment. I wasn't sure how thorough I was with cleaning up evidence of my stay, having been caught off guard. Did I leave anything behind in the bathroom?

And then there was the BMW I had spotted. If it was just a random Uber, then so be it. But if the car had been driven by Frank Rossi and he happened to also be watching Wendy, how long before he would catch sight of me trying to follow her?

Then there was Wendy herself. I still needed to get the tracker on her car. I didn't trust myself to follow her home in my pick-up, especially with Rossi possibly stalking her as well.

Stalking her. Just thinking the words filled me with dread. Is that what I was doing? As I continued biding my time in the cabin of my truck, I scrolled through a few of her Facebook posts. It was strange seeing the warmth of a mother in those photos, while knowing the monster who stood in the shadows behind her.

I decided that I needed to do something, anything to advance my cause. If I continued sitting in some back alley for too long, then I would risk Wendy driving off into yet another evening, with me no closer to finding out where Rossi's children lived. And it was the children who I knew would end up being the key to everything.

I'd always kept a spare baseball cap in my truck, although I didn't make it a habit of wearing one religiously, the way some people did. Add to that a change of shirts, plus some sunglasses, and I figured it was going to be the best identity change I could manage at such a short amount of time.

Climbing down into the heat of the day, I looked up and down the street to make sure I still hadn't drawn too much attention to my ride, then turned back towards the main road. About half way down, I changed my mind after considering my destination. If Rossi had returned to the same spot he'd been parked at previously, then he would see me attach the tracker to the car. Realizing I needed to exercise a little extra caution, I did a U-turn and headed back passed my truck and out the opposite end of the alley. I went the long way, reached Liberty Avenue and turned left.

Instead of turning left again the second I reached Pearl Street, I slowed right down, paused before crossing the street, then took my butt over the road while scanning the cars parked by the curb. From what I could see, there was no sign of the white BMW, and again the whole Uber theory returned. I put my excited overreaction down to nothing more than an overactive brain, seasoned by the previous month's activities.

I didn't hurry along the sidewalk as I began to make my way closer to the grey Mazda sitting a few hundred yards ahead of me. With hands in the pockets of my jeans, I felt the tracker, rolling it through my fingers again and again as I kept my eye on the target. A few pedestrians dotted the sidewalk, but most were either staring at their cellphones, or were too focused on where they were going to pay attention to random strangers passing them by.

The closer I got to the car, the harder the beating in my chest took over. Passing out could have been a real possibility and I slowed my breathing down to try and lessen the chances. Thankfully, the sunglasses meant nobody could see my eyes anxiously darting from one person to the next as I tried to time my approach perfectly. The act of securing the tracker to the car would take me less than a second, but it had to be done personally, with me fixing the device to the vehicle's underside by hand.

If I had been asked a year ago as to whether I could bring myself to attaching a tracking device to a stranger's car in broad daylight, I would have laughed at the idea. Now, I took on the task like a seasoned amateur. I wasn't perfect, but I wasn't about to pass the opportunity up and by the time I came to the point of following through with my intention, it happened in the blink of an eye.

A black RAM had parked itself a few yards behind the Mazda and as I passed it and made sure nobody was sitting inside, I made out as if I was crossing the street.

Taking a final look behind me as I stepped off the curb, I angled myself in such a way as to pass within inches of the small hatch back. I leaned down at just the right time to pull down the leg on my jeans with one hand, while the other slipped under the rear of the Mazda and secured the magnetic tracker with a dull thump.

Nobody paid me the slightest attention, despite me expecting someone to shout for me to stop. I felt my body tense as a car started up a few dozen yards ahead, but it was facing the same way as the Mazda and the driver wouldn't have been able to see anything.

With the second part of my plan done, I headed back to my own truck and prepared for the next chapter. Affixing the tracker to the car had just been the beginning. The time had come for the wheels to finally begin rolling.

CHAPTER 10

After making sure the connection to the tracker was linked to my cellphone, I headed home. In short, there was one thing I craved more than finding Wendy Ranch at that moment, and that was having a shower. The scent coming off me couldn't have been the best and I must have stood under the stream for close to a half hour before I had satisfied my need.

The other thing I needed was a nap. I could feel my energy levels low and at first thought it was nothing more than a lack of proper food, but when I checked my blood sugar and then followed up with a couple of hard-boiled eggs, I realized it was nothing more than fatigue. Sleeping on a hard floor wasn't my thing and after setting the alarm for four, I jumped into bed.

The sleep I had was over way too quickly and when the alarm woke me, I first had the feeling I had slept through until the next day. It took me a few minutes to remember where I was and the reasons for the afternoon nap. The realization came to me in a rush of excitement and I checked the signal on the tracking app. The car was still parked just where I left it, something I figured wouldn't change, as long as Wendy repeated her usual routine.

By ten minutes to five, I had set myself up on the couch with a pen, some paper, a bottle of mineral water, plus a fully charged cellphone. To get myself more in the mood, I also streamed the feed directly to my television with the Chromecast.

Bang, at five o'clock, the car began to move, slowly at first as Wendy turned the Mazda around. But once it faced the right way, she shot up towards the intersection with Liberty Avenue. I knew how heavy traffic could get by that time and so wasn't surprised when she began to crawl along at a mind-numbing pace.

It took her close to an hour to finally reach a destination I knew would most likely occur. It was a home, but not one I thought of as hers. I watched in anticipation as the car remained on the side of the street instead of pulling into the driveway. When it began to move again just ten minutes later, I knew why.

I noted the address down on my piece of paper and wrote "After school care" beneath it. I wasn't sure how likely it was that Rossi would show up there, but if he was desperate enough, I didn't think anybody would be out of his reach.

Wendy continued on for another five minutes, eventually turning into Lynnbrook Avenue as the car slowed and almost immediately turned into an adjacent driveway. It paused, then slowly moved forward another few feet which I assumed was her driving the car into a garage.

Just like that, I had the information I needed to close off the third part of my quest, with three separate addresses in my hot little hand. Her work, her home, as well as the place her children stay while their mother worked. The last one was still just an assumption, but it made sense, given what I had already learned about her.

The next thing I needed was to set up some sort of surveillance on the woman as well as her home and business. I also needed to find out just how much contact Rossi had had with her and for that, I knew I needed help. But who? Bringing in an outsider meant exposing myself, or at the very least, opening myself up to a potential blackmail. Crooks had a way of working their advantage, regardless of the price. If someone was to do that to me, I would need to protect myself. How far would I go to keep my activities a secret?

In another life, I might have had a few people I could have brought in, but not in my current one. The truth was, I didn't trust anybody. Maybe that lack of distrust was due to fear, but I couldn't be sure. It didn't really matter. I had a secret and I wasn't in a position to share it. That's all there was to it. I wasn't about to tell people I was planning to murder those who had managed to escape justice. If I did, I would be vulnerable.

As strange as it sounds, I knew there was just a single place where I knew I could go to get my thoughts back into order. Sitting by Tess and Charlie's final resting place had a calming effect on me and gave me the opportunity to deep dive into my own consciousness and rediscover my true purpose.

I waited until the next morning, waking up early I then headed out into the morning traffic. Sitting amongst hundreds of people also gave me a sense of belonging to something. They might have been strangers, but in some weird way, it was them I was ultimately doing my work for. Cleansing society of the evil amongst them, was how I liked to think of it. Did I sound crazy? Maybe, but I didn't care. If I get caught, it will give me a reason to plead insanity.

The cemetery was completely deserted by the time I arrived, a good thing for a man wanting a bit of solitude. This was one of those mornings where I hoped Frank Dunn wouldn't show up. The sun had already burnt away most of the dew, so when I dropped down onto the grass, I didn't get that awful wetness through the seat of my pants.

I wasn't there to talk, but I did give each of my girls a brief greeting and a rundown of the latest events. After a few minutes of one-sided idle chatter, I withdrew into myself and went quiet, simply staring at the headstone displaying the most beautiful smiles in the world. Thoughts ran through my mind, each caught in a jumble of options, misconceptions, and confusion. I didn't try to fight them, simply letting them work their way through the shadows of one man's brain.

I had just a single target I wanted to focus on, a hitman with one hell of a history. There was his ex-partner, a young mom who wanted a fresh start for her and her young family. There were the girls, two young souls lacking the maturity needed to understand the situation for what it really was.

Ten minutes of quiet reflection was all it took for me to make the most important decision of the morning. Could I murder a father to two young girls? The answer was a resounding yes. My reasons? They were young enough for the grief to fade away into the darkest recesses of their imagination. I doubted they would even truly understand the reality when it happened. If I played my cards right, I could do it in such a way that he would simply disappear. That way, none of them would ever need to know the truth. The pain in Wendy Ranch's life would just…be gone.

What I did need was the old alibi I had become so fond of, the DNA, used in a way which would completely throw the authorities off the path. I tried to think of the inmates who I saw on a regular basis, the ones with a history I could use for my own dark purposes. I'd already catalogued a few, but did they suit this specific situation? I didn't think so, but that didn't mean the end. It just meant I needed to go back to the drawing board and find someone appropriate.

CHAPTER 11

The rest of my week off, work flew by with little advancement in my plan to get close to Rossi. There was still a certain hesitation on my part, which kept me from getting too close to Wendy Ranch and her home. Now that I knew where she lived, I wasn't sure how to proceed without using the help of someone I brought onboard.

It was the fear of getting caught which dogged me for days and as I returned to work, I still found myself trying to find a way of getting over the next obstacle. What I needed were eyes on her life, her home, her work, all the places where I knew Rossi would show up.

Actually, I was scared. The truth was plain as day, I just struggled to fully accept it. Frank Rossi was a very bad man, someone way over my head and far more cunning than the judge ever was. This was the man many paid to get rid of their problems, and right now, I was trying to become *his* problem, in a sense.

Up until that day of my return, I didn't know whether I had ever truly believed in fate. I know many people would often quote it as being responsible for sheer coincidences.

So, when a substantial event happened to me that very first day back, I couldn't help but wonder.

The nudge came around eleven that morning and was almost a mirrored event from a few weeks earlier. The on-duty guard was walking through the unit calling out random names to come forward and collect their mail. One of the names called was Ray O'Neil. He called it a number of times before one of the inmates currently in the middle of receiving a murder one called out to him.

"O'Neil was released day before yesterday." And then perhaps as an afterthought, he added, "His forwarding address should be on file."

"Forwarding address," I thought to myself as I paused near the inmate. I'd been slowly walking back and forth, tired of standing in the corner watching on. Did guards really go to the extent of hunting for a released inmate's forwarding address? I'd always assumed guards couldn't be bothered with following up on anything prisoner related.

Before I had a chance to fully absorb the revelation, something warm splashed across my face. The sensation caught me off-guard, that was until a familiar smell filled my nostrils. As shouting erupted somewhere behind me, I felt my legs freeze, the knees refusing to bend as I found myself unable to move.

Time is a curious thing, even more so when caught in the midst of conflict. The blood sprayed across my face a second time as I finally had the presence of mind to see what was happening. Looking down to my right, the inmate, Cooper Dunn, who had been so helpful just a few moments before tried to rise out of his chair, with one hand held to his throat as he met my gaze with eyes wide enough to pop out of their sockets. The mouth trying to verbalize his shock never quite rose, a thick gurgling holding them down in his throat.

He been stabbed, and not just once. The one who attacked him had hit and run so fast, the blade punched through into the man's neck four times within just a couple of seconds. The final one hit the mark, the carotid artery letting go as bright red blood sprayed across the mirror. Each time he moved his head, the fountain turned with him, a wide arc of mist raining down across the floor as the commotion hit fever pitch.

While Cooper Dunn tried his best to apply pressure to a wound which would never stop spewing, guards tackled the attacker to the ground, while the inmates backed up to the walls with their hands in the air. When they were ordered down on the ground, nobody hesitated.

Dunn remained conscious for another twenty or so seconds before enough blood had leaked from him. His movements slowed as he dropped back into the chair, his skin a pasty white that would never return to the way it was. A few seconds later, he looked at me a final time as his hand slid from the wound and dropped beside him.

He died staring at me, his eyes simply glazing over as he held my gaze. I could still feel the blood run down the side of my face, a horribly slow sensation which I tried to rub away. The man had been alive just the minute before, and before anybody could react, someone had stabbed him to death right in front of me.

When I arrived home just a few hours later, I think it was the closest I came to having a drink since swearing alcohol away. I almost stopped a couple of times along the way, each time contemplating buying a bottle of Jack Daniels and taking it home for a night of one-on-one with my old nemesis.

The next best thing was the shower, and I jumped in a little too quick, almost tripped on the edge of the tub and grabbed the curtain for balance. Three of the hoops let go, tearing off with repetitive pops, one after the other. By the time I managed to catch my balance again, my hands were shaking so bad, I thought I was going to drop down to my knees.

Standing in the stream of that heat, I closed my eyes, the coppery scent of blood still as strong as when it first sprayed across me. I wanted to give in, to sit down on the edge of the tub and just cry, the way I might have done back when I was still just a normal man. But I wasn't normal anymore.

What happened next felt as if someone else suddenly stepped forward, took control of my body and forced me to listen the way a parent might scold a toddler.

"Pull yourself together, you coward," a voice said from somewhere inside me. Before I knew what was happening, I stepped out of the tub and walked to the basin, wiped the mist from the mirror and stared into the eyes of a stranger. "This is the business you chose," the voice continued. "The smell, the warmth of another man's blood, it is what it is. Get used to it, trooper. Because it is the only way you know you've succeeded."

I felt like a man in a cinema, watching a scene on screen which felt so real, I could mime the words along with the actor. Only the actor was me and the words my own. None of it made sense as a new kind of fear washed over me. My first thought was that I had somehow developed a split personality. Was it my alter ego staring back at me?

I squeezed my eyes shut, sure that I was experiencing the first clear signs of madness. I felt my head, wondering if a fever had snuck up and somehow changed my perception. When I opened my eyes again and saw me staring back at myself, I didn't have the answers I needed.

While it took considerable effort, I eventually made it back out into the living room, and instead of a bourbon, I made myself a cup of coffee; hot, black, and strong. As I slowly sipped from the cup, I could feel my fingers still trembling just the slightest bit, a mere hint of the previous shakes.

"Stay strong," I whispered to myself as I remembered my promise to Tess and Charlie. This new life was as much for them as it was for me, a promise to give others a chance for redemption. And that was when I knew my next move.

CHAPTER 12

The plan, once I ran it through my mind a few times, was simple. I was going to forward the envelope I'd already intercepted back to the prison and cross my fingers. But instead of including Wendy's note, I would include one of my own, one which was going to give him the complete opposite message to the one she had intended.

I needed Rossi to make an appearance and so I figured I would use a bit of a white lie. In short, I would send the man an invite on Wendy's behalf for a sit down and chat, something I assumed he would jump at. If given the option for a one-on-one chat with an ex holding his children, I figured it was a proposition any estranged father would jump at.

As I typed the note on my laptop, the white BMW came back to me, the car sitting on the side of the road with the occupant doing nothing more than staring into the distance. If it really was an Uber, then I figured my brain had taken an unnecessary detour. But the more I thought about it, the more I convinced myself that it was my target, the man I intended to end.

I kept the message to a minimum, not wanting to delve into issues I knew nothing about.

We have to talk about what's best for our two girls, and if you're willing to have a mature conversation, then come over to the house next Friday night at eight.

Just as she didn't sign off on her note, neither did I on the fake one, mimicking her style, so to speak. After printing the brief message out, I carefully folded it together with the drawings, then pushed all three sheets into the envelope. As I sealed it with a small strip of tape, I looked at the address she had written on the back and wondered whether he knew her home address.

There was a possibility he didn't, but thinking about him parked near her work, I figured if he followed her there, then there was every chance he'd already followed her home. Controlling creeps like him had a way of slinking their way through the shadows to find what they couldn't let go.

Wanting to keep the ruse going, I drove down to a post box near Wendy's work the following morning and dropping the envelope in felt like something of a relief for me. It wasn't just the fact that I had effectively set the wheels in motion to finally meeting the man himself. A sense of excitement yes, but also a hint of fear mixed in.

I worked at Pine Grove that Monday, a prison I would consider one of the easier ones in my itinerary. It held a larger population of younger offenders, and it felt a little like visiting a local college with bars and armed guards. The thing was, I couldn't stop thinking about what I had done, about how I was effectively baiting a hitman. It wasn't something I could have ever imagined myself doing.

Thankfully, the shift went by without a hitch, and apart

from a couple of verbal confrontations happening between some of the inmates, the rest of the day was nothing more than routine. Driving home, I wondered at what stage the letter was. The downside to my plan was that I wouldn't know if he would ever actually receive the letter, which is why I made it a certain day and time. It would give me a specific window of opportunity to make contact and I could then begin my surveillance of him.

Just as I arrived home, my cellphone vibrated in my pocket and when I checked, saw a message from someone I wasn't expecting to hear from. I wasn't exactly known for having a huge circle of friends and so receiving any random texts felt a little weird to me.

Her name was Linda Loy, a new guard who started at McSweeney the previous week. She'd been something of a breath of fresh air in the place, the kind of woman who didn't take shit from nobody, but managed to maintain a certain sense of maternal presence about herself. Some of the inmates were somewhat intrigued by her. During that initial shift where I first met her, the crooks would approach her with all manner of questions and the wink she shot me after sending one of the prisoners on his way was enough to tell me she was different. I liked Linda from the get-go.

Her message was brief and to the point. The spare set of clippers the prison kept on hand for inmates to use during the day had been damaged and she was wondering when I would be in next so I could perhaps take a look at them. It was an odd request, but I put that down to mild inexperience.

I was due there the very next day and when I sent her my reply, got a response back almost immediately. Thanking me, she said she was in as well and would talk to me then. I smiled reading her words, but didn't think about them again until I walked into the unit the next morning.

Just as she had promised, she was there in the unit already working her way through a number of requests from needy inmates. As I walked past carrying my tool chest, she again shot me a wink before continuing on with her task.

I didn't see her again for almost an hour, by then my usual crew already busy working their way through several heads of hair. She was carrying the box of clippers and held them out to me.

"I wasn't sure whether these would just be replaced, or what," she said as I took them.

"They don't have much of a lifespan," I said, rolling the set over in my hands. I could already see what the problem was, the blades twisted enough to end their lives prematurely. "My guess is someone dropped them a bit too hard." I looked at her and smiled. "Administration will just order a new set."

"I figured as much," she said.

What followed was half an hour of the kind of conversation I actually missed. It was an exchange between adults, talking about random things while getting to know another person. Romance wasn't what this was about, rather just a meeting of the minds.

Linda told me about her previous role at Florida State Prison, working as a guard there for almost ten years. Far from new into the role, hearing about her past didn't surprise me and it was something she spoke about with a certain degree of pride.

What I gathered from listening to her was that she wasn't that different from me, not in the way I might have initially assumed. The tipping point for me came when a prisoner named Mark Watts walked past us. I saw her expression change when she saw him, her words suddenly stopping mid-sentence until he was gone again. What she said next, once he was out of earshot was something of a revelation for me.

"Lucky he didn't commit his crimes in Florida," was what she said. Watts had committed an armed robbery a few years before, which had resulted in the shooting deaths of three people, one of whom was a four-year-old boy and his mother. The felon received twenty-five years, down from life after his lawyer provided a winning argument for his client.

It wasn't the words she said, as much as the look in her eyes. Something about her demeanor told me she harbored the same sorts of feelings I did about inmates beating the system, of that, I was sure. Of course, I would never tell her, but it was good to see someone with a similar soul to my own. What I didn't know at the time, was that Linda Loy thought the exact same thing about me.

CHAPTER 13

The Friday I had chosen for Wendy to meet with her estranged partner held another important aspect, one to me personally. It was my birthday, a day which in recent years had meant a day off from work to spend with a bottle or two of the finest bourbon I could afford for myself. The day would begin at the gravesite of my lost family, followed by an afternoon and evening of wild weeping, drinking, and downright sorrow.

I hated my birthday now that I was alone. It didn't hold any significance for me, no special occasion marked by celebration the way most people did. But this year was different, completely different. I had come by a renewed sense of purpose, and through that, it gave me reason to continue on. Not only go on, but also keep myself in a much better frame of mind so I could conduct business. Dealing vengeance wasn't exactly an amateur sport.

To mark the day, not only because of the birthday itself, but more so because of the distinct change in my life, I decided to treat myself. I told myself that I deserved it and what I decided on was something I would never have considered in my previous life.

The Barber Shack was the kind of place only a true barber could ever truly appreciate. The way a car enthusiast might lose themselves in a Mopar performance store, or a bargain hunter will spend an entire day at Walmart. The Barber Shack served the Pittsburgh community of barbers with all the tools of the trade and then some. And by then some, I mean specialty stuff which needs to be seen to be believed.

When I say I wanted to treat myself, I wasn't kidding. I had seen the kinds of gear some barbers used, especially those working in some of the fancy salons out west, California way, for example. They knew quality and that's what I wanted.

There had always been a memory of mine when it came to my early days as a barber. Money hadn't been easy to come by back in those days and so I had managed to put myself an initial tool chest together with bits and pieces I purchased when either on sale, or even second hand for the more expensive gear.

Money wasn't exactly an issue for a man living alone, with minimal weekly commitments and I had managed to save quite a bit, enough to treat myself for this birthday. The item I wanted wasn't hanging on some store shelf where anyone could molest it with their grubby fingers. No, the thing I wanted sat in a display case behind lock and key, with a couple of small spotlights lighting it up like some sort of showpiece.

To the normal person, they were nothing more than a pair of scissors, but given their $599 price tag, they stood for so much more. With a Japanese name, made of genuine Damascus Steel, and an appearance like something out of a movie, these were the kind of gift someone received just once in their lifetime.

The Saki Shears felt as incredible as I imagined, light, and yet harboring a solid feel to them. My fingers slipped into the handles with ease and mimicking a few cuts, I felt as if I had somehow mastered the art of cutting silk. An intricate pattern of dragon scales covered the finger loops, fading out halfway up the blades.

The woman behind the counter watched me with suspicious eyes, as if expecting me to run at any moment. I knew I was being judged, but didn't let it worry me. I was in love from the moment I first opened and closed them in mid-air.

"I'll take them," I whispered as I carefully slid them off my fingers and saw the look of surprise turn to astonishment.

"Shall I gift wrap them?" I almost said yes, but then held back. Call it a hint of arrogance, or perhaps a need to prove to the woman that I was indeed buying them for myself.

"No, that's fine," I said, offering her a warm smile.

They came in a cool leather snap case, the rich black case was punctuated with a distinctive red stitching around the edges. It was about the size of a sunglasses case and I simply carried it in my hand back to the truck. Once I was back in the quietness of my pick-up's cabin, I did the unthinkable. After opening the case again, I took out the scissors and flicked the case over to the passenger seat like a discarded wrapper. I had no intention of using it again, and stared at my prize. A moment later, a grin birthed itself I was powerless to avoid and as I slid the scissors into my shirt pocket, I began to laugh.

CHAPTER 14

The street Wendy lived on proved to be a painful one to try and stake out. Her house sat close to the corner, just the second house in, which meant it gave Rossi three possible directions to come from instead of the usual two. Being alone, I had to make a choice between sitting on the actual street, or near the intersection, on the corner street. Thankfully, it was a T-intersection. A cross road would only have amplified my precarious position.

The upside to my little debacle was a playground which sat on the opposite side of the road, with a small parking lot fronting it. From what I could gather, some of the locals already used it to park their second vehicles, which gave me the perfect place to "fit in", so to speak.

I reversed into a spot between a couple of other pickups a little after six, with the light fading fast from the sky. The street lights had already kicked in, adding an air of mystery to the scene for me. I knew I was early, but didn't know what kind of man Rossi was. If he was the punctual type, then I had a long wait ahead of me. Somehow, he didn't strike me as a man who stuck to timetables, when it came to people beneath him.

Once parked and the engine killed, I sat back and sank deep into my seat until my eyes barely saw above the steering wheel. I also had my window down a touch to ensure I could hear approaching cars. If the man of the moment showed up, I wanted to know about it.

It wasn't a busy part of the neighborhood, with vehicles rolling by maybe twice a minute. The whole area was effectively a dead end, which meant it lacked the through-traffic of most other places. Only those with specific business rolled through, and looking at the homes, I could tell the area was made up of what I considered nice families.

I was in the middle of admiring an old-school Volkswagen Kombi parked in the driveway of a home three or four down from my position when I saw headlights approach from the right, slow, then turn down Lynnbrook. Something inside me awoke as I saw the distinctive shape of the X5 as it disappeared from view on its way down the street.

Was it white? The thumping in my chest told me it was, although a shadow of doubt remained, telling me to ease up a little. I checked my watch, saw it was still a good chunk before seven, and figured it was just coincidence. I mean, how many X5's lived in Pittsburgh alone?

"*Sure, it was silver,*" I tried to tell myself, but the uneasy tightening around my middle told me otherwise. Logic suddenly flooded my mind as common sense took over, aware at that very moment that an Uber driving an X5 was extremely unlikely. And that was when I saw the two neat headlights come back into view, visually rolling down the street at walking pace.

I sank down a little lower and raised the binoculars,

taking a quick peek to either side of my truck to make sure I was still alone. Once sure, I focused my attention on the vehicle and while I could only make out the barest of shadows inside the cabin, I confirmed the color once and for all. It was white, the same white as I had spotted the morning at the salon.

"Son of a bitch," I whispered to myself as the X5 came to a stop directly outside the house. Only one of the front windows in the home appeared lit up, with the curtains blocking the view. I knew she was home, but was he going to take advantage and show up early?

Before I had a chance to fully prepare, the BMW suddenly accelerated towards the top of the street and turned left without indicating. I had to think fast and before I really understood what I was doing, had my own ride started. This was an opportunity I couldn't pass up and so I took off after him as fast as I could.

Thankfully, I drove a shitter of a car, which didn't stand out, as such. The kind of dumpster on wheels, there are dozens just like it in any crowded parking lot, unlike the car I was trailing. Making sure to keep enough distance between us, I caught up with him before he turned onto Brookline Boulevard, and maintained my tail with half a dozen cars between us.

The thoughts running through my mind were anything but controlled. He'd thrown me a complete detour by not only turning up early, but also leaving again. I couldn't decide whether he just wanted to prep himself for the confrontation, or whether he had decided to ignore the invite completely. I know I had a habit of checking a place out ahead of time when due for a meeting.

We continued through the evening traffic, eventually turning onto Liberty Avenue and headed south. Another ten minutes later and the X5 turned onto Gilkenson Road, with my slowing down to try and keep a bit of distance. There was far less traffic on this road, which didn't give me any cover.

He slowed about half a mile down and pulled in beside what looked like a pizza shop of some kind. I didn't react in time and ended up driving past, catching a glimpse of the man himself as he stepped out from the car. The sternest look on his face wasn't lost in the dim light and I could see how he carried himself, even when alone.

I waited until I was a quarter mile down before popping a U-turn and slowly heading back the other way. There weren't exactly a million places to park and as I neared the pizza shop a second time, panicked at the prospect of not finding anywhere suitable to stop. That was until I spotted a small parking lot immediately across the road. It looked like it belonged to the city, with a few orange cones and line markers sitting at the far end, alongside a couple of mounds of road gravel.

Once parked in the shadows, I shut off my engine and turned off the lights, hoping for the night to swallow me into it. I grabbed the binoculars and zeroed in on the store to finally catch Frank Rossi in full for the first time.

He stood a lot taller than I imagined, his face chiseled into the kind of stern appearance only men in power exuded. The suit he wore screamed money and while I couldn't tell the label, I knew it didn't come from any mass-produced store. His arms looked solid; his shoulders broad for a man that tall.

Another customer stood before him in line, the man behind the counter looking old and tired as he worked the register. I figured Rossi was simply biding his time, perhaps grabbing a pizza before his meeting later that night. It wasn't unheard of. Even I wasn't unaccustomed to craving food when nervous. This was about the man's children and if he was that kind of father, then I figured he was trying to calm himself.

When the customer finally paid and took his food, Rossi suddenly turned away from the counter and walked to where the drink fridge stood. He opened the door and appeared to look for something specific as the other man left the store. A few moments later, his car started up and he pulled out into traffic.

Still training the binoculars on him, I don't know how I missed the signs, but before I knew what was happening, he closed the fridge, walked back to the counter and said something to the man behind the counter. When he walked up to answer his question, Rossi pulled a gun from under his jacket aimed, and fired. The brief splatter of blood I saw streak the wall behind him had barely begun to run when Rossi calmly turned and walked to the door.

My stomach did cartwheels as I tried to fathom what had just happened. Rossi climbed back into his car and before I could make sense of it, he disappeared back the way we had come, leaving the scene before anybody else showed up.

The shock gripped me tighter than anything and I struggled to comprehend what happened. If it wasn't for the sudden scream from the store, who knows how long I would have sat there paralyzed. Looking back inside, I saw an old woman and a much younger man standing behind the counter, both looking down at the floor. When the woman screamed a second time, it was enough for me to finally get my butt into gear.

CHAPTER 15

The grim reality of what I had just witnessed burnt into my brain on a never-ending reel of horror. It felt unreal, like the climax to a bad movie I was powerless to escape. He'd killed someone, and from what I could tell, the event was premeditated. As I raced to try and catch up to the X5, I wondered whether I had just witnessed an actual hit. Did the man take time out to drive past his ex-partner's house before going to murder someone?

I couldn't find him, the frustration fueled by a lot more than anxiety. His actions hit me in a way I wasn't expecting and it wasn't as if I had ever experienced them before. I knew what it felt like to kill someone, but seeing another die was a completely different thing. Unanswered questions plagued me, peppering my brain in a barrage of wild thoughts. Who he was, what he did, who had ordered the hit; endless questions I didn't ever hope to answer.

Traffic appeared denser than when we came earlier, but despite me going well above the speed limit, I couldn't spot the distinctive taillights of Rossi. I'd hesitated for a moment too long and because of it, lost contact. In other words, I'd blown my one shot to follow him.

With no other place to go, I returned to where I had initially caught sight of him, the playground near Wendy's house. Given his original drive-past, I figured he'd return for the orchestrated meeting and with just under half an hour to go, it was the best chance I had of catching back up with him.

As I sat in the darkness with my eyes focused on the home of a single mom, I imagined her sitting inside, completely oblivious to the uninvited visitor who was about to knock on her door. I imagined there would be a moment of shock from her, and then of course the argument when one tried to defend his actions to the other who hadn't asked for them. Yes, I'd feel guilty, but I also knew the endgame would benefit her in the long run, especially with what I had just witnessed myself.

Time continued to pass and as the minutes wound down to the final few before eight o'clock, I found myself breaking into a sweat. The nerves were something I hadn't ever experienced before, the heat of the truck too much to bear. I wound the window down all the way, hoping for the night air to cool me down before I passed out.

A car approached, the sound reaching me long before I saw it. The beating in my chest rose to new heights as I heard it slow down to take the turn and I imagined Rossi behind the wheel. This was the moment I couldn't screw up, my one chance to hopefully follow him home after a brief interaction with Wendy. If everything went according to plan, I would have his home address within the hour.

The car finally came into view and turned into Lynnbrook, but it wasn't an X5. Instead, the Camry looked more of a disappointment to me than the innocent car. I was so sure it would be Rossi; I think I even held my breath, only noticing as I drew in a deep breath to make up for it.

It wasn't him, and neither were the next half a dozen cars which came and went over the next hour. I checked the time every few minutes as I grew increasingly frustrated with myself. At one point, I turned on my radio for background noise and when it began sharing the hourly news, found myself captivated by the news of the shooting death of a seventy-six-year-old man earlier in the evening in what authorities called a professional hit.

The man he'd killed was none other than Mario Traiforous, the father of a local drug kingpin named Alphonse. According to sources, the hit had been in retaliation for a long running feud between warring drug factions and I just happened to witness the latest.

I snapped the radio off again, feeling my insides churn from the news. What had I gotten myself involved in? This wasn't just a person who'd killed someone in the course of their day and managed to evade the law. This was a paid professional who specialized in death itself and I had taken it on myself to end him.

By ten o'clock, I considered ending my watch and returning home to regroup. I'd have to try and figure out another way to find out his details, or even just pay someone for information. I knew there were plenty of people at the prison willing to divulge information for enough cash. I just wasn't sure I wanted to open myself up to such things.

Retreating wasn't something I really wanted to do and rather than leave, I sat tight to try and figure out my next move. Out on the street, the traffic slowed to just a car or two every fifteen to twenty minutes. The night grew and with each passing minute, I came to the realization I'd failed.

"It's not like you're on the clock," I whispered to myself, and of course I was right. Time wasn't against me. It wasn't as if I had a timetable to stick to. If nothing else, I stepped back and started again.

Happy to accept my own advice, I reached out to start the truck. My eyelids hung heavy and after the extra stresses, I knew that I would sleep well. But just as I prepared to turn the key, a scream suddenly rose into the air from somewhere across the street. A new level of pounding filled my insides as I froze and looked over to the house. Nothing had changed, the same window still lit up behind the thick curtains. There was no sign of the X5 and from what I could tell, the house appeared untouched.

A second scream rose, this one more intense than the first and when I took another look at the house, saw the curtains violently pull to one side, before a third scream erupted. Without thinking, I jumped from the truck and broke into a sprint, crossed the street and in a moment of horror, I saw the front of the BMW parked a hundred yards down the street.

Feeling beaten for the second time that night, I didn't slow when I reached the door, and shoulder charged it with all of my two-hundred and twenty pounds. The door splintered before me with an almighty crash and I stumbled into a living room of a complete stranger, trying to catch my balance.

It took me all of a second to see why she was screaming. The woman whom I had only ever seen working inside the salon, lay on the ground with Rossi sitting on top of her chest. Blood ran from the side of her mouth, one eye almost completely closed over as the other one appeared to lose the life behind it. Rossi had both hands clasped around her throat and I finally understood why he had waited. The man had no intention of negotiating anything.

"Rossi," I screamed and launched myself at him. He tried to keep his hands on her throat, but my body weight coming at him was never going to let that happen. He let go at the last instant and tried to deflect me, but it was too late. I shoulder charged him off, the pair of us rolling over into the back of the couch. Trying my best to get the better of him, we began to throw and block punches like a couple of school kids, with both of us on our sides. I added a couple of knees to the mix, figuring that any preconceived rules had gone out the window the second he attacked a woman barely half his size.

"Who the hell are you," he sneered at me as he landed a punch. It had some strength behind it and for a brief second, I saw stars.

"Someone who's come to stop you," I snapped back, launched a flurry of punches and missed with all of them. He was good, and I struggled to get through his defenses. I couldn't be sure how Wendy was doing, but I did hear a child's cry just before another punch caught me in the ear. The pain exploded with a blinding light and I felt numbness run all the way down my legs.

Thinking I needed something, I reached into his jacket and fumbled around for what I knew would still be sitting. Just as my hand closed around the grip of the gun, Rossi pulled himself back just a fraction and elbowed me in the stomach. The wind effectively left me, and no amount of gasping filled my lungs as I struggled to remain conscious. Another punch to the side of my face and he had me beat.

I could barely keep my eyes open as he grabbed me by

the shoulders and rolled my carcass over before climbing on top of my chest. With the very breath still evading me, I couldn't do anything but wait for death as Rossi finished pulling the gun out himself.

"Time to die, hero."

It was over, with me unable to move as my lungs refused to perform their most basic function. I watched in horror as he snapped the slide of the pistol back, the bullet snapping into place for the second execution of the night. Time slowed as his weight denied me the very air I needed to survive. A veil of faintness descended over me as I stared up into the eyes of a true killer, his face remaining just as stern as before. Emotion wasn't his forte and as he lowered the barrel of the gun down into my face, I knew my time had come.

Just as I closed my eyes, a lone vision filled my mind as I prepared to meet death head on. The vision was sitting in the cab of my truck, and I was laughing, laughing because it had been the first time in my life, I had purchased something for me without any reason behind it. It was the scissors in my hand, and I was laughing because of the expensive pair of barber shears which I had no actual reason to own.

Just as I prepared to die, I had a final moment of revelation and remembered the steel blades still sitting in my shirt pocket. In the blink of an eye, my escape came to me as an instinctual reaction, a sudden move I hadn't been expecting to make. I bucked myself to the left, with the barrel of the gun violently swinging right. At the same time, I reached into my shirt pocket, felt the cold steel hiding inside and closed my fingers around the handles. Bringing them out, I thrust upwards in a single motion. Even when I felt my hand make contact with the man's soft flesh of his neck, I pushed on, not stopping until I felt the familiar sensation of warm blood.

Rossi tried to scream, but it was a scream which would never take flight, the blood already filling his throat from the inside. He dropped the gun as he tried to grab the wound, the blood jetting across the room when I pulled the scissors back out. When I met his eyes for the only time, I could see the only emotion I would ever see in the man's face. Fear.

He was dead before he hit the ground, with me pushing him off the final bit as I tried to free myself, finally able to roll out and onto my side. A few feet away, I could see Wendy groggily trying to get up as another stranger ran into the room. He went to her and after making sure she was OK, kicked the gun away from Rossi who had begun to convulse, his body ridding itself of the final few nerve signals.

"You OK, mister?" I looked up and nodded, trying to make sense of what had just happened.

Another couple of people came in through the front door and as I staggered towards them, waved their attention to the young mom and children. Both girls had been in the room during the scuffle, too scared to make a peep as they watched their mother fight the attacker.

I made it outside and despite a small crowd gathering, nobody paid me the slightest attention as someone called for an ambulance. Making sure nobody was following, I made it back to my truck and only began to breathe again once I reached the safety of the adjoining street.

CHAPTER 16

The next few days were a mere blur in the scheme of things. The authorities couldn't make sense of what had happened between Rossi killing the father of a known drug dealer, and his ex-partner whom he tried to kill. While initial reports spoke of a mystery man coming to the woman's rescue, eventually the lack of evidence led to him disappearing from the story completely.

It wasn't big news, as such, Rossi's death. Yes, he'd been a piece of scum on the streets of Pittsburgh, but there were plenty more to take his place and while he made it as high as Page 3 of several newspapers, he never achieved the coveted front page of any.

As far as I knew, Wendy ended up moving home the very next day and when I saw a very brief interview with her on the six o'clock news, I did not see the kind of grief that I was hoping to avoid. From what I could see, she had been finally granted her family's freedom.

Unable to take any more time off, I returned to work the very next day myself and while sporting a decent cut above my right eye, as well as a couple of bruises, I explained them away with an excuse as old as the hills. Falling down some stairs wasn't exactly the best I could have come up with, but it was enough for most people to give me a brief laugh and a head shake. I could only imagine what they must have thought about a man many considered nothing more than a drunk, despite him being a few months sober already.

The one thing I did decide, was to move the main operation away from my house. While the cellar had been a great place to start my journey into the world of vengeance, I always knew it wasn't smart to keep that kind of evidence in my own home. If a fire broke out, or something worse, and authorities needed to get down there, I would have way too many questions to answer.

I ended up buying a block of land on the outskirts of Elderton, another town which held a significant place in my heart. I was lucky enough to find a decent-sized block of land a couple of miles out of town and given its remoteness, I was going to turn it into my own personal bat cave. A couple of shipping containers and a large hole and I could effectively take my operation as far underground as I needed to.

As for the scissors? To me, they had served their purpose, a purpose I knew which could never be superseded. Not only had they saved my life and that of a young mom and her children, but they had also proven to me that sometimes, the best tool against evil is the one you don't see coming. They were my blades of justice and they had dealt out a new kind of vengeance I was still busy trying to learn.

I took them to Keystone Lake and threw them into the water from the pier on its southern edge. It was a clear windless day and when they hit the water, I watched as the ripples expanded in all directions, imagining how far I had come in such a short amount of time. The number of people I had saved through a single act was something which I knew couldn't be ignored. And while Wendy and her daughters would never know the stranger who had taken away the biggest threat of their lives, it didn't really matter, because for me, this was nowhere near the end.

FADE INTO THE SHADOWS

CHAPTER 1

Watching him writhe about with a bullet in his back awoke something within me I did not know I had. It felt primitive, a fundamental trait almost caveman like as I watched this man, this piece of trash, squirming in agony because of something I had done to him.

The thing was, it should not have happened, the attack was nothing more than a spur-of-the-moment event I felt helpless to ignore. He had gotten under my skin, too close to the emotional turmoil my brain recognized as being a little too familiar. I guess that's what happens when a man willingly shoots a child while high on some substance he had purchased from his dealer.

Melvin Foster was not a name I had been too interested in when it first crossed my path in early November. The case had not even made front-page news, just a small column on page six of most of the papers I saw. But it had not been the first of its kind, and not even the first for that month. It felt as if children had become the easiest pawns for warring parents to use against their former partners, a bargaining chip to get what they wanted.

Where Melvin Foster's path took a sharp turn into the completely unbelievable, was the reason he had grabbed the little boy in the first place. For most domestic battles involving children, it was normally the child who they fought over, trying to get that little bit of access a court might have granted them. A few precious minutes a week to spend with their loved one. But not for Foster.

The reason this piece of garbage came to his ex-girlfriend's house one miserable November night had nothing to do with the boy at all. What Melvin Foster wanted was cash and he held a gun to his child's head to force the mother to give it to him.

Already as high as a kite and on steroids, Foster had not bothered coming into the home on the quiet, which is why the situation spiraled out of control so fast. He had kicked on the door for a good five minutes before launching his entire two-hundred-forty pounds at it, the frame splintering under the weight of the assault. The sound was enough to alert neighbors who didn't hesitate to call the cops.

What followed were ten of the most confrontational minutes in any human's existence, with Foster grabbing the six-year-old child into his arms and holding him up like a mini shield. The pistol he had, a snub-nosed .38 that he had stolen from a friend, already had a hair trigger, a fact unbeknownst to the crackhead. With a screaming mother, an armed and wound-up junkie, a couple of protective neighbors, and two on-edge cops all in the same room at once, it was a situation which was never going to end well.

The newspaper report stated that Foster barely understood the killing, the event lost in a cloud of confusion as the cops brought him down with four of their own bullets once the child had been shot. He had been rushed to hospital, another fact lost on me, considering what his existence would cost the system if he was saved. They did save his life and it was from there the child killer escaped during a routine changeover of his police guard.

Which brings me to the moment I found him crossing my own path late one night as I was walking through Hazelwood Greenway. I had not been doing so well myself at that point, having spent a couple of hours pre-dusk at the gravesite of one Judge Ferris. Call it reflection, call it soul-gathering. I do not know why I stood in front of his site for so long, but before I knew it, the sun had slipped over the horizon, the shadows had arrived, and I was still a long way from having resolved my issues. I wanted to walk, and Hazelwood Greenway was where I ended up.

Imagine my surprise, walking along those walking tracks with nothing but moonlight for company, when a dumb-ass crackhead named Melvin Foster tried to rob me while pretending to hold a gun in his jacket pocket. It was the old "point-a-finger-and-hope" kind of trick, and it might even have been a bit humorous were it not for my own state of mind.

"Gimme your wallet, fool," he hissed at me a second time when I did not react to his initial demand. Feeling something inside me snap, I initially mirrored him, pointing a finger at him inside my own jacket pocket. There we stood, face to face, like a couple of stooges about to throw pies at each other. The problem for Foster was that I was not just pointing a finger at him inside my jacket pocket.

I shot him without a word of warning, something primitive in my brain wanting to make him suffer more than I had made anyone suffer in my life. The bullet struck him in the gut and at first, he simply stood his ground with a dumbfounded look on his face. I do not think he quite comprehended what had just happened and to bring him up to speed on the situation, I shot him a second time.

After a few moments of staring at each other in the light of a full moon, he finally dropped to his knees and looked up at me as if he was about to propose. Hazelwood was not an area amiss of regular gunshots, which is why I did not run the second I shot him the first time. I could stand my ground long into the night without fear of someone calling the cops.

The groan began once he fell onto his back, his legs twisted underneath him at an unusual angle. His hands went to the wounds and tried to plug them, but I knew that was an unlikely outcome. Blood wept through his fingers as a deep guttural moaning rose and fell from him. I remained where I stood, hands in pockets, watching him with a strange fascination.

Looking back on that moment now, I think it was the first time in my life I felt a sense of satisfaction I had not ever experienced before. It was his suffering which was driving the sensation, his moans of pain only adding to the sweetness of it. Knowing he was going to die by my hand was just the tip of that emotional iceberg, the real pleasure coming from the pain and torment itself.

It took almost twenty minutes for the groaning to stop, by then a neat puddle of blood had accumulated beneath him. The final twitches took a few more minutes to fade away and once I knew he was dead, I stared at him a little while longer. I do not know why. If anybody had come along at that moment, I would have been caught. The shadows of the night would have still given me some sense of security, but I would have been directly linked to a murder, a risk I should not have taken in the first place. And yet I did.

Melvin Foster had died by my hand on a spur of the moment decision which I could have never imagined happening. Fate had ensured his path crossed mine in the best way possible and I had managed to take full advantage. It also gave me a horrifying insight into the evil which lived inside my own soul, a frightening glimpse into the man I knew I would eventually become if I continued to fade into the shadows of society.

As I finally turned away from the body and began to make my way back towards where I had left my pick-up parked hours before, two things had happened which I still did not know about. The first was that I had finally crossed the threshold from apprentice killer to full-on murderer. The second was that I had not been the only one to watch Melvin Foster die. Somewhere in the shadows, someone had been watching.

CHAPTER 2

Foster's murder didn't reach the newspapers for two days, and I must have read the initial article more than a dozen times. As brief as it was, it told me everything I needed to know, with the main point being that the police had no solid leads and no suspects.

No solid leads. These three words were what stood out to me the most, not because it meant they weren't on to me, but for something much more sinister. I actually saw it as a missed opportunity. Killing Foster had been a spur-of-the-moment killing, but a killing nonetheless. It should have taken up a spot on my trophy board, and yet, it couldn't because of one major detail.

It was the part about no solid leads which kind of summed it up. The police had no solid leads because I hadn't left any, not by accident and not on purpose. While most would have seen the murder of Melvin Foster as a success, given the social ranking of the man, I saw it as a failure.

What had been playing through my mind over the previous few weeks, was my identity. Who was I? Was I just another killer walking the streets; a self-groomed avenging angel who killed on impulse? It wasn't what I set out to be and the more I thought about it, the more I understood my purpose.

Quantity over quality was an old adage that many people lived by, but the more I thought about it, the more I came to understand that the opposite would be more beneficial in my line of work. What I wanted was quantity over quality. I wanted to implicate as many people as possible with each and every murder. I wanted to ensure that I managed to involve more than just one criminal in each crime, hence why I saw Foster as a failure.

Foster died without ever implicating anyone else. To me, he was like a caught fish which, instead of being taken home to be turned into a meal, had instead been left lying on the riverbank to die. So much potential, for little reward.

That thought was still running through my head when I returned to McSweeney a couple of days later. The roster had given me an extra day off and I wasn't about to complain. Once back in the unit and watching inmates go about setting up for the day, I let my mind wander again, back to the night of a random killing which just happened to cross my path.

Harvey Knight, one of McSweeney's more popular guards, had the honor of watching our part of the unit for the day. After the stations had been finalized for the eventual clientele to come through, he took up a post close to where I normally spent my time. Being the one to oversee everything that went on, I liked to remain vigilant for any signs of violence. Incidents could happen in the blink of an eye and often without warning.

"Getting ready for Christmas, Vic?" Knight asked me

as he stood a few yards from me. Despite the festive season already creeping into a lot of stores, I hadn't spent a single moment thinking about it.

Christmas didn't hold the same excitement for a man living alone, especially when that man had lost his family. I knew Knight didn't have family either, although he once told me it was through choice. He couldn't imagine being tied down to just a single person and then be forced to provide for them for the rest of his life. He said he loved his freedom too much.

"No, you?"

"Bought myself a new fishing rod. Hoping to get down south for a couple of weeks in February."

"How far south?"

"Mexico's the plan, but we'll see. Kinda thinking Australia might be on the cards as well."

"Can't get much further south than that," I said as one of the younger inmates called me over to help with some blocked trimmers.

"Had a friend who visited the Great Barrier Reef a couple of years ago. Said the fishing was spectacular."

"Yeah, right," I said, as I switched the clippers over for a new set.

Personally, I wasn't much of a fisherman. The thought of sitting on some river bank for hours on end while hoping for something to give my bait a bit of attention just didn't appeal to me. I already had a hobby, and that one kept me intrigued around the clock. It may not have been something I could share with friends over a couple of beers, but then, I didn't have many of them either.

The morning went by at a fair pace, with plenty of inmates wanting haircuts that December morning. Perhaps it was because the first of the month gave people a sense of self-care, or maybe to prepare for the upcoming festivities. Whatever it was, all I know is that all six barbers worked non-stop on multiple heads of hair that morning, and without so much as a single raised voice.

It wasn't until Linda Loy arrived just before midday that anything significant changed. First, we had midday muster to contend with, something which the two guards did with relative ease. Once the count was called correct, Knight headed off for his break, while Loy remained behind to take his place.

Linda Loy was an OK guard, as far as I could tell. Quiet, she tended to let others do the talking, spending most of her time monitoring from a distance. Whenever we crossed paths with each other, she would often pass by with a warm smile, an extra glint in her eye when I gave her a wave. But not this day.

Unlike normally, on this day she barely looked at me, and when she did, the usual smile appeared lost. She wasn't quite stand-offish as such, but rather more withdrawn than usual. In her hand, she held one of the daily newspapers which looked as if it had been read a dozen times over.

Once Knight had gone, Loy took up position near the middle of the back wall, a place perfect for not only watching the inmates in the actual barber section, but also out in the adjoining common area. There were another two guards out there, with an extra one in an upstairs control room monitoring all the various cameras.

She must had stood silently leaning against the back wall for a good twenty minutes before she spoke to me and that was only when I happened to pass near her on my way to help the first station in line.

"How was your weekend?" I gave her a smile and said

it was OK, nothing specific really. She took it as an answer and went quiet again until I finished replacing a blunt set of shears. As I went to walk back to my previous post, she held out the paper for me. "Here, you want this? I'm finished with it."

I didn't make it a habit of reading newspapers at work, but I wanted to be nice and so accepted it.

"Thanks," I said and shoved it into my back pocket. "Anything of interest in there?"

"Nah," she said. "Just the usual depressing stuff. I got it from the staff room." She lowered her voice a little and leaned in. "Someone left it on the table in there. Figured they finished with it."

I thanked her a second time and before I could get any further, voices erupted at the far end of the stations. The screaming hit fever pitch by the time Loy reached them and called for calm. Behind us, two more guards burst in through the door.

Thankfully, it was just an altercation, sorted the way inmates usually preferred. Loud voices were a front, a shield so to speak. Prisoners used them to try and sound more threatening, when in fact, they used them to alert officers. Some inmates just knew how to play the game and the guy sitting in the chair, Justin Richards, had a rep for squealing, which is why he made all the noise.

By the time Richards was escorted from the unit, Knight returned from lunch, with Loy giving me a brief wave before heading back out into the day. A few hours later, after a fairly non-eventful afternoon, I followed her, relieved to finally head home.

CHAPTER 3

The drive home took a lot longer than normal thanks to an accident, and while I did try for a detour, it didn't help. I ended up walking into home near five o'clock, famished and in need of a hot shower.

First, I checked my blood sugar and seeing it was fairly low, decided to take care of the more serious problem first. The last thing I fancied was an episode and knowing how easily it was fixed, put the shower off until later.

There was still a nice piece of steak in the fridge, and by adding fried mushroom and onion, I turned it into a gourmet feast for one. Some sweet potato fries gave me the carbs I needed, and I opted for a tall glass of milk to wash it all down. Given steak was so easy to cook, it was less than twenty minutes later that I sat down to eat.

I had almost forgotten about the gift Loy had given me and as I sat down, felt something still sitting inside my back pocket. Pulling it out, I set it down beside my food, unfolded it and began to scan over it as I ate.

The front page wasn't anything special, just political crap I had no interest in and so immediately flipped to the next page. The usual line-up followed, like which celebrity had just broken up, or who had scammed people via some lucrative real estate deal.

For the most part, I simply skimmed over the words, more focused on my food. The steak was damn fine and I enjoyed every bite, the twist for me the fried egg I always sat on top to add sauce. It had been a trick I learned from Tess when we first met and sunny-side-ups had been my new "steak gravy" ever since.

A knock on the door broke my interruption and when I went to answer it, found a man there wanting to sell me some new cellphone plan. I politely declined and as I watched him turn and leave, wondered what the world had come to. Cellphone plans…of all the things.

There were only a few mushrooms left on the plate when I returned to the table and feeling the moment had passed for me, scraped them into the trash and headed off for the overdue shower. The water always had a way of cleansing the prison residue off me and I couldn't imagine going without it after a day inside.

As I stood under the stream a few minutes later, my mind turned to another project which had taken up a lot of my spare time. Because of my own insecurities about keeping evidence about my hobby in the home, I purchased a decent-sized property on the other side of Elderton. Two hundred acres, with enough distance between me and my neighbors to ensure prying eyes wouldn't trip me up.

The idea for what I had planned for the place came from an unlikely place, but made so much sense to me at the time. I've never been much of a DC Comics fan, but one night a couple of weeks before, I found myself face-to-face with a late-night screening of Batman, the one with

Christian Bale. My opinion on whether he had been the best of all the movie versions doesn't matter, but what does, was the immediate light bulb which went off in my brain when it came to the bat cave.

Superheroes always needed somewhere to hide, a place where privacy and seclusion went hand in hand. Whether anybody would consider me a superhero per se could be up for debate, the final decision perhaps down to a matter of perception. But nonetheless, I needed privacy to conduct my work and what an amazing idea then, to build my very own bat cave.

I must have spent close to four hours that night, planning, drawing, weighing up options, all with the one purpose of constructing this place within a couple of months. It needed to be hidden from view, with no chance of anybody finding it. Otherwise, I might as well keep everything at my home instead.

It took maybe another week for me to come up with a plan I thought would work a treat, during which time, I set aside my previous DNA collecting activities. While I still had every intention of making that my mainstream purpose, I needed somewhere safe to store it, and some half-baked plan wasn't going to cut it.

What I eventually came up with was quite simple, and if given enough time and the right equipment, manageable for one person to complete. That was the other part I had to remember. Help would be non-existent, so anything I couldn't do alone was out of the question.

It did take a few days, but finally the plan went ahead and I began with a giant hole. I had hired an excavator which I used to dig up a massive hole right in the middle of the property. It wasn't a hole, as such, but rather a trench about a hundred feet in length, moving down enough to where the final forty-feet sat at a depth of around thirty feet, which would ultimately become the base of my cave. This way, I would be able to drag the two containers down into position without too much trouble, or without damaging them.

The good thing about my surrounding neighbors was that neither side lived on their properties. The nearest home, so to speak, was close to a mile away and with a thick tree line dividing us, it meant I had enough distance to cover up what I was doing.

The week before I hired the excavator, I purchased seven shipping containers, each one forty feet in length. Three of them I would eventually join together for a small house, the kind architects sometimes designed for unique homes. Two side-by-side, with the third sitting across the top. Two others, I used for storage, one at the bottom of the property, the other off to the side of the house. I thought of it as a kind of garage for a small motorbike I used around the place.

All five of the containers would be nothing more than a ruse, with the final two the only ones to serve their real purpose. These I dragged into the hole with the excavator. It was simple enough, with a long cable hooked up to one end of the containers, and the big machine parked on the far side of the hole. It worked a treat and just forty minutes after starting, both containers sat side by side and ready for the next step.

I didn't like having the containers exposed like that for too long, in case some snoopy neighbors decided to check the place out while I wasn't there, and so intended to take the following day off from work and head down to finish the welding, so I could fill the hole up again. Considering I was rostered on to attend the store in Indiana for just a few hours of book keeping, it wouldn't inconvenience anybody.

Back in my shower, it wasn't until the water began to run cool that I realized I'd taken my sweet-ass time and needed to hop out. Long, unnecessary showers had always been one of Tess's pet hates and I felt a surge of guilt as I turned the faucet off.

"Sorry, babe," I whispered to myself as I stepped out and dried myself.

I felt like a bit of rest time once I was dressed again, and crashed on the couch for a bit, but after channel surfing through dozens of options, I couldn't find anything worthy of my attention. An old war movie did grab me for a few minutes, an oldie called The Great Escape, and feeling like ice-cream was needed to further enhance the experience, I went and grabbed a tub of Ben and Jerry's. That was after I first checked my levels.

It was on the way back to the den that I spotted the newspaper and figuring I still had a few pages to go, grabbed it as well. I already knew my mood wasn't suited for the movie and despite sitting there eating chocolate fudge ice cream, the dopamine I was chasing just never hit. After half a tub and an hour of watching Charles Bronson dig three tunnels, I called time on the exercise.

Instead of turning the TV off, I simply hit the mute button. Having the screen continue to play out in the background gave me a sense of company and once I grabbed the paper, took up from the page where I previously let off.

My night took an almost immediate turn the moment I turned to Page 5 of the paper and saw the red pen mark. The circled article wasn't a major one, just a narrow one-inch column on the inside part of the page. A small photo sat beneath it, showing the face of a man I had seen in a more recent setting.

It wasn't the article which chilled my blood, not even the photo itself, nor the neat circle someone had drawn around the article and photo combined. What sent goosebumps breaking out across my arms was the little cartoon someone had drawn beneath the head of the man in the photo.

Whoever had drawn the set of electric clippers under Foster's head possessed a real sense of artistry. The dimensions were bang on, with them positioned in such a way as to make them appear as if they were actually running across the man's throat. The artist even added a few tiny flecks of blood shooting off Foster's neck to mimic the cut. While not exactly graphic, it did have the touch of flair to make it look more than a little morbid considering the man was already dead. But using a barber's main tool; could that have been a message for me?

Knowing how many people would have had access to the newspaper, it could have been possible for any number of guards to have chosen this part of the newspaper to share their artistic talent. This could have been nothing more than a an idle doddle created during a moment of boredom; the five minutes before they were due back on shift. But as I stared at it, I couldn't help but wonder...had the drawing been made by Linda Loy?

I tried to think back to the time she almost completely ignored me, watching me with some sort of protective shield. But then again, she *had* been the one to give me the newspaper in the first place. Me...specifically. Was that in itself a somewhat confession for "Hey, I know what you've been up to?"

Impossible, I thought to myself as I stared at the photo

again. There was no way she could have known the truth, or anybody else for that matter. I had been alone when I ended Foster, and not only that, it had been in an isolated place, with night already falling. There was no way anybody could have witnessed his end.

I put it down to me just being paranoid, a common trait amongst amateur killers and I knew it to mean one thing. I had a long way to go when it came to perfecting my art. If I was going to become some big shot avenging killer, then I would need to step up my game considerably.

The idea that someone could have been watching me remained in my head until I was lying in bed a short time later. I stared at the ceiling for a long time, lying there in the dark with a million scenarios playing in my mind. And despite thinking that I had been careful to cover my tracks, I still couldn't shake the undeniable feeling that somebody knew as I finally drifted off to sleep.

CHAPTER 4

Sleep must have worked its magic on me because when I awoke the following morning, none of the suspicious thoughts remained. I put them down to nothing more than late-night jitters, the kinds of crazy thoughts people had the moment daylight left them in darkness.

After phoning McSweeney with my need for a day off, I set about packing supplies for the day ahead. While a normal person could just grab a few things and run out the door, the same couldn't be said for a diabetic. As I began throwing things into a backpack, I compared it to packing for a day out with a small child, needing to ensure I had all the right things before I left the front door.

The only thing I didn't need to worry about was insulin, thanks to a new automatic pump I had been fitted with a couple of days prior. It took constant readings of my blood sugar throughout the day and released insulin accordingly, all without me needing to worry about it. Compared to how things worked before the pump came along, it felt like an extended vacation.

With food and drinks packed, I jumped in the truck

and drove the twenty-minutes to Elderton, before heading south on the 210. After another few miles, I turned right off the main road, trekked down a narrow dirt road before pulling up in front of the gate leading into my very own property. I still had the manual gate fixed in place and thought about shopping around for an automatic one as I shoved it open.

The relief came when I found everything just the way I had left it a few days before, right down to the welder and generator which I had locked up in one of the shipping containers. Knowing how much people liked to snoop, and even worse steal, I kind of placed my bet on maybe thinking the universe would throw me a bit of a bone. It did, and seeing the unbroken padlocks still securing the container's doors drew some much needed relief.

Not wanting to waste time, I returned back to where I had finished the previous visit to the place. I had already set about cutting a massive doorway from one container through to the other and continued using the oxyacetylene torch to trim off the final few pieces. Once done, I fixed a thick rubber strip to the edge, giving the archway a kind of trimmed appearance.

Next, I worked the cutter into the roof and cut out a neat hole for the ladder. Since the floor of the containers sat close to thirty-feet below ground, I needed a safe way of getting down into the bat cave. I had already prepared a three-foot wide piece of pipe which I welded to the container to act as the shaft.

I couldn't completely relax as I worked. A distinct fear of being discovered continued to hang over me and not even music was enough to distract me. I didn't think headphones would be appropriate, nor playing music loudly over speakers, and so I worked in silence, with just the sounds of my work for company, along with whatever wildlife chose to watch me.

By lunchtime, I stood back and checked on my progress. Needing a better view, I walked out of the hole, then circumvented around to the far side where the end of the trench sat. This was where ground level remained and the place where my eventual front door would live. It meant I needed to return a lot of soil back into the hole, but with the excavator also doubling as a front-end loader, it wouldn't take me too long to fill it back up.

It looked odd to see the length of pipe sticking straight up into the air, appearing like some kind of phallic salute to the gods. If anybody had arrived at that very moment, there would have been plenty of questions raised, which is why I returned back to the machine and immediately set about filling in the hole.

I didn't bother taking a break for lunch. Instead, I ate as I worked, if that's what you could call it. Work wasn't exactly considered sitting on one's butt while manipulating a machine around an empty hole. It felt a like a driving simulator and if it hadn't been for the occasional shaking, it might have passed for one.

Again, I felt vulnerable sitting in the machine as I continued working the dirt back to its original position. Enclosed in the cabin, I had no chance of hearing anybody approach and so worked feverishly until the entire area looked almost back to normal. The only thing I did have, was a couple of tons of leftover dirt which I spread out until it had faded into the landscape.

Once finished, I stood back and checked out my handiwork and thought I'd done pretty good. The next part of the job wasn't going to be as easy, but I knew it had to be done. Without some sort of solid foundation beneath the rest of the shipping containers, things could potentially sink and move and that wasn't going to help anybody and so, I made an on-the-spot decision to bring in some concrete.

There were two options open to me; the first being bringing in professionals to pour it and create a proper slab. But because this would also bring with it inquisitive eyes, I didn't want to open myself to that kind of exposure. Which left me with Option 2, not only the one which would guarantee me a little more privacy, but also prove the backbreaking choice of the two.

With no help, I would effectively need to cart several tons of dirt, gravel, and cement mix from a mixer to the slab, a job which I figured would take me a decade to finish. But there was one aspect which gave me hope and that was the fact I would be building an integral part of my bat cave. The idea filled me with a kind of hunger tinkerers felt when they were about to finish a pet project, like those finishing a classic car they'd been working on for years, or an artist about to add the final few brush strokes. The slab would be part of a series of steps I needed to ensure I did it right, with the finished product my very own masterpiece.

It was four o'clock by the time I managed to sit down and begin making phone calls and by the time the minute hand had completed another trip around the clock face, I had secured myself enough bags of concrete and materials to build what I needed. The cement place even agreed to throw in a free cement mixer rental because of the size of my order.

Thankfully, the forecast was for clear skies across the weekend, another sign that somewhere in the cosmos, fate had decided I was doing the right thing. With my deliveries due the next morning around eight, I finished locking up and headed home just as the sun touched the far horizon.

Just before I climbed back into the truck, I took a final look back at my handiwork and felt a surge of excitement. This was going to be a pivotal moment in my career, a career which up until a few months before, had been nothing but built-up frustration in my soul.

The last thing I did was put a cover on the pipe. If rain did somehow happen to fall, the last thing I wanted was my cave to fill up with water. Despite the sky clear as far as the eyes could see, I knew rain could sometimes appear out of nowhere and wasn't worth the risk.

By the time I reached home, night had fallen and while my body felt like I'd run a marathon, I knew it was nothing compared to how it would feel in the next couple days.

CHAPTER 5

By the time I returned to McSweeney that Monday morning, my body felt as if it had grown muscles in places I didn't know muscles existed. I could barely walk and even received a couple of comments from passing guards as I headed to the unit, asking whether I'd been on holidays due to my sun tan.

With not a lot of building experience, I managed to finish my goal in just three days of uninterrupted work. By the time I headed home that Sunday night, the foundation had been laid, which left me with just another couple of days left to relocate the remaining shipping containers into their final positions.

Once I set up the stations and watched the inmates take up their positions, I settled into the morning by running the next part of my pan through my head. Despite watching the prisoners go about cutting their clients' hair, my mind was barely there, caught up in a daydream of crane work and welding as I created a two-story shipping container home, complete with a secret entrance down into a bunker where the hub of my operation would live.

Fearing myself becoming a little too distracted by my thoughts, I tuned into a conversation between one of the inmate barbers and his current client, a man named Dolby Wilson. Wilson had spent the majority of his adult life inside, convicted of killing his wife and her lover when he was just twenty-two. The inmate once told me that she had cheated on him with another man and the pair tried to kill him for insurance money. I remember thinking at the time how that story had been repeated endlessly in both real life and Hollywood plot lines forever.

Wilson was a nice enough guy, the kind who seemed comfortable with prison life. I don't quite know how else to explain it, but whenever I saw him, he just appeared relaxed the way a tradesman on his way to work might look when stopping at a random gas station to pick up a snack. Wilson just looked like a man who had accepted his fate long before I ever met him.

It was Roland Tucker who was in the middle of giving Wilson a Murder 1, the kind of hairstyle which took very little imagination and even less skill to perform. And because of the lack of concentration needed, it gave their conversation much more depth.

From what I could gather, the pair were discussing another inmate named Angus Weir, and it didn't take an expert to read the body language from either man. Neither of them appeared to like Weir, much less respect him. Given the way they screwed their faces up during the conversation, it was pretty clear Weir had been rubbing people up the wrong way, a feat not hard to do when not playing by the rules.

Weir wasn't a stranger to me, and while it did take me a moment to recall where I had heard the name before, once I did, I understood the two men's reaction to the subject of their conversation. Given my new line of work, so to speak, it was also the reason why my ears pricked a little higher than usual, with their own disgust at the forthcoming events not proving popular among inmates.

The reason why the name Angus Weir was familiar to me was because he'd come up during one of my many research sessions. New names for me to follow up didn't exactly fall into my lap. They took effort, with me spending considerable time scouring newspapers, as well as online news resources for just the right criminals who had earned my attention. Angus Weir was just such a man.

Men who beat their wives normally had one of three reasons, or at least as far as I could fathom. The first and perhaps the most obvious was alcohol, with drugs also making a surge in numbers. The more research I did on the matter, the more I found that the drink was responsible for perhaps the majority of spousal abuse, closely followed by jealousy. A lot of the time, the pair went hand-in-hand, with one almost guaranteed to amplify the other.

The third reason I could find which explained this common form of assault was more of a character trait. Narcissism proved quite a common form of abuse and often went further than just physical assault, crossing boundaries into emotional, sexual, financial, and other forms of abuse. These were also the ones I loathed the most and did my best to try and find.

Angus Weir was none of them. From what I could gather, the man didn't drink, had never shown any evidence of drug abuse, and from what I could tell, sounded like a normal husband. That was until the night he went home and physically beat the brains of his wife out for no reason other than he'd received a speeding ticket on the way home. Or so people thought.

There weren't too many stories about him which I could find, with just a couple of news reports on the story. Neighbors described him as a quiet man, someone they would wave to out in their front yards. The couple had no children and mostly kept to themselves. But that was where the nice part of the story ended.

Angus Weir might have appeared like a normal, loving husband to those around him, but as if taken straight out of a Hollywood film, the man had secrets, with the number not fully known. He not only lived a double life, but also a double life from his double life. He appeared to be married to three different women, with his other families living in Ohio and West Virginia, and they were just the two authorities managed to track down.

To me, it read like one of the old Stepfather movies, especially once you added the fact he murdered his wife for what appeared to be no justifiable reason. Despite doing their best to try and find more, the authorities gave up with just the three families.

Weir had initially reported the death of his wife to authorities, calling the police when he walked into the home after a day at work. He claimed that he found his wife in their bedroom. She had still been alive at the time, although barely, but died shortly after and according to the defendant, she was unable to name her attacker.

When police arrived, they took the husband's statement and began their own investigation and it wasn't long before discrepancies arose. For one, investigators found a single splatter mark on top of Weir's work boot, a sign he must have been in the house when his wife was still upright. Forensics proved that the splatter pattern showed it to have landed from a distance of greater than four feet, which made it impossible if he had been kneeling next to his wife.

It wasn't just the crime scene forensics which didn't corroborate his story. For one, his boss claimed Weir failed to show up to the last client of the day, while a neighbor also stated to have seen him come home earlier than normal. Another neighbor also said she heard a short scream coming from the house, but didn't report it because she wasn't quite sure once it finished.

Weir ended up arrested and the more police probed, the more strange evidence they came across, including links to two cases in the early 2000s which appeared hauntingly familiar. While there weren't any specific links to Weir other than similarity, a couple of photos linked to the cold cases looked an awful lot like the man in their custody.

As I listened to Wilson and Tucker talking about the Weir case, my ears pricked more and more as I heard words like "getting off on a technicality" and "freeing a killer". Normally, inmates tended to support one another, especially when it looked like someone could be beating the system, but not always. There were still certain morals even prisoners hung to in such a god-awful place and murdering women was one of them.

I don't know why, but listening to a man who beat his wife to death talking about another inmate who had beaten his wife to death awoke a sense of urgency inside me. It was as if the very crux of my own operation sat right before me in plain sight, staring me in the face with both hands held out for me to grab.

From what I had gathered, Weir sounded like the kind of man who needed my attention, someone with a history of bringing misery to those around him. While I still needed to do a bit more background research, I was almost sure he would measure up to somebody I needed to focus on and the irony of the situation was that Dolby Wilson just happened to be another wife beater.

The idea of using DNA evidence in my murders wasn't a new one. My initial intentions had been to use the evidence to offer the police a distraction, to throw them off my tail. But as I stood listening to Wilson and Tucker exchange views on Weir's situation, I couldn't help but wonder what it would be like to give the cops a definitive curve ball. What if I started planting evidence which made no sense, and eventually led them to people with no direct connection to the victims?

Maybe out of habit, or perhaps from my subconscious taking over, but at one point, I found myself sweeping up the hair from around Tucker's station. It was his hair I wanted, the short, stubbly tufts swept into a neat pile by my feet. This was a man with a history I could use and instinct drove me to shove some of them into my pocket. And that was when the answer hit me.

A lot of my accumulated evidence had been ascertained through the prisons I worked in, while the knowledge behind the inmate's crimes nothing more than guesswork and many hours of research. Eavesdropping on conversations between inmates had proven effective, but it left me vulnerable to false information. What if the prisoners were only speculating? This would open me up to the kinds of mistakes I didn't want to risk.

Then there was the research itself into each prisoner. I could spend hours upon hours trying to find the details of their crimes, which weren't always as accessible as one might hope for. Newspapers and online resources only provided a limited amount of information. What I really needed was the foolproof stuff, like access to their criminal records.

It was during the usual lunchtime changeover of guards that an idea struck me, one so ostentatious that I wondered whether it was worth the risk. The prison's own database had everything I needed to know, with every inmate's record on file, right there waiting for me to take it. All I needed was access to it. But how could a non-custodial employee like me get myself close enough to a terminal, let alone access to the database itself?

I watched Knight and Loy exchange a couple of flat pleasantries before one disappeared from the unit, leaving the other to watch over the proceedings. Loy took up a post near the middle of the back wall, just like she usually did. Our eyes met and she shot me a wave, the kind lacking most of the emotion behind it. I sent a wave back and turned my attention to the line.

I must have spent the rest of the afternoon in a near catatonic state, because I don't remember too much about it, save for the thoughts running through my mind. There was something about the idea of getting my hands on a database which I couldn't throw and by the time I walked out through the front gate at the end of the day, I was no closer to finding an answer.

CHAPTER 6

McSweeney released Angus Weir the following day while I was working at the shopfront in Indiana, a fact I didn't find out until the following day. And while I did spend a little bit of time running things through my head, it all vanished in the blink of an eye when an incident occurred which ended up with one of our own thrown out the front door.

The shopfront's main purpose was to give recent-released inmates the opportunity to learn a trade and use it in a retail environment. Learning the skills was just one side of a career which for many could be set up almost anywhere. There wasn't a lot needed to cut a person's hair, with nothing but a pair of scissors the best starting tool.

A lot of the ex-cons who had managed to get a spot in the program lauded their chance, using the opportunity to their advantage as much as possible and I had nothing but praise for them. It takes confidence to take a significant step in one's life, as well as a bit of faith. Most of the men working for me would often comment about how significantly their lives had already changed in just a few short weeks, and to be honest, hearing it gave my heart a bit of a squeeze.

It was that morning when I was sitting in my office doing the books and I happened to look out through my viewing window. It was the only window I had and the truth is, my mind was a long way from the numbers sitting on the pages in front of me. The thoughts running through me were of a certain database, one which I still needed to gain access to if I wanted an inside view of the men who I would use in my after-hours activities.

Only four of the stations were in use that morning, with two of the assigned barbers calling in sick, one of whom still sounded like he'd taken a bath in a tub of ale. Perhaps it was because of the fewer stations operating that I spotted the deal going down, but whatever it was, it happened and I saw it.

I must have jumped out of my chair so fast because the next thing I knew, I was standing face to face with Jackson Roach, the newest of our barber brigade. He'd only joined our crew the previous week and as I stood there staring into his surprised face, I remembered the suspicions I already had about him back then.

"There's no dealing here," I snapped, my volume running away with emotion. Jackson turned to look at me and initially tried to talk it down. I think he must have seen something in my face indicating it wasn't going to work and so he went a different route.

"I ain't dealing," he finally said. "I don't do that stuff."

"I saw you," I said, but before I could add anything else, powerful hands suddenly grabbed me from behind and shoved me aside. Oddly enough, the shove wasn't in a malicious kind of way, but rather felt as more of a courtesy. The next thing I know, Barry Walker stepped past me and grabbed the much smaller Roach by the throat and pulled him back the other way where the other big guy was already waiting. Sam Clark reached for Roach's arm and twisted him against the wall. Both of them stood well over six-foot, a good head and a half taller than the would-be drug dealer, who at that point began screaming to be released.

Clark and Walker didn't listen to Roach's protests and began going through the man's pockets until they found what they were looking for. More than a dozen small baggies sitting inside a bigger bag, together with a few hundred-dollar bills. Despite the screams, neither man slowed until they went through every single pocket and when Roach tried to pull an arm free, Walker reacted in a way which ended the fight-back in an instant. He reached out, grabbed the smaller man by the throat for the second time and slammed his head into the wall behind him. His own face never slowed, propelling forward until the two men stood nose to nose, with one staring into the other's eyes with menacing vibes.

Roach froze, his arms kind of melting back down beside him until he was simply standing before the two men like a stunned scarecrow. His mouth hung open in shock, his eyes filled with fear. Walker could have snapped his neck in a heartbeat, if he wanted to, but the larger man held back. Instead, he held the gaze right up until Roach snapped his mouth shut.

I stood my ground and just watched as the men took care of their own. There would be no police called, of course. This was an in-house matter and would be dealt with accordingly. The rules from inside the walls of their previous home followed them out into the world and I think Roach knew that the ramifications from his actions out here would be far more severe of he didn't listen.

"Get out," Walker sneered into Roach's face and the man didn't hesitate to get distance between himself and the other two, kind of shuffling towards the doors while keeping his eyes on them. Not watching where he was going, he hit the edge of one of the barber chairs and managed to tangle his legs in a mass of confusion before tumbling to the ground. He hot the floor hard, but barely noticed as he jumped back up. By then, Walker and Clark had taken a couple of steps after him and when Walker stomped one foot onto the floorboards, Roach turned and ran.

Once the former barber vanished from view, Walker turned and looked at the client who had managed to purchase the final bag of meth sold in our building. The man briefly stared at the two then got to his feet and followed his dealer out the door. Once he was gone, a kind of silence hung in the air for a few seconds before Clark turned to me and held out the bag of drugs.

I don't know why, but in the seconds before I reached out and took it, something told me this was more than just a bag of dope being handed to me. A feeling in my gut trend to warn me that this was a test of sorts, a moment where I was being watched just as much as they watched their own.

Nobody moved as I took the bag from Clark. I thanked him and Walker for their help, then turned for the bathroom. I wasn't a stranger to the ways of cons, the rules which controlled the lives of millions around the world. As I walked to the bathroom door, the silence remained behind me and I could feel their eyes watching me. They wanted to know whether I was one of them, or just another man thinking he was in charge.

I had never been much of a drug man and so have no idea how much the bag of meth was worth. For all I knew, it could have been tens of thousands of dollars worth, or perhaps just a few hundred. Whatever it was worth, it still ended up floating momentarily atop the toilet water before the flush sucked it from the world and out of this story.

By the time I got back to the storefront, the men had returned to their clients and the former jovial conversation which hung in the air had come back. Barbers and clients engaged in smalltalk, while one took care of the other's needs. Would I have called the cops? Police tend to complicate things in these types of instances and I had no doubt, the matter was over with.

When I got back to my desk, a bundle of hundred dollar bills sat on top of my ledger and I stood in my doorway for a few seconds staring at it. I don't know which of the men put it there, but I knew they all would have agreed. Part of me wanted to take them and flush them down the same place as the drugs, but I wasn't completely stupid. Instead, I dropped them into petty cash and made a mental note to use it for buying lunches for the barbers over the following few months.

Finally, after a bit of drama, I finally managed to get back to my previous train of thought about the database and how I was going to get access and I think it came to me within a few minutes. I wasn't sure whether it was going to work, but it was worth a shot.

The other part of my thinking that day was about the DNA I had continued collecting and how I could utilize it in a better way. I knew *why* I wanted it, why I thought it was a great way to implicate others in the murders, but not how the police would see it. I wondered how they would react to finding evidence of people who had no earthly way of being present in those locations. Many would still be in prison.

A thought suddenly hit me, hard enough to make me smile. In a way, what I had been doing was a form of payback; a service to the community for the abysmal failures of the justice system set up to protect them. The system itself appeared broken to so many, while others defended it without question. What if I found a way to show just how incompetent it really was?

What had crossed my mind was me somehow getting my hands on the DNA of not only those locked behind bars, but also those who had been executed. While none of the prisons I had access to had capital punishment, there were enough spread out around the country. What if I found a way of getting hold of some?

For the next couple of hours, I thought about everything from digging up coffins, to writing letters to death row inmates asking for their hair. Of course these thoughts were nothing more than a warped fantasy, of sorts. Death row inmates would never send me pieces of themselves, and even if they did, prison staff inspected every piece of mail going in and out of their facility, which would defeat the purpose.

I understood my business was still in its infancy, a growing baby which would eventually mature into the sort of operation I could still only imagine. When I had first begun, it was nothing more than a vendetta against a man who killed an innocent child. Now, it had already. Blossomed into a full-on avenging-angel kind of operation. Who knew where it would eventually end up?

Finally, as each man finished with his current client,

they came in to bid me farewell, another day done and dusted. When Walker came in, I thanked him for his help with Roach.

"We don't need that crap here, Boss. Most of these guys are trying their best to stay away from that side of the tracks, if you get my meaning."

"I do," I said.

"Don't worry, he won't show his face here again; that I promise." I didn't doubt him.

"Hey listen," I began, then told him about my plans for the cash he'd left on my desk. When I finished, he nodded.

"You do with it what you want," Walker said, then wished me a good night. He disappeared out into the fading light, leaving me alone to finish up and shut the place down. Ten minutes later, I followed him out the doors and headed home.

CHAPTER 7

For many, crime is nothing more than an impulsive reaction to a moment of opportunity. Finding an open door, a left-out power tool, a lonely woman walking down a dark street at night. Most would normally cross the threshold into criminal activity of it wasn't for those moments, a split-second thought process where the person believed they might actually get away with it given the circumstances.

That's exactly what went through my own mind two days later while at McSweeney, when I was presented with an opportunistic glimpse at the answer I had been searching for. And the man who made the whole thing possible was none other than Harvey Knight. If it hadn't been for a procession of decisions, the opportunity may not have shown up at all, but once it did, I had just a split second to decide if I was going to take advantage of it.

Technically, it all began with me needing to take a detour home from Indian due to a road closure. The cop redirecting traffic mumbled something about a tree blocking the road, the result of a wayward truck taking it out. From there, I ended up him a little later than usual, which put me on the back foot due to a late doctor's appointment I had.

The appointment wasn't anything serious, just a basic check-up and a prescription for some new insulin for the pump I'd been wearing. Because of my long days, I had continued to push the appointment off until I managed to dwindle my remaining supply down to visually nothing, meaning I now had no choice but to get my meds.

By the time I came out of the doctors, the local drug store was already closed and aside from a twenty-four hour one almost forty minutes drive away, my only other choice was to wake up a bit earlier and get to the drug store on my way to work. A great idea, but when Murphy is listening, Murphy happens.

It was Murphy's Law which made me forget to plug the charger into my cellphone, and then for my cellphone to go flat halfway through the night. It was Murphy's Law which caused me to sleep in the following morning and leave the house almost an hour after I had intended to. I think it was Murphy who I grumbled about by the time I finally left the house.

Because I knew my insulin pump would run low during the day, I packed some of my old variety into my lunch pack; just in case. For a diabetic, back-up insulin was never frowned at and I tended to pack extra as a matter of course.

I contemplated ducking into a drugstore along the way, but of course the morning traffic was never going to be my friend on that front. Was it yet another instance of old Murphy coming along for the ride? With time slipping away, I gave in and kept my focus on getting to work on time. Despite nobody actually paying too close attention to me, I knew there would still be eyes on me, especially with my previous drunken state still fresh on many people's minds.

Managing to make it to the prison on time, I hurried to the unit after getting processed in and although I had to race to get things set up, everything was back on track by the time the first lot of would-be barbers showed up. Knight had been assigned to guard duty in my part of the world and the morning took off in its usual direction. So far, so good.

For the next few hours, I supervised the crew as they worked their way through several clients, with just a single altercation messing up our routine. Someone made a joke, someone else didn't like the joke, an exchange took place, before one lashed out at the other and before we knew it, two grown men were rolling around on the ground in each other's arms while shouting what they hoped was a better insult than the other's.

Personally, I never got involved with physical altercations. Not only was it not my job, but it also put me at risk of interfering with the officers who's job it actually was, and believe me when I say, you do not want to stand between those guys and a couple of inmates going for it. The term steam train comes to mind.

Once the officers managed to get the two back under control, they escorted them from the unit, giving everyone else a chance to get back to work. The excitement did give me somewhat of an adrenalin boost and I think it was this boost which somehow numbed my internal diabetic sensors, the ones my body had depended on since the beginning of time.

The alarm bells began to go off for me about half an hour into Knight's lunch break. His replacement, an officer named Drew Bates, was the first to notice my flushed appearance, something I didn't feel until he mentioned it. When I checked, my levels were quite low.

You can be forgiven for thinking it happened due to my insulin running out, but that would be incorrect. Insulin's purpose is to give my body the ability to absorb the energy from food and drink, which means f I run out of insulin, my levels would skyrocket. This was the opposite. In my haste to get out of the house that morning, I had grabbed a quick bite to eat, then ended up only eating half of it. The morning had also offered up repeated distractions and before I knew it, I had missed all the signals telling me to eat.

"My blood sugar's low," I said and asked Bates if he could cover me for a few minutes. He more than agreed and even asked if I needed a medic to come and check me. "No, I'm fine," I said. "Just need to get myself a soda."

One of the officers in the control room buzzed me out of the unit and I found myself slowly walking up the hallway towards the main corridor running around the inside perimeter of the prison. Each three units shared a common staff room between them, sealed by a locked door only accessible to staff with a swipe card. Not being an official prison staff member, I didn't get the privilege of one. It was the one on this side of the prison I happened to be passing when Knight emerged through the door, saw me and stopped.

"You look like crap, Vic. Everything OK?"

"Just need a soda," I said. "Blood sugar's low."

"Yeah, OK. Here, go in and grab one from the fridge. The two Cokes on the bottom shelf are mine. Help yourself."

I thanked him and expected the man to follow me

inside, but it appeared he had other places to be. By the time I reached the fridge and turned to thank him again, he was gone. I couldn't see the door from this side as the room was kind of an L-shape, but I did hear the door click shut.

The coke did the trick a lot faster than I had anticipated, tasting cool and refreshing as a bonus. It was while I was leaning against the table with my butt that I noticed the computer terminal on an adjacent table. The screen was still on and what's more, the session still logged in.

My brain took off like a bullet, with images of Knight sitting at the terminal working the keyboard as he checked his email, or roster, or whatever other access he had. And when he was done, instead of logging out, he did what so many lazy people did, and simply walked away, knowing that eventually the session would time out through lack of input.

The screen suddenly went black and I must have lunged at the keyboard like a man possessed. My fingers smashed the space bar repeatedly as I hoped to catch the computer before it went into standby mode. I must have held my breath for an eternity as I stared at nothing but blackness. Imagine my relief when the previous screen suddenly reappeared and I stared at some plain background with a couple of program icons scattered across the blue sky.

There were already two tabs open that I noticed, with one being the email program, while the other had the word "MCF" underneath it, which I knew to stand for McSweeney Correctional Facility. I checked it out first and thankfully, Knight had left his session in the database open. From what I could tell, he'd been reading up on one of the men employed as a barber in my unit and his file was still open.

From my many years inside the system, I knew officers and guards had two levels of access when it came to computers and the outside world. Most of the new staff members had limited access to internal stuff, with zero access to the outside world. Management had removed access to the internet for nearly everybody a couple of years prior when too many instances of porn surfing were discovered.

Only a few of the older heads retained their internet access, which they sometimes passed onto their colleagues. From what I could tell, Knight appeared to have been granted access by someone higher up and I knew instantly, that I was going to take advantage.

I don't know whether it was my nerves, excitement at having access, or just downright fear, but as I began to type, my fingers looked as if they were dancing across the keyboard in a near blur. They appeared possessed and I could barely keep up as they came alive and navigated through a string of menus and selections.

The database wasn't complicated to understand, a fact I put down to yet another indicator that fate had stepped in, and it took me less than a minute to build a list of violent criminals with charges for dangerous assaults, rapes, murders, and serious drug offenses. The numbers continued to build and once I had close to fur-hundred names, I download them into a single file, compressed it down into a zip-file, then emailed it to a dummy address I always kept handy. This was a free one I set up some months before and used it whenever I needed anything remotely to do with my alter ego. This seemed like just the job it had been meant for.

I was about to close the email again when I heard the familiar ding of a swipe-card reader and before I had a chance to react, the door into the staffroom opened. With just a split-second to react, I rolled out of the chair, dropped to the floor and tried my best to hide under the desk. Thankfully, it was the kind with a fully-enclosed underside, giving me a near-perfect hiding spot. That was, unless they decided to take a seat and use the computer, in which case their legs and my body would definitely meet.

As the boots of the new arrival clip-clopped along the floor and out into the main area of the room, I held my breath. I was trapped, unable to move, and it was at that point I wondered why I just didn't simply stand up and...

Oh my God, the Coke, I thought to myself. In my haste, I had left it sitting next to the mouse, a sure giveaway of someone snooping. Before, I had a reason for being in the room. Now, I had given myself a reason to get caught... and fired.

Feeling paralyzed, all I could do was listen as someone first went to the fridge, rummaged around, then set something down on the counter. When the mystery person opened a cupboard directly behind my hiding spot, I slowly pulled my legs in a little tighter, my lungs feeling compressed as beads of sweat broke out.

A door suddenly swooshed open; not the main door, but a different. I tried to think about the room about and when I heard it squeal shut again, with the footsteps on the other side of it, I guessed it must have been a small bathroom.

I was up in a flash, not bothering to wait for the new arrival to catch me. First, I got into the Sent folder and deleted my email then closed both tabs. There wasn't much I could do about deleting the files I had accessed and I wasn't about to sit there and worry about it. Once I was sure I was done, I grabbed the coke and left the staffroom.

My chest felt ready to explode as I hurried along the corridor and just before I turned the corner towards my unit, I thought I heard the door to the staffroom open, but I couldn't be sure. I wasn't about to stop and check. Instead, I continued on and didn't slow again until I was back in the unit.

Harvey Knight was already back at his post and he gave me a once over when he saw me.

"You're still looking a bit peaked there, buddy," he said.

"Yeah, 'cause your dumbass left the computer logged in and I used the opportunity to hack the database and use a dummy email to send them out to myself," was what I wanted to say, but didn't.

"Hit me a lot harder than usual," was what I did say. "It'll be OK soon."

"I couldn't imagine how tough it must be living with that."

"Ah, you guessed used to it," I said.

It took close to an hour for my heart rate to drop to normal levels again. I couldn't believe how close I had come to getting caught, but knew that once I got my hands on the information, it would be totally worth it.

CHAPTER 8

It wasn't until the next Saturday that I actually began to check the file I had sent from the prison database. While I could have accessed it at home the night I had initially sent it, the close call in the staffroom had again reminded me of just how delicate this operation really was. I wasn't sure how many more times fate would let me off.

Instead, I went out and purchased myself a brand new laptop and left it in the trunk of my car until I finished the rest of my plans for the bat cave. I spent the entire Saturday from morning till night, using the loader to position all three final containers into position. It wasn't easy and I could have used help along the way, but they were in position by lunchtime and by four that afternoon, all three were welded into place.

The final act which I knew was also probably the most important, was setting things up in order to hide the entrance to the cave. It was no good building a secret cave if everyone walking through the front door could see it. Plus, I had already pre-fabricated the set-up ahead of time.

My shipping containers had been set-up in such a way

as to look like a home and the one hiding the entrance was also where the kitchen was situated. One end of the container was where the entrance sat and it was there where I set up the sink cabinet. All I needed to do was undo two small hooks located on either side, and I could swing the set-up out from the wall to reveal the small entry way. Once I stepped down onto the top decking, I grabbed hold of the top of the ladder, took a couple of steps down and pulled the sink back into its original position.

I took a small breather once everything was in place and only once I was sure there were no forgotten tasks I needed to do, did I climb down into the pit for the very first time. The lights worked brilliantly and the tunnel lit up when I snapped the switch, although the climb down wasn't as easy as I had hoped. As I carefully took each step, I wondered how well a metal pole would work. They seemed to do well for firefighters.

"Just your luck to lose grip and drop on your head," I mumbled to myself as the tunnel opened up into the main cave.

Thankfully, I had had the presence of mind to pre-stow all the furniture and major equipment I'd need down there before filling the hole in again. I wasn't exactly going to get a couch down the narrow tunnel and knew I had to make sure I thought of every possible need before closing off the possibility to add more.

Everything was still stacked against one wall, but I took care of the more important stuff first, including setting up the desktop computer which would display the security feed on two monitors. I couldn't very well spend my time below ground without knowing what was happening topside. Four cameras sat around the place, including one which I hid near the very front of the property, kind of like an early-warning system. I did have plans for an electric gate and intercom system, but until I had more money to waste, put that idea aside.

Once the computer was set up and I had everything plugged in, the two screens showed me several views from around my property. When I was happy with the way things looked, I spent the next couple of hours setting up the rest of the equipment, including a couch, a bed for those nights I wanted to stay here, plus the very jewel of my operation, the safe holding my DNA evidence.

Still too excited at what I had built, I couldn't sit still and rest once I was finished and so, I decided to start my investigation into my latest target almost immediately. Angus Weir had already been released from prison and I didn't want to give him too much of a head start. Knowing how difficult it was to pick up trails from previous targets, I hoped this time I could make things a little easier for myself.

I could have sat at the desk and used the desktop, but instead, I opted for the laptop and couch. For one, my back ached from the amount of work I'd done for the past couple of days, plus I know it sounds weird, but I actually liked the way the camera feeds looked on the two monitors. I couldn't bring myself to change a thing and so, dropped down onto the couch and opened the lid of the laptop. A few minutes later and I found myself lost in the world of yet another killer, a man who'd been hiding secrets across the country.

Angus Weir had been arrested for murder almost a month before he was released on a technicality and while many called for him to remain in custody, the judge turned down each and every request.

Rather than look through official reports and media articles, I dove deeper into the social media side of things. What I wanted was a personal insight into what Weir had done; to get to know the people who he had hurt and betrayed.

It didn't take long to find the other two cases law enforcement believed him to be a part of, but to date, they hadn't put together enough evidence to warrant further action. It took me about two seconds to see a photo of the husband of one of the past victims and know that it was him.

From what I could tell, Weir had married no less than six times, with three wives dead, one dying beside her three-year-old boy. A fourth wife committed suicide a few months after their separation, but the details for that one were more than a little sketchy and I couldn't determine whether Weir had been responsible for that one. Even still, four dead wives is still significant and I knew he needed ending.

Retracing his steps, and then following his trail since his release, it looked as if he had crashed at a friend's house in nearby Wexford and it was there I decided to begin my tracking. It didn't need to be much, just a drive-by to scope the place out and see if I could spot anything worthwhile. After the sheer luck of Melvin Foster crossing my path, I was more than open to another similar coincidence, hence why I made sure to carry my new handgun permanently. I say new because each time I use it in a case, I bury it in a random place.

It was already dark by the time I locked up the cave and headed out into the night, feeling more than a little excited. It was cold, yes, but I wasn't going to let that deter me from what I was believing to be a much higher cause.

Who knew how many unfortunate women I could save by taking a man like Weir out of the picture?

On my way through Kittanning, I stopped by home and grabbed a jacket, as well as a freshly-filled thermos of coffee. Who knew how long I would decide to be out for? With no definite confirmation that Weir was even in the home, I figured I'd go a little better prepared. This was, after all, an official field trip and I would be expecting some sort of result.

The first thing which I noticed when I turned into the street the friend of Weir's lived on, was the cleanliness of the place. It looked as if the neighborhood was home to some well-off middle-class families. Well maintained yards sat beneath glowing street lights, with the vehicles mostly relatively new, not the kinds of junkers a lot of the poorer neighborhoods sported.

I had already done a little homework about the home, having checked it on the street-view side of Google Maps. While it might have been dark, I could still make out enough landmarks to guide me to the home I was looking for. And just as I had hoped, the home itself was lit up, giving me a small glimpse inside through an open window.

There were people inside, two sitting on the couch, with a third standing up beside it. All three looked as if they were looking at something playing out on the television and I couldn't quite make out if any of them was my target. I had slowed to almost a complete stop and one of the men on the couch suddenly turned to look out through the window.

"Damn it," I hissed, temporarily forgetting that the window sat slightly open. I did notice it when I first neared it, but being too busy trying to identify the people, the small detail quickly slipped my mind.

I hit the gas, but not enough to appear to be escaping. Instead, I hoped to give the impression I was simply looking for a specific home and just a few yards down the road, I saw the man turn his attention back to the TV.

Two things almost immediately ran through my mind and both needed attention. The first was that there were three vehicles at the house; two in the driveway, and one sitting on the grass to the side. I needed to get a shot of the license plates on my second pass, so I could run a check on them.

The second part was the street itself, an issue I couldn't see past. There was nowhere to hide, when it came to scoping the home out. From what I could tell, all the homes appeared occupied and with the street itself too narrow to park on, there was nowhere for me to sit and wait for a better opportunity. The only thing I could do was come back either later that night, or very early in the morning before anybody was up.

I was still thinking about this second problem when I noticed something ahead of me, something which at first didn't make sense. It was a car, parked maybe a hundred yards further along the street and sitting in such a way that it appeared as if the person was trying not to be seen while keeping an eye on the road. Doing less than twenty-miles per hour, I couldn't see anyone inside from where I was, but I did feel the unlikely itch of recognition in the back of my head as I got closer.

The vehicle's headlights suddenly came on, practically blinding me in an instant and before I had a chance to readjust my vision, the car roared past me in a brilliant blaze of light. I had to pull slightly to the right to avoid a head-on collision and only caught sight of it leaving through my rear vision mirror. But the tickle of recollection felt almost overwhelming.

While the red Mazda 3 wasn't exactly a unique vehicle by any means, there was something about it which did grab my attention and I must have only caught sight of it at the last possible moment before I was blinded. It was a doll hanging from rearview, a doll which hadn't been around in a very long time, save for a few nostalgic collectors. The Troll hung with its distinctive hairline in clear view and Imagined it swinging wildly from side to side as the drive maneuvered their car towards me in an effort to get away.

There had only been one person who I knew to drive a red Mazda 3 and have a troll doll hanging from the rearview. I knew because I had walked past the very car dozens of times and each time, seeing it had made me grin. Trolls were ugly; old; a toy from the past when people craved individuality, almost as much as the different types of trolls on offer. And as I turned for home to decide on what to do next, I wondered just how much Linda Loy actually knew about me?

CHAPTER 9

Seeing Linda Loy's car come at me in front of a home I believed Angus Weir to be living in, shook me up in a way I wasn't expecting. It freaked me out, not only because t appeared as if she somehow expected me, but because I had arrived at a completely unplanned moment in time, almost as if she somehow guessed my arrival.

As I returned home, questions screamed through my mind, questions which I desperately needed answers for and yet somehow knew I wouldn't get no matter how much I tried. She knew about me, that much was clear. If not, then it must have been one hell of a coincidence to have her in the very same street as Weir.

What frightened me more than her knowing what I was up to, was her telling someone else. What if she herself was a kind of vigilante and I just happened to be the type of person she hunted? After all, murdering bad people came down to a matter of perception.

The question of whether it had been Loy's car never crossed my mind, that's how confident I was that it had been her. The troll just sealed the deal for me and the only confusion which I had, was about how much she actually knew about me. It was because of that very question, that I knew exactly what I was going to do next, on that front I had very little question.

My line of work, or should I say my *other* kind of work, involved risks, risks which numbered too many to keep track of. Even just a suspicious mind could bring me down, with one single phone call enough to raise suspicions of law enforcement and once they turned their attention in my direction, I knew it would just be a matter of time before they hit pay dirt. Which left me with just a single option when it came to Linda Loy. Shut down my operation until I was absolutely one-hundred percent sure she wasn't suspicious.

To begin with, I headed home, where I set about conducting a room-by-room sweep of anything and everything which had ever been remotely connected to my other life. Anything from hair sample bags, maps, surveillance equipment, old receipts, random writing pads, it all ended up in pillow cases. I didn't want to use plastic bags in case they tore. I knew pillow cases would hold everything safely inside. Not wanting to risk the slightest chance, I even threw in my trusty laptop, the one which had been serving me well, right up until I purchased the new one which now lived at the bat cave.

Only once I was sure that I had absolutely everything did I take it all out to the truck and sit it in the passenger side footwell. Not wanting to leave them unguarded, I jumped into the driver's seat and immediately turned for Elderton. Despite the time of night, a new matter had taken top priority in my life and it wasn't something I could set aside for another time.

I drove in silence, focusing on the road ahead, as well

as the headlights behind me. Something inside me refused to let me relax and every now and then, I randomly pulled over to let trailing traffic pass me by. To say I had my guard up was an understatement. Panicked wasn't quite there, but it was close. Jail felt like a real possibility and I knew it wouldn't take much to lose my hold on secrecy.

It was almost ten by the time I pulled up at the property and as I pulled up in front of the gate, I again waited until passing traffic had gone by before I jumped out to open the gate. Being a quiet country road, traffic was virtually non-existent and the only vehicle which had passed by me wasn't a Mazda 3, of that I was certain.

The act of opening the gate, driving through, and then closing it again took me less than a minute, but before I climbed back in, I paused at the back of the truck. I listened for the sounds of approaching traffic and gazed at both ends of the road to look for any sign of headlights.

The country silence hung heavy over the landscape and perhaps it felt a little more homelier that night than I was expecting. It wasn't so much the quietness of the moment, but more the sense of isolation. The longer I stood there, the more I felt at peace.

Instead of heading straight underground once I did eventually reach my base of operation, I parked the truck, then took the pillowcases to the side of the building to where I had added a little patch of relaxation in the form of an open fire pit. It wasn't much, just a hole with a few natural stones lined up around the outside and a single chair.

Rather than keep the things I had brought with me, I burnt them, destroying them with the kind of finality this work needed. The laptop I set aside, but everything else went up in smoke that night, leaving my life once and for all. My thinking was that the less I kept, the less chance I had of getting linked to anything in my past and if I could only be connected to my current case, then murder wouldn't be part of the charges.

Something I had always known about the line of work I got myself into was the fact that it would continuously evolve the longer I remained at it. I mean, it had to, or else I would constantly continue to make the same mistakes over and over. What was needed was a person with an open mind and a willingness to adapt. In other words, learn from mistakes, make the necessary changes and move on.

The one thing I knew I didn't need were trophies, one distinct detail which brought down many past serial killers. Trophies in a nutshell were direct connections to murder, something to mull over, to hold close while letting the memories of the moment flood back. I didn't want that.

The people I already had and would kill in the future weren't the kind of people I wanted to remember and therefore, I certainly didn't need trophies. Whatever links I had to the dead (I couldn't even bring myself to call them victims. They were anything *but* victims), whatever evidence which could be used against me, needed to be destroyed the moment I finished with it.

The longer I sat by the fire, staring into the flames and letting my mind wander, the more my continuing plan evolved. I would wipe all written notes from existence, destroy all evidence, and cleanse my operation of that particular person. I also decided that each piece of DNA could only be used a single time, left while working just one case. If I needed to use at two locations, it would only be ok if used for the same target, not subsequent ones.

I must have sat staring into the flames for more than hour, just sitting still while the fire hypnotized me with its allure. By the time I did finally extinguish the flames, the only question which remained was how long I would need to back off. The prospect of Linda Loy knowing about my operation hadn't changed and so neither had my intentions of pulling back for a bit.

After taking the rest of the gear down into the cave, I had a moment of conflict, with part of me wanting to remain for the night. I actually liked the feeling I got from the place, plus with the serenity of the countryside, it just felt a little too homely.

If I didn't have work the next morning, I might have given in, but instead, I made the trek back to Kittanning. It was late, my eyes hung heavy and I felt like I had achieved a few things in the previous few hours.

Once I pulled up into the driveway, I hopped out of the truck and halfway to my door, paused. The sounds I heard contrasted everything from the property, from the hum of traffic to the occasional siren. Dogs barked over each other, a helicopter flew by somewhere out of view, the sounds of the town far more invasive. I grinned as I turned for the front door, knowing where I would have preferred to be at that moment.

"Maybe we need to talk," a voice suddenly said from behind me and despite giving me an awful fright, I didn't need to turn to know who it was. A huge load of adrenalin sent my heartbeat into overdrive and it did take me a few seconds to calm myself enough to respond, but once I did, I made myself sound calm.

"I was wondering if you were going to show up," I said and slowly turned.

Linda Loy stood in the shadows of the hedge which

straddled the edge of my front yard. She slowly stepped out, looking every bit as stealthy as I felt when on assignment. She could have passed for the female version of me.

We stood staring at each other for a few seconds and I honestly didn't know what to say. Nerves gripped me, yes, a real fear of having been caught. What I didn't know was her intentions. Thankfully, she took the cue, but instead of putting me out of my misery, sent chills running through.

"How long had you been tracking Melvin Foster before you put him out of his misery?"

The question hung in the air for a long time before I knew how to answer it. Goosebumps broke out across my body as visions of her watching me kill him filled my mind. How could she possibly know? Had she been following me all the way back then?

"I know he was a piece of shit," she finally added, then held her hands up in a kind of surrender. "Don't worry. I'm not here to turn you in."

"Then why *are* you here?" It was all I could think to say, the words coming out more out of reflex. What she said next left me with even more questions.

"If my suspicions are correct, then you might just be the one I've been looking for."

CHAPTER 10

Rather than remain out in the cold and darkness of night, I invited Loy into my home. Knowing no evidence of my other activities remained, I felt a lot more at ease, and once inside, guided her into the living room.

Offering coffee was one of those deep-seated habits most people had and we ended up sitting at the kitchen table instead of the living room. It also felt a more suitable setting, the kitchen chairs keeping us upright and guarded instead of laid back and relaxed.

The coffee somehow brought the tension down for me personally and Loy took a couple of sips before she finally let me off the hook.

"Look, I didn't come here to bust your balls, so you can relax."

"Bust my balls?" She grinned slightly.

"Sorry, been hanging around the boys at the prison too long."

"Go on," I said.

"I was there the night you shot Foster." Hearing the words struck me harder than I had anticipated. I thought

I'd been clever, keeping myself out of public view and yet there I had been, giving someone a front-row seat because of my spur-of-the-moment decision. Again, she held her hands up and said, "Probably not what you want to hear, but your secret is safe with me."

"Why?"

"Well, for one, Foster was an asshole, a piece of shit who killed a child, and he certainly deserved what he got."

"You're not here because of Foster, or to tell me you forgive me for him." I could see more in her eyes, but couldn't for the life of me think what it was. Loy hesitated to answer, took a sip of coffee and looked down as she rested her cup on the table top.

"I'm here for someone else," she finally said, about to shock me for the second time of the night. "I need your help."

I felt like a puppy as I tilted my head a little sideways, squinting in curiosity at what she could possibly want.

"Help with what?"

She was about to start talking when a grin suddenly formed on her face and it was enough of a distraction for her to pause again.

"Before I tell you, I need to ask…aren't you curious how I knew you weren't just a once-off killer?" The question hadn't crossed my mind, but now that she mentioned it…

"Go on," I said.

"You know, you should really think about using a different cologne."

"My cologne?"

"Creed Green Irish Tweed, right?" I was stunned and my look of surprise was answer enough for her. "Can't go past those hints of lemon and peppermint." Her grin grew as she took another sip.

"But how…"

"My father used to wear it. It's perhaps one of the most vivid memories I have of him." Her grin faded again. "I knew it was you hiding in the staffroom when I came in. You're the only man I know at the prison who wears it and believe me, the sell has a way of hanging heavy in a room like that. Anyway, it didn't take much to connect the dots and when I found out Angus Weir had been let go, I knew if my hunch was right, then it wouldn't be long before you showed up."

She had played me like a fiddle, or at least that's how it felt. I had been tracked all along, watched from the shadows until the right time of approach had come.

"But, like I said…I ain't here to bring you down. Instead, I need your help."

"Help with what?"

"Help with killing Harvey Knight."

I don't what part stole the words out of my mouth, but I again found myself unable to speak. Hearing the name at first numbed me into silence as my brain tried to assimilate the words surrounding it. Murdering a prison guard hadn't been something on my radar and there I was being asked to do exactly that.

"Harvey Knight?"

"Yes, the guard who's been watching your back at McSweeney."

"But why would I want t-"

"Because he murdered my family."

Again, I found myself speechless, caught off guard by the revelation. Her words kind of hung in the air, almost as if I didn't want to fully accept them. My mind raced with wild thoughts of confusion, and I tried to answer, but when I opened my mouth, nothing came out.

"Look, I know it's not something you would probably believe from someone you hardly know, but it's the truth. Fifteen years ago, I watched as he killed my family in cold blood. I was six at the time and it was only because I had been hiding at the time that he didn't kill me as well. He used a knife and hearing him stab people I loved to death is a sound I can never forget."

"Why were you hiding?" I know it was the least important question I could ask, but it was the only one which came out.

"My brother and I used to play hide and seek after my parents had gone to bed. We figured it was better than during the day." She smiled as the memory played out. "I'd been hiding under the couch and that's where I stayed as he came in and killed them all. My parents, my brother, my twin sister."

"I'm sorry," I said, genuinely shocked. "I can't imagine how that must have been for you."

"It was enough to send me into a mental institution for a few years. I didn't speak a single word until I was fourteen and by then, he moved on to other victims."

"Other victims?" The shocks continued hit me.

"Yes, three more families since then."

"So, you're telling me that one of our work colleagues is actually a serial killer who murders entire families and has been for…how many years?"

"At least fifteen, or at least that's what I think. I tried finding more from before my own run-in with him, but haven't found anything."

"I…I just can't fathom it," I whispered, genuinely shocked. The thought of a man like Knight, someone whom I had trusted enough with my life while standing inside a unit with criminals…it just didn't sink in the way it should have.

"I assure you, it's all true."

"And that's why you're here?"

"Yes," she said. "I need you to help me kill him."

A couple of things crossed my mind at that point, with one standing out far beyond the other. If she knew about Foster and Weir, then she knew what I was doing, or at least what my end-goal was with both. And if she knew about those two, she would have probably put two and two together and perhaps figured out other victims of mine. That made her a liability for me, so if I decided against helping her, it left me vulnerable. In short, she had me by the stuff of the neck and could effectively end me with a single phone call.

The other thing which stood out to me was the fact she wanted us to work together. This wasn't her hiring me for a specific job, not that I offered such a service, but the details felt the same. She wanted me to help her and by that, for us to join our forces and bring a common enemy down. I say "common enemy" because the more I heard her tell me about Knight, the more I realized just how much he resembled the rest my targets. He fit right in, down to the finest detail.

"Why haven't you just gone to the cops?" I asked, thinking it was the most logical way to get rid of him.

"And have them make mistakes the way Foster and Weir were let go? Uh-uh…no way. I'm not risking that scumbag getting off on a technicality. I want him dead."

I leaned back in my chair and looked up at the ceiling for a few seconds, one thought repeating over in my mind. Up until that moment, I still hadn't confirmed more denied her accusations of me, or what I had been up to. My secret wasn't exactly safe, but she still had questions unanswered and I hadn't given her a single indication of the validity of her assumptions.

If it wasn't for the fact she had me cornered good and proper, I could have denied what she thought she knew, spun it into something else entirely and told her she was crazy for thinking so. I could have…and yet I didn't.

There was too much at stake for me, and given what she already knew, I would have a hard time trying to change her mind. Even if I wanted to, I couldn't come up with a different explanation on the spur of the moment, and nor did I want to. The truth was, what she proposed was exactly what I had already been doing and Knight sounded exactly like the kind of man I wanted dead.

The only question which I hung on was the one about cooperation. What Loy suggested was us working together and I had never so much as considered the option. Trying to keep my activities a secret was already hard enough for me alone. I could only imagine the challenge of there were two of us running around. Loy must have sensed my questions and answered them for me.

"I've been tracking Knight for almost two years now and in that time I haven't tripped his suspicions at all. I know how to keep myself in the shadows and if we do this, I can promise you I want compromise you; not with Knight and not with whatever else you have going on."

"How can I be sure of that?" The thought of us working together made me nervous. Sure, it intrigued me, but it also gave me bad vibes.

"Because I don't care about what else you've got going on. All I care about is getting Knight off the streets…permanently."

It took a lot for me to come up with an answer and even as I prepared to verbalize it, I still wasn't a hundred-percent convinced it was the right one. And yet as I spoke, it felt more than a little neutral, almost as if it was meant to be.

"Alright, I'll help you," I said and rather than simply accept it, Loy held out her hand. What she wanted was the handshake to close the deal.

CHAPTER 11

With the night getting late, we ended up postponing our follow-up meeting for the next night. We both had work the next day and I was already tired before I headed out to Weir's house and that had been four hours before. Loy agreed and I walked her to the edge of my front yard, then big her farewell and remained until her taillights faded into the night.

I don't know whether it was something of a likeness to contentment, or just lain old fatigue, but sleep took me a little too easy that night. The second my head hit the pillow, I zoned out and the next thing I knew, dim light shone in through the edges of my curtained window, with close to eight hours having passed.

The morning rolled by in a cloud of distraction, with my shower, breakfast, and preparing for the day ahead all melding into the same sequence of events. It wasn't until I caught sight of Loy at McSweeney later that morning that I stopped for the first time to consider the future.

We passed each other down a hallway with nothing more than a sideways glance and a restrained "good morning". There was nobody else within ear shot but we both must have felt the urgency to keep ourselves separated, or at least at a distance most already recognized as normal for us.

The moment which *did* create a definite reaction was a few moments after running into Loy in the hallway, when Knight appeared in the unit to oversee the day in the barber area. He greeted me just as he normally did, with a warm smile and a nod of the head. I returned it and hoped he couldn't see my hesitation. Now that I knew who he *really* was, the man appeared to me in a whole different way.

For the next couple of hours, I found myself staring at Knight each time the man turned his back to me. I couldn't help myself, no matter how much I tried. For one thing, I couldn't see the evil in him. He looked just as he always had, a friendly face, inviting smile, keen for a chat whenever someone approached him. He didn't carry himself the way so many other guards did. There wasn't any sense of superiority in him, the man's appearance as someone on the same level as everyone else. And yet…

If he really was a killer, then he hid his dark side well. His eyes, the windows to the soul, as some called it, didn't reveal anything. Not even when I approached him just before lunchtime break, asking about his planned weekend, there wasn't a single indication of the evil Loy said lived behind them. As far as I could tell, the man appeared normal.

It wasn't Loy who came in for Knight when he headed for his hour off, but a new guard named Felix something or other. This one *did* portray everything one expected from a new guard, along with the arrogance to boot. A couple of the inmates tried to bait him with a fake argument and he took the ruse, threatening to lock them up in isolation if they didn't knock it off.

Throughout that day, I couldn't get away from the fact I didn't see Knight as a threat. It wasn't that I didn't believe Loy, but it was hard when there had been no evidence presented, no clear signs, and definitely no indication of the monster she made him out to be. When he came back and took up his previous position, I must have spent the rest of the workday more focused on him than the inmates.

It wasn't until I was sitting back in my truck at the end of the day that I took time to let everything sink in for real. I must have sat in my truck for close to forty minutes before I finally fired up the engine and headed home. Up until that moment, there hadn't been a chance to really weight things up in my brain, not with everything else which had been going on.

Food was the last thing on my mind, but I ended up stopping at a McDonalds on the way home because I knew there wouldn't be time for dinner once I got home. Loy had already agreed to drop by at seven and I didn't want any interruptions once she arrived, not from my empty stomach, not from my diabetes.

A Big Mac, some fries, and a chocolate shake kept me company for the last part of the journey home and just as I knew it would, the food made me feel like crap. It always did, but thankfully, the feelings quickly subsided once I jumped into the shower to wash the remnants of prison smells off me. By the time I hopped out and got dressed, it was already ten minutes to seven.

Loy showed up bang on time and this time, she came carrying a bag which I guessed would contain all the evidence she needed to convince me off her accusations.

She greeted me with nothing more than a smile and headed straight to the kitchen ahead of me, before setting the bag down and removing its contents.

"I figured you might need some extra convincing, so I brought these."

Amongst her stash were newspapers, a couple of small folders, photos, plus a diary of some sorts. She pushed them all into a neat pile, then sat down before them.

"Shall we?" The look on her face wasn't exactly joy, but I could see that this was a matter she took serious, and from what I could gather, she wanted to get this part of our conversation out of the way as quickly as possible so she could turn her attention to the more important bits quicker.

"Of course," I said, sharing her sense of urgency.

Loy must have spoken uninterrupted for close to two hours, taking me through som baby details, I couldn't help but admire her for the efforts she put in. Her research looked remarkable, her information both in-depth, as well as accurate. Aside from multiple newspapers showing the murders she had previously mentioned, Loy also managed to get hold of multiple police reports, all of which sharing one common detail; none of the murder scenes held any sort of forensics evidence.

Only one case offered a hint of something different fro the others, and that was a secondary victim near the scene of a horrific murder in Kentucky. A family of five had been slaughtered in their home, including two children and a grandmother.

The strange part about the cases...in *all* the cases...was that in each instance, the killer cleaned up the murder scene. He didn't just *clean* the murder scene, but also washed each of the bodies, dressed them in their finest clothes, then lay them on top of their respective beds. The fathers in each case, had been dressed in suits, with neckties knotted and straightened accordingly.

Some of the photos Loy showed me included those of the victims and if one didn't know the truth, could have been forgiven for thinking that the people were simply sleeping. There were no signs of violence, no indications there had been a struggle. The furniture all looked to be where it should be, nothing was stolen, and even the pets remained unharmed.

But then, there was Harvey Musk, the neighbor from the family in Kentucky, a man who had been beaten to death and left in a pool of blood while he struggled to suck in life-saving oxygen for almost fur hours. His tongue had been ripped out and despite still being alive when paramedics did eventually show up, he couldn't identify his attacker before he died.

The more I read, the more I felt my repulsion grow for the man. He'd been hiding in the shadows and butchering families, and all the while continued living his life as if nothing had been going on. As far as Loy could tell, his last murder had been six months before she picked up his trail, and she had been following him for almost two years. It was only the previous year that she became a prison guard in Florida when she learned about who the killer of her family actually was. She managed to win a position at McSweeney just four months before our eventual meeting.

"I'm ready to end this," she finally said once her pile had been shared with me.

I sat for a few moments staring at the paperwork before me. Silence hung over us and Loy just looked at me as I tried to get everything right in my brain. Not only was Knight the exact sort of filth I wanted to rid the world of, but here he was being handed to me on a silver platter. When I finally looked over at her, I just had a single question.

"How do you want me to kill him?"

The question must have hit her the wrong way, because I saw her twitch a little before she leaned back in her chair.

"I don't want *you* to kill him at all," she finally said. "*I* want to be the one to end him. I *need* to be the one to end him. Knight is my nightmare. He murdered my family, remember?"

Her tone sounded almost confrontational and I wasn't about to get into an argument over it.

"I'm sorry, I thought that's what you were asking of me."

"No, not at all. Yes, I need your help, but when the time comes, I want to be the one to actually pull the trigger."

"So shooting, then? That's how he goes?" She grinned, something I would have thought impossible given the strain the conversation had had on her, but she was a lot stronger than I had given her hope for.

"Listen, Vic. I've been dreaming about this moment for longer than you could possibly imagine. I've lived a life focused on just one thing; to end Harvey Knight. I've gone through years of mental anguish, years of living in institutions; I've changed my name, my identify, all so I could one day come face to face with the man who killed my family. I have no wish to prolong this ay longer than I have to. Is a bullet too quick for him? Maybe…maybe not. Perhaps I could stretch his suffering out over minutes, or even hours, but that's not who I am. I simply want him dead, gone, unable to do this to anybody else."

I didn't answer her immediately, but I think she knew what I was going to say, and that was because she already knew who I was long before this night. There wasn't a shred of doubt in my mind that she had investigated me just as much as she had Knight himself. She had most likely been following me for longer than I was aware of and that gave her a definite upper hand. In the end, there was just one thing I could say and when the words left my mouth, they seemed to give us both a sense of relief.

"OK, I'll help."

CHAPTER 12

We must have spent almost three hours getting ourselves prepped for the upcoming weekend and the start of our operation. Loy's demeanor changed considerably once I gave her my assurance that I would help. Gone was the unsure, almost timid persona, replaced by a woman who would have felt at home doing a high-pressure job in some corporate environment. This was the person I expected her to be, but up until then, she had kept the alter ego shielded behind a wall of insecurity.

Loy took the lead as she led me through what she already knew about Knight, everything from where he lived, to who he knew. She had his current work roster printed out, plus a list of social activities he undertook. His car, license, home address for his mother, social security number, she had it all, right down to who he voted for in the previous election.

"Linda, this is impressive," I finally managed, once she gave me an opportunity to interrupt.

"Thank you," she said, a genuine smile of gratitude

growing across her face. "I know it's not perfect, but it's a decent start."

"Decent start? What else could we possibly need?" I asked, flabbergasted that she would even think what we had wasn't enough.

"A place to kill him," she said with a matter-of-factly tone and I grinned.

"Of course," I said. "That part's always the toughest."

"It wasn't for Foster," she said and I grinned again.

"No, that one just happened to fall into my lap." I chortled slightly. "Still can't believe someone watched me from the bushes."

"Don't feel bad, I just happened to catch sight of you seconds before you disappeared behind the undergrowth. It was already late and there wasn't anyone else around."

"Did you know it was me?"

"Aha…if nothing else, my eyes are perfect."

"Well, I hope my actions didn't traumatize you too much."

"They didn't," she said. "I've witnessed much worse, remember?"

Of course she had, I thought to myself and not only that, she had witnessed her own family murdered. I couldn't imagine seeing a piece of filth like Melvin Foster getting his ticket affecting someone.

"So, where to from here?"

Our plan was simple, or at least to begin with. Loy would drive me around and show me the places where she had followed Knight to, and then to the house he lived in with a flatmate. The woman owned the home and from what Loy had been able to gather, she had lived there ever since her husband passed and she sold her much bigger house in Philadelphia and moved to Indiana. The town must have proven to be a huge change for her.

"She doesn't leave home much and has all her groceries delivered," Loy said about the landlady. "My guess is Knight prefers to stay incognito as much as possible. Maybe that's why he doesn't rent a place of his own." I tended to agree.

"Less paperwork, less connections for him. Do we know if Knight is his actual name?"

"No, he's changed it a number of times from what I could gather." Again, her answer made sense.

"Sounds to me like he's really got himself into a routine." I thought about how to proceed and wondered how much I could use Loy. A small part of me wondered whether she would make a worthwhile ally after we'd finished with Knight, but I wasn't ready to put forth such a suggestion. For that to happen, I would need to build a hell of a lot more trust than what we currently had.

"He's working tomorrow, so once we confirm he went to work, we can start heading to some of the places without fear of him catching us." I agreed and given the late hour, we both decided that a good night's rest was on the cards.

"Want to come back around ten?"

"Sure thing," Loy said and just before she walked out the door, turned to me and smiled. "You know, I always had a hunch you were into something, but I could never have guessed this." I grinned and nodded my head in a single bob.

"Thank you," I said. "That makes me feel so much better." She laughed at that and before I knew it, she was gone, her taillights again fading into the shadows.

I didn't bother cleaning up once I was back inside, my

eyes barely open as I checked my BSL's for the last time of the day, then headed to bed. In short, I was beat and without a clue for how the next day would end up, I wanted to make sure I was rested and ready. I had been on enough stakeouts to know how things could turn on a dime and without knowing exactly who I was beginning to track, I didn't want to take unnecessary risks.

CHAPTER 13

I don't know how long the banging on the door had gone of for, but by the time I awoke, it sounded fairly impatient, as if the person behind it was losing hope of getting an answer. Checking my watch as I rolled out of bed, I saw that I still had close to two hours before Loy was due, which meant whoever was trying to wake me, had other intentions.

My brain still felt wrapped in dusty curtains as I opened the door and scratched my head. Surprisingly, it *was* Loy and she didn't look happy.

"He didn't go to work," she snapped and pushed passed me.

"Come in," I muttered, checked the front yard for anyone else, then closed the door.

"Think we can still check out all the places?" She had walked through to the kitchen and surprisingly, began to make us coffee.

"I can do that," I said, but she shrugged.

"It's just coffee, Vic."

"Give me a sec," I said, leaving her to the job, while I

went to take care of my bathroom needs. Being awoken was one thing, but interrupting my routine another thing entirely.

The coffee was already served by the time I came out, feeling much better than when I left. For one thing, the smell coming off seemed a lot more social, and I always felt better with freshly-brushed teeth.

"How did you know he didn't go to work," I asked, expecting her to tell me something like her doing a drive-by.

"I've tapped his phone," was what she did say, nearly knocking me off the chair.

"Wait...what?"

"I've tapped his phone?"

"But how did-"

"I had a friend who was a bit of computer nerd back at the hospital. He used to use a cellphone to cause all manner of havoc amongst the nurses, including sim swaps, email hacking, hell...he even managed to crack the fire alarm at the hospital and would activate it whenever someone annoyed him."

"Sounds like he knew what he was doing."

Yeah, well...Rick knew how to get what he wanted."

"And he showed you?"

"Kind of," she began, but then stopped when I noticed color flush her cheeks. It was a sign for e to change the subject.

"So, you heard him call?"

"Not exactly. His cellphone sends me a readout of everything he says on it."

"Every call?"

"Yup, every call." I made a mental note to ask how I could do that for future targets. It sounded like a skill worth having and I didn't want to pass up an opportunity to learn it.

In my mind, I had already made the mental decision to push Weir aside and save him for a later date. Not only did Knight sound like much more of a threat than Weir, but he also needed our utmost attention. I couldn't risk getting distracted by one to the detriment of the other.

"Let's take my truck," I said once we were ready to go. "Less recognizable." She did look little dubious, but I assured her a bright, red Mazda 3 with a troll doll dangling from the rearview mirror was far more recognizable. "A rusty shitter like mine sits parked on almost any street in America and they all look the same."

We turned onto Route 422 just before nine and drove mostly in silence. What little chat we did have was mostly about the the places she intended to show me, wanting to give me a visual insight into his life.

"You know, I wish there was a way to prove his connections to the past murders," she said as we neared Elderton and I pointed out that doing so would jeopardize her own interests. "I know," she whispered, almost melting into the landscape as she sank deeper into her seat. And then, catching me completely off guard yet again, she pointed to an upcoming turnoff.

"How's the new property going? Your underground bunker finished yet?"

She continued staring out through her window as I eyeballed her, stunned by just how much she knew, and not just about me. It was if she had ace'd me at just about everything to do with surveillance and tracking someone. I felt like a damn amateur.

"Just how long *have* you been following me?"

"Long enough to know you need help," she said

without looking at me, and the sad fact was that she was right. I was about to say so when I felt the very air in the cabin of the truck turn serious. I saw Loy straighten in her seat, while her eyes remained on the road ahead. I looked at her and was taken back by the change in her expression.

"What's up," I asked, expecting her to tell me that she'd had a pain or something, perhaps needing the bathroom.

"It was him," she whispered, her voice barely loud enough to hear over the road noise.

"What was-"

"He just passed us," she said, but didn't turn to look. "That pick-up truck that just passed us...it's him." I risked a look in the rearview and just caught the tail end of the Tundra before it disappeared over a rise.

Without waiting, I hit the brakes, pulled the truck to the side and waited for an approaching semi. Once it drove by, I pulled a quick u-turn and hit the gas.

"He's going to recognize us," Loy whispered and I could see her fingers shaking as she gripped her cellphone.

"No, he won't," I said. "Typical, nondescript pick-up, remember?"

I couldn't exactly give chase, not while we remained behind the huge truck blocking our way, but as it turned out, we didn't need to. Loy suddenly pointed across the landscape.

"There," she snapped. "He's turned off. Should we follow?"

Before I could answer, the Tundra appeared to turn again, this time into what looked like a farmer's field. Something inside me screamed for me to stop and when I spotted the Shelocta Car Wash, I did.

"What are you doing?" Loy asked and I steered the

truck into one of the self-serve bays and rolled forward just enough to hide us from view.

"Wait here," I said, reached into the glove compartment and pulled out my binoculars.

"Vic?"

"One sec," I said and jumped out of the truck.

I slowly crept to the very edge of the bay and looked across the gully towards where I last spotted Knight driving. The other side sat a hundred-yards or so higher than where we were and gave anyone up there a good view over the small township. I scanned the line of trees, searching for any sign of him and when I did, felt my skin prickle.

Knight stood beside a tree with a pair of binoculars to his face. I couldn't see his truck, parked somewhere behind the thick mass of undergrowth. The dense bush was at the very edge of the tree-covered hill and gave the man just enough coverage to hide him from prying eyes. All except someone specifically looking for him.

The home he seemed focused on stood at the very edge of town, nestled amongst homes in the last street on that side of the creek. On the other side sat some train tracks and further up, the farm's fields began.

"What can you see," Loy suddenly whispered from behind me and I stepped back.

"Have you ever seen him around here?"

"Once or twice, sure. Why?"

"Because I think he might be scoping a house out."

Loy held out her hand for the binoculars and I gave them to her, then told her where to look. She slowly made her way to the edge of the wash bay, then held the binoculars to her face, but after a few seconds of scanning, pulled back.

"I can't see him," she said and when I took the binoculars back and looked for myself, Knight was gone.

We couldn't risk him spotting us and so I asked Loy to jump back in the truck while I did the unthinkable and began to wash the truck. It wasn't as if it needed it, but with Knight missing, I didn't want to risk him driving past and seeing us looking for him. Much better to try and for in with the surroundings.

We pretended to do what normal people at wash bays did and once I finished, climbed back into the truck and turned back for Indiana. I wasn't quite ready to give up entirely, and the drive gave Loy a chance to tell what she knew about the place.

"He's been to the town twice that I know of, but he's never gone up there before."

"Where *has* he been?"

"The tractor dealer and the vacuum cleaner store."

"Vacuum store?"

"Aha, and both times he stayed for at least an hour."

"Think he knows someone there?" Loy nodded.

"I did read a transcript from a call with the owner of the tractor dealer. They did sound chummy, but it didn't give me much else."

"Run a check on the owner of the place," I said. "Let's see who we're dealing with."

Before she finished, I pulled into a random gas station and filled up. Once done, I went inside grabbed two cokes and then drove us around the side into the parking lot where we sat and reset ourselves.

It didn't take her long to find the information we needed. Taylor Walker, aged thirty-three, had purchased the tractor dealer four years prior. The man was married to Imogen Walker, thirty-one, who worked at the vacuum cleaner store owned by her father. The couple had two children, aged six and four.

"Wait a second," I said once Loy finished sharing the details. You got the details of the other victims?" She pulled them up on her cellphone and held them out.

"They're eerily similar," I said as my eyes scanned the information. "All the victims had been in their early thirties, young children, living comfortable lives."

"You think that's why?"

"Why…what do you mean?"

"I mean why he kills them…because they look so happy."

Loy pulled up some social media accounts and just as she said, the couple looked more than happy. Every post showed a loving family who appeared to be enjoying life.

"Maybe that's it," I said. Loy must have seen my expression change.

"What is it?" When I didn't answer, she lowered her cellphone. "Vic? What is it?"

"I think we need to take him out sooner rather than later."

"You think he's preparing to strike?"

"I don't know, but I'm not prepared to risk their lives through hesitation."

I sat back and watched as Loy continued going through a few of the wife's posts, many showing images of the two children. There was no denying the happiness those photos showed and I wondered whether Knight's main driver was jealousy. Perhaps each of his victims had what he desperately wanted and he'd made it his life's mission to steal it away.

"I could go and find him right now and kill him," I finally said. My tone must have sounded a lot more dedicated than I had intended because the way Loy turned and looked at me gave me goosebumps.

"Think that's a good idea?"

"No, I don't, but I'm not risking losing these people because we were too slow to act."

"How do you know he's coming tonight?" A valid question, but I didn't think it needed answering.

"I don't think it matters when he's got planned. All I know is what you've told me and from what I can tell, it's been quite a long time since he's last killed and this happens to look like the kind of victims he favors. Take him out before he has a chance to strike is my suggestion."

Loy looked to be considering it and I'm sure I saw the moment she agreed with it.

"Just so we're clear," she began, "I'm not against offing him right here and now, but I want to be sure we can go through with it." Part of me believed her, but a small part of me wondered whether that was the whole truth. Thinking about how long she had spent tracking this guy, I understood that the ending the way I suggested didn't hold the weight of a grand finale. I think personally, she wanted more.

"We just have one problem," I finally said.

"What's that?"

"We can't leave these people alone now. If he happens to come back before we find him, he might pull a fast one and beat us anyway."

"What do you propose?"

"I know you're not gonna like it," I said, "but we have to split up."

"No, no way." She looked almost panicked. "Vic, I have to be the one, I told you that. It has to be me, for my family's sake." The sad reality was, I understood what she meant, but this wasn't going to work out of he didn't come back.

"Look, I know, but one of us has to go back to his house and pick up his trail. The other needs to remain here and keep an eye on the home."

She knew I was right, I could see her demeanor admit to it. The question was, which one of us would go hunting?

CHAPTER 14

Just like most professional hunters, we ended up deciding through the ancient form of Rock, Paper, Scissors, with me on the losing end with the scissors.

"I'll go after him," Loy said, " and you wait here."

"OK, fine." I thought about the place where Knight had stood and decided it would probably be the best place for me, given how it had the perfect view over the street. "Remember where he hid in the tree line? That's where I'll wait."

We swapped places and Loy took the wheel. As she returned us back to Shelocta, I grabbed the binoculars, my pistol, as well as my jacket. Who knew how long I would be out there for.

"Just take sure to keep in touch with me," I said as she pulled over near the train tracks. "And don't be leaving me out here all night, you hear?" The smile was enough to tell me she understood, and if I had known it would be the last time I saw it, I probably would have commented on it.

"I promise," she said and once I jumped out, I watched her turn around and head back the way we came.

Not knowing whether Knight was still around, I didn't waste time getting my butt away from the side of the road and down towards the dense foliage near the tracks. Midday traffic had built up considerably and if Knight wanted to, he could have mingled easily amongst the continuous flow. Just like red Mazda 3s, white Tundras were a dime a dozen.

I found my place a couple of hundred yards in, with thick vegetation not only giving me a cushion, but also some cover. For the most part, I lay on my stomach sniper style, scanning the horizon with the binoculars for a long time.

Minutes turned to hours and before I knew it, the sky began to grow dark. I checked my cellphone repeatedly, but by five o'clock, still hadn't heard from Loy. I began to wonder whether she hadn't tricked me and had instead, been planning to rob me of everything I owned while I was stuck hiding on some make-believe stakeout.

The phone finally began to ring just before six and I answered with a less than enthusiastic hello.

"He still hasn't come home," Loy whispered into the phone. "I've been sitting here for hours and nothing."

"Well, he's not here," I said, "so, I'm sure he'll show up eventually."

"I hope so," she said. "I just want this over with." She paused, and I could hear fidgeting before she came back on the line. "Oh my God," she whispered. "He's just pulled up. I gotta go."

Before I had a chance to answer, Loy hung up and just like that, I was alone again, this time with no idea of what was about to happen. I knew she intended to take him out, but would it happen right there and then?

With no choice but to wait, I sat up and leaned back

against a tree. I saw movement along the street and began to run the binoculars up and down, watching as people began to come home from work and what not.

The home we knew to be the Walker's, was three doors down from where I was sitting and I watched as an SUV pulled up into the driveway, followed by two children jumping out from the back seat. The mother followed and after a brief wave to the neighbors, all three headed inside.

Daylight continued to fade and eventually, the streetlights came on, followed by more lights in the windows of the streets. The traffic on the streets also began to show up via their lights and soon I was the one sitting in darkness, while the rest of the world were safely inside their homes.

Time continued to pass and by eight o'clock, I phoned Loy for an update. I figured it must have been enough time for her to make a decision one way or another. The first call rang for maybe ten seconds before getting diverted to a message bank and so I waited another ten minutes before trying again. Subsequent calls all went straight to message.

"Great," I muttered, figuring her phone had died.

I got to my feet and stood in the darkness as I felt the familiar sting of a mosquito on the back of my neck. I slapped at it in disgust, realizing I had managed to completely isolate myself with no way home, and now, clueless as to Loy's location.

"I told you not to work with anybody," I reminded myself and thought about my options, which I saw as two. I could either call myself an Uber and consider the whole thing a loss, or stay where I was and wait things out.

I opted for the second, although wasn't too happy about it. My hope was that Loy would show up soon and give me the good news that she had gone through with it.

Knight was dead and we could go home. Could it be that easy?

Before I had a chance to answer my own question, headlights suddenly appeared at the end of the street beneath me. Normally, they wouldn't have mattered much, but something about them seemed awfully familiar. The beam on the right side shot off slightly to the edge of the road and pointed down a lot more than the left. I noticed this because that was exactly how the lights on my own truck appeared.

I held my breath as the truck slowly rolled down the street and when it passed underneath a street lamp, I felt chills run through me, a massive dump of adrenalin kick-starting my heart. The truck rolling down the street was mine.

"What the hell," I whispered as I thought about what to do.

Something seemed off about the way it was moving and rather than aim for a driveway, the truck kind of continued straight, failing to follow the natural bend in the road. It never slowed and with a very faint clunk, it hit the front fence of the Walker's neighbor's home, got deflected back out onto the road, and then hit the opposite fence.

I stood my ground as the silence returned, with just the faint hum of traffic from the main road. The truck had come to a stop between street lamps, which meant it sat mostly in darkness, with the home itself appearing empty.

Rather than stand there contemplating life, I pulled out my pistol, cocked the hammer and carefully made my way down the small hill. When I reached the tracks, I jumped across them, then slowly maneuvered through the last patch of undergrowth. Crickets continued chirping in the dark, and I took it as a sign that maybe this wasn't what it looked like.

I approached the truck with the pistol held out and saw the driver's side door hanging open. The cabin was empty and I stood in the dark for a moment trying to get my bearings when I heard the moan from behind me.

She was lying in the back, the smile long gone from her face. The handle of a buck knife stuck out from her chest and when I jumped into the tray with her, Loy looked up at me with the last expression her eyes would ever portray in this world.

"Please, Vic," she croaked, her voice struggling against the blood in her lungs. The hope remained in her eyes, but I knew it was too late.

"I'll get him," I said. "I promise."

I like to think she heard me, but her eyes glazed over before I got them all out. Feeling a bolt of rage rip through me, I looked over to the house where we knew he was headed, but before I reached it, a single gunshot rang out, followed by a scream louder than any I'd ever heard. Lights began to pop on at various houses and curious people came out to investigate.

The Walker's house was where the noises had come from and I ran as fast as my feet carried me. The front door to the place sat ajar and I burst through, pushing the heavy door out of the way like a seasoned quarterback. Before I had a chance to react, a gunshot exploded n front of me and I felt something rip past my ear.

"Wait, wait, wait," I screamed, holding my hands up. "I'm on your side."

I nearly tripped over the body laying just inside the entrance, my focus on Taylor Walker as he stood near the back of the room, his hunting rifle aimed straight at my head. We locked eyes for a split second and as I let the pistol swing from one finger, he lowered his gun.

It took the cops less than five minutes to show up and by then, the mess which Harvey Knight had left behind was far from sorted. The strange thing was that Taylor Walker knew about Knight's intentions all along. He told me had just gave off that kind of vibe and had shown up at the house multiple times. Not only that, but he had shown up to both his own and his wife's place of work.

"Piece of shit took stalking to another level," was how he put it to the officers who first showed up.

Of course, I was interviewed as well and with Linda Loy dead in the back of my truck, had no choice but to give them the truth. I explained how she had come to me for help because she knew who he was and what he had done. They initially found my story hard to swallow, but when I told them about the pile of evidence she had shown me, they kept an open mind.

I would eventually be called in another two times to answer questions, but with each subsequent visit, the officer's demeanors became more relaxed, until they eventually believed every word. My only concern was that Loy had somehow kept information about my own dark side at her home, but nothing was ever mentioned.

I know fate should have had Linda Loy murder her family's killer, but in a cruel twist, the opportunity had been taken from her at the final hurdle. I remember lying in bed for many night, staring at the ceiling as I wondered what her final thoughts would have been.

If this had been a Hollywood crime thriller, then I would have been the one to finish her job, to take down a man who fit the bill of my targeted enemy in every way. He should have been in the home, about to slash the throat of the beautiful wife when the stranger burst in and shoots him dead. That way Linda would have had her dying wish fulfilled, I still got to be the hero and the villain meets his usual demise.

This wasn't Hollywood and the real world seldom follows the glorious path of the perfect story. I felt empty as I lay in bed most nights, empty and sad for the way things ended. She should have at least had the chance to know that he died.

I ended up going to Linda's funeral the following week, attended by maybe five or six dozen people. Most were from work, a few from outer state where she had worked before McSweeney, and a few who I didn't recognize. I mingled amongst them and when people asked how I knew her, I would say that she watched my back in a place filled with monsters. It wasn't far from the truth.

She ended up buried next to her father in Pittsburgh, in a place not far from where got to see some of my handiwork. I've visited her a few times since and often sit and talk to someone whom I only knew a short time. Unlike many in my life now, Linda Loy was one of the only people who truly knew me and the things I did. And while she didn't get to experience a win for herself, I like to believe that in some small part of this universe, she knows that she helped bring him down.

For me, I took a break from my activities for a while, just to be sure nobody had managed to follow up some further enquiries from what they had found in her apartment. But each time I visited her grave, I reminded her that our work wasn't done. People like Angus Weir remained in this world and what they needed was a visit from the one man who had made a promise to right the wrongs of a system many deemed broken.

Time was ticking until my return and it wouldn't be long before I was back to doing what I believed fate wanted me to. And with each passing moment, my list continued to grow with the names of those the crime collector would eventually come to visit.

Thank you for reading the Collector series. If you enjoyed this book, would you mind helping out a new author? Reviews really are important to us and if you could spare just a minute or two and leave one fore me, I would be forever grateful. Thank you.

AFTERWORD

Thank you for taking time to experience this relatively new author. I hope you enjoyed The Collector Series. This series has been locked away since 2008. It has been long over due to be released. It all started while I was working behind the wall of Pennsylvania's prisons and working with some of the most dangerous inmates. I have had many conversations and interactions with coworkers and inmates which gave me a clear insight on how our judicial system works. I realized that sometimes it is not always fair.

Working in a prison is unlike any other work environment. Throw in fifteen fully tooled barber stations, fifteen inmate student barbers, and 50 inmates waiting for barber services then lock yourself in a small room with them. Welcome to my prison barbershop. It will make a man or break a man, not just the prison staff but every man in that room.

This series clearly shows how one-man transitions from a regular everyday man on the streets, to a man heavily influenced by his work environment. Victor's vengeance is giving his life purpose again. Even though it doesn't bring his wife and daughter back. He becomes alive through the calculated exterminations of these immoral offenders. Please join me in this series as we watch Victor Controne's skills become more honed, like the very razors in his barbershop. As he develops his skills, is he a vigilante or just a cold-blooded killer?

Please take time to leave a review on Amazon or wherever you have made your purchase. Please like and follow me on Facebook at RC Blaides Author.

Take care and look for the good in the world.

RC

Made in the USA
Middletown, DE
12 December 2022